"You're really not a second-class woman."

Marlowe's words shocked Cinnabar so much she forgot to struggle in his arms.

"A...a what?"

"A second-class woman," he repeated. "Despite your claims, I doubt you've ever been in love...mainly because you have absolutely no confidence in your powers of attraction. Hence this need to be the aggressive career girl...."

Cinnabar's eyes glared into his, so close...so dangerously close.

"I'm aggressive, but only with men of your type. And I do have self-confidence...in every way." It wasn't true, but she wasn't about to admit it. "Now will you please let go of me. I don't need your comments or advice. I don't have to prove my powers of attraction to anyone. Certainly not to you."

"Oh, you're right there," he growled. "So very right...."

The Chrysanthemum and the Sword

Annabel Murray

Harlequin Books

TORONTO • NEW YORK • LONDON
AMSTERDAM • PARIS • SYDNEY • HAMBURG
STOCKHOLM • ATHENS • TOKYO • MILAN

Original hardcover edition published in 1983
by Mills & Boon Limited

ISBN 0-373-02596-3

Harlequin Romance first edition January 1984

For my Mother

CHAPTER ONE

'OH no, Mr Lamonde! Why me? Why can't Gary go to Japan?'

Cinnabar Forester made her protest with vigour, her wide, blue-grey eyes imploringly on her employer's face.

Vyvyan Lamonde waved aside her words with one white, languid hand, his deep-set eyes already longingly on the new sketches before him, anxious, Cinnabar knew, to get back to the creative side of his work, haute couture fashion design.

'Why me?' she repeated.

'Because, my dear Cinnabar, Gary is covering the Spanish assignment and I can't wait for him to come back. We must get started on the Japanese portfolio right away. Now, be a good girl, hmm, and say you'll go, without any more fuss?'

As Vyvyan Lamonde regarded her anxiously, Cinnabar prowled restlessly about his workroom, for once unaware of the sketches crowding the walls, the luxurious fabrics piled high in every available corner.

In reality, she knew that she had little choice but to accept the Japanese assignment, since the alternative was to risk losing an interesting and profitable career, and she enjoyed working for the House of Lamonde, one of the foremost fashion houses in London, with branches in Paris and New York.

Vyvyan, though temperamental and a little precious in his manner, was a generous employer and the work was absorbing, often exciting. She would have had no qualms about this proposed trip, but for one thing . . . or rather one person.

She turned to him in a final appeal.

'But four months! Four whole months of Magda Llewellyn. You know I can't stand her . . . and neither can you, if you're honest. Why you employ her, I can't think.'

Vyvyan sighed, running an agitated hand through over-long, waving grey hair.

'Simply because she's a marvellous clothes-horse and she photographs divinely.'

7

Cinnabar and her colleague ... and boy-friend ... Gary Reid were both highly trained and competent photographers, with a particular flair for photographing fashions; and, since Vyvyan Lamonde liked his creations to be set against exotic backgrounds, they were, necessarily, involved in a great deal of foreign travel, visiting places that otherwise they might never have seen.

Their often separate assignments meant that they did not see much of each other, but Cinnabar found that this did not trouble her unduly, though Gary tended to be less complacent. He wanted to get engaged, but though Cinnabar was very fond of him, she was in no hurry for marriage. At present her career was still far too new and absorbing to abandon for mere domesticity.

Now, Cinnabar was torn between her very real desire to see Japan and her dislike of Magda, the House of Lamonde's top model, whose company she would be forced to endure.

Conscientiously, she had always tried to hide her own feelings, but Magda, who in any case was always bored in female company, made no secret of her own antipathy for Cinnabar, never missing an opportunity to belittle the promising and attractive young photographer; and, since Cinnabar's temper was of the volatile kind, which often accompanied red hair, the whole situation held a promise of more than potential explosiveness.

Far better if Gary had been Magda's companion on this trip. The model was always syrup-sweet to him ... to any male; but Gary was the only man Cinnabar knew who saw through Magda's hard, porcelain-like shell.

While Cinnabar brooded, Vyvyan Lamonde leant across the tooled leather of his desk top.

'Well, what is it to be?' His precise tones were a little impatient.

Cinnabar sighed.

'O.K., Mr Lamonde, I'll go.'

The designer smiled his satisfaction.

'It won't be so bad. Four months will soon pass, with all the ground I want you to cover; and although I say it myself, the Oriental collection is my best work yet. I shall be expecting a simply brilliant portfolio from you.'

Cinnabar's retroussé nose wrinkled with worried intensity.

'That's all very well, but I don't see how we're to manage

... the language problem, I mean. Neither of us speaks a word of Japanese.' She smiled, a mischievous smile, which, although she did not know it, many men considered utterly enchanting. 'I don't suppose "Ah so" will get us very far!'

Vyvyan Lamonde laughed too, relaxing now that he was sure of the young photographer's co-operation.

'Many Japanese speak English. But in any case, you'll be well looked after. The arrangements have been made for weeks.'

She looked at him accusingly and he tossed his leonine head a trifle defiantly.

'I knew you wouldn't really be able to resist the lure of the Orient, my dear Cinnabar.'

She smiled ruefully. Vyvyan was more perceptive than his artistic, rather distrait manner led one to suppose.

'So, what are these arrangements, then?'

'Well ...' He leant back in the expensively upholstered swivel chair, becoming expansive. 'You know that, in my modest way, I am a collector of Oriental antiques?'

She nodded, amused. Vyvyan's modest collection amounted to several rooms in his luxurious flat being crammed with chinoiserie and other valuable items.

'I negotiate all my purchases through a firm of importers and exporters in Tokyo ... Messrs. Hirakawa. I've had several long telephone conversations with their managing director, with whom I am personally acquainted; and he is arranging your hotel accommodation ... and the supervision of your itinerary.'

'Supervision?' she enquired, her hackles rising defensively.

Only one contention ever arose between herself and Gary, and that was Cinnabar's conviction of her own self-sufficiency, her ability to organise her own life and her work, without interference or direction from men.

'Women are just as capable ... if not more so ... than men,' she often reiterated.

'Supervision,' Vyvyan repeated firmly. 'Although things are slowly changing, Oriental customs are not ours. Women play a far more subsidiary role in the East. You will allow yourself to be guided absolutely by Mr Hirakawa.'

We'll see about that! Cinnabar thought darkly, but she knew better than to actually voice the thought to Vyvyan, who was, after all, her boss; and now that the die was cast ...

Magda or no Magda . . . she felt it would be unbearable to be taken off such a challenging assignment . . . her most exciting to date.

The designer thrust a thick sheaf of papers across the desk top. Flicking through the schedule of scenes against which Vyvyan wanted his model to be photographed, Cinnabar whistled soundlessly. The next four months would indeed be full.

'So, when do we leave?' she asked.

'The day after tomorrow.'

Her delicate brows rose in horror.

'Thursday! But we can't possibly be ready by then.'

'Oh yes, you can,' he assured her suavely. 'The collection is already crated up and on its way. Magda is standing by. All *you* have to do is to pack.'

Ten minutes later, Cinnabar left Vyvyan Lamonde's office, feeling that she had been skilfully manipulated and stampeded into her present position; and, at four o'clock on the Thursday afternoon, she and Magda Llewellyn left London, by Japan Air Lines, en route for Tokyo.

As soon as they met at the airport, Cinnabar felt the usual irritation welling up in her. Always honest about her own emotions, she had to admit to herself that it was partly envy of the model's striking good looks and poised grace which inspired her antipathy, making her feel commonplace and awkward.

Cinnabar's self-confidence in her own abilities did not extend to her appearance. She was totally unaware that to those men who saw beyond superficialities, her square, mobile face, often alight with irrepressible mirth, was far more appealing than Magda's sulky sultriness.

Comfortably clad for the journey in a safari shirt and matching jeans in a light shade of rust, which complemented the dark bronze of her curly hair, Cinnabar had been reasonably pleased with her own trim, workmanlike appearance until Magda had entered the departure lounge, with her swaying model's walk, wearing an understated but sophisticated silk suit in chartreuse green.

Fashionably thin, with a peach-bloom complexion, Magda's elegant long neck seemed too slight to support the deliberately windblown hairstyle she affected. Her greeting to Cinnabar was barely polite, her manner one of languid boredom.

As Magda did not seem to be any more inclined for conversation than Cinnabar herself, and as the model immediately adjusted her seat into the reclining position, Cinnabar too relaxed and prepared to make the most of the experience before her, despite Magda's uncomfortable presence.

She still found it incredible to reflect that, only four years previously, she had held an ordinary secretarial position in the city ... photography then only a hobby ... spending her lunch hour gazing in shop windows at cameras she could never afford.

Then, incredibly, she had won a competition for amateur photographers, run by a well-known firm of camera manufacturers. In a fit of wild optimism she had given up her job and embarked on a course of photo-journalism, with the aim of taking up a career of some kind in photography.

On her own in the world since she was seventeen, she had no family to shake their heads over her impetuous decision, and then, at a party, a chance encounter with Gary Reid, already working for the House of Lamonde, had given her the opportunity to show her work to Vyvyan. He had instantly recognised her talent and employed her on the spot. Since then she seemed to have lived her life in a whirl of glamorous top models, exotic fabrics and foreign travel; but this was going to be the longest, most challenging assignment to date.

To her disappointment, after all her expectations, the journey itself was long, tiring, uneventful and, owing to Magda's uncommunicative manner, slightly tedious.

Although, when surrounded by male adulation, she was capable of remarkable animation, with her own sex Magda Llewellyn was poor company, for she had no conversation, being fretfully concerned only with her appearance; and, on this occasion, she was plainly aggrieved that Cinnabar and not the attractive Gary Reid was her companion on the trip. Gary, though impervious to her wiles, was tactful enough never to let the model suspect his true opinion of her.

Nor was Magda enthralled, as Cinnabar was, by the prospect of their stay in Japan.

'I would much rather have gone to Norway or Sweden,' she complained. 'Scandinavian men are fantastic. Even Spain would have been better than this. I simply adore tall, dark men. There's something so ... so *animal* about them!'

Cinnabar forbore to remark that neither Scandinavia nor Spain would be exactly in keeping with Vyvyan Lamonde's Eastern designs.

Consequently, it was a relief to the young photographer, when the aircraft touched down at Tokyo International Airport at five-thirty on the Friday afternoon.

Vyvyan Lamonde had assured her that they would be met at the airport, so it was no surprise to hear their names being called on the tannoy system.

At reception, they were handed over to the care of a bowing Japanese chauffeur and escorted out to the luxury of a silver limousine, with pale grey upholstery.

'Now *this* is what I call a car,' Magda purred with satisfaction. 'If we're going to travel like this all the time . . .'

'Oh, I shouldn't think so,' Cinnabar said hastily. 'This is probably the managing director's personal car.'

She had not revealed to the fastidious model that part of their itinerary included travel by train and dreaded her all too predictable reaction.

She had expected to be instantly aware of the Eastern flavour of her surroundings, but the scenery from the airport to the city proper was disappointing, a vista of grey factories, power lines and petrol pumps; and approaching the city itself, the monstrous Tokyo Tower, taller even than the Eiffel Tower of Paris, dominated the view. Where, she wondered, was the famous cherry blossom, said to be so much in evidence in April?

The streets of Tokyo itself were narrow and choked with traffic, claustrophobically enclosed by tall buildings with their flashing sky-signs. Soon they were driving through the Marunouchi, the main business district of Tokyo, a seething mass of jay-walking humanity and traffic, which seemed to hurtle along at a crazy rate, swirling in and out with apparently suicidal abandon. Their ears were assailed by a cacophony of honking horns, clanging bells, screeching brakes and blaring loudspeakers, the din of pneumatic drills and concrete mixers.

After one particularly close encounter with another speeding vehicle, Cinnabar drew a shaky breath and attempted to laugh off the tension.

'Did you know, Magda, that all Japanese taxi drivers were frustrated Kamikaze pilots?'

Magda's blank, unresponsive stare attested to the success of this conversational gambit, and Cinnabar relapsed into silence, wondering instead about their forthcoming meeting with the managing director of Messrs Hirakawa.

Vyvyan had reiterated once more the necessity of their deferring to Mr Hirakawa.

'He is an extremely astute business man, but also a great connoisseur of beauty ... as one might expect from someone who deals in objets d'art,' Vyvyan commented. 'I'm sure he will be of great help to you, in choosing the most aesthetically pleasing backgrounds and compositions.'

Cinnabar had chewed hard on her full lower lip, to prevent herself from breaking into angry protest. *She* was the photographer and she would compose her own shots. Just let this Mr Hirakawa try and interfere!

Oh, she must not be rude, she reminded herself. After all, as Vyvyan had stressed, Japanese women deferred to their menfolk; Mr Hirokawa could not be expected to understand a European woman. But she would be politely firm and with any luck he would be far too occupied with his business affairs to waste time in fruitless persuasion. After all, if the Japanese were as courteous as Vyvyan had said, Mr Hirakawa would scarcely try to order her about. No, she felt she could cope quite easily with any unwanted advice.

According to the display panel in the lift, the seven-storey Hirakawa building, an anonymous, functional structure of white concrete and steel with its own underground car park, housed, as well as offices, the main distribution warehouse and several private apartments.

At the office level, the chauffeur handed the two girls into the care of a courteously bowing male secretary, who led the way into an office which surprised Cinnabar by its ultra-modern appearance and conformity with Western standards.

'Well,' Magda drawled, looking about her, 'at least we shan't be expected to sit on the floor. That's a relief!'

As the model adopted one of her many studiedly elegant poses in a comfortable armchair, Cinnabar prowled around the room, examining its appointments with a feeling of considerable disappointment.

'Filing cabinets, telephone, drinks cabinet, dictaphone,' she enumerated. 'We could be in any office, anywhere in the world.'

'I'd rather be anywhere else in the world.' The model's drawl was irritating. 'Japan just isn't my scene ... and why couldn't Vyvyan have sent a male model with us, as he did for the Paris assignment? At least it would have been company for me in the evenings.'

'I think it's just as well he didn't,' Cinnabar said drily. 'We're here to work.'

With a man on the horizon, it was always difficult to keep the model to a rigorous schedule, such as that laid down by Vyvyan Lamonde. Cinnabar had experienced trouble of that kind on past trips with Magda Llewellyn. The lack of male distraction could be a decided bonus to this assignment.

'Talking of men,' Magda complained fretfully, 'where has this Hirakawa person got? I'm dying to get to a decent hotel and have a bath ... put on fresh clothes. I feel utterly dishevelled!'

Magda might feel dishevelled, Cinnabar thought, but she certainly didn't look it. The green silk suit had stood up well to the long journey, and constant attention to her face throughout the flight had ensured that Magda's make-up was as impeccable as when she had left England.

Cinnabar wished she could be as confident about her own appearance. The cinnamon-coloured safari suit was decidedly wrinkled, and she made a mental note to complain to the manageress of her favourite boutique, who had assured her that the material would not crease.

As though on cue, the deferential secretary appeared in the doorway, his bespectacled face creased in smiles.

'Hirokawa-San now coming.'

Both girls looked towards the door, Magda in languid indifference, Cinnabar with a certain amount of apprehension; for on the man they were about to meet depended a great deal of the success of their trip. Without his goodwill and co-operation, it would be difficult for two women alone to visit some of the places she hoped to photograph; then too, there was the difficulty of diplomatically rebuffing any actual interference in her work.

Expecting Hirokawa-San to be of comparable height to his employees, Cinnabar fixed her eyes at about five and a half feet from the floor, encountering, consequently, only the centre of a crisp white short-sleeved shirt, concealing an extremely broad chest, while revealing strong, muscular forearms, their bronze slightly darkened by a fine layer of hair.

Puzzled, she let her eyes travel upwards and heard her own tremulous gasp of surprise echoed by Magda, who was already uncoiling herself with deliberately supple grace, to rise, her slender hand outstretched to the devastating-looking man who had entered.

He must be all of six foot three, Cinnabar decided, aware of an unaccountable weakness in her legs, as she studied his powerful physique. Dark brown hair, not too long, waved around a square, determined face that was certainly not of an Oriental cast.

Her enquiring gaze met the amused, impersonal stare of wide-set hazel eyes, the humour in them echoed in the quirk of a firm but sensuous mouth.

By now Magda had reached his side, and as he looked down at her, his eyes widening with the instant appreciation that the model's appearance always evoked, Cinnabar thought with disgust that yet another man had fallen for Magda's apparent charm, the public image which the other girl could adopt at will, particularly if there were men present.

With the wry humour which, fortunately, always asserted itself, she reflected that it was going to be exceedingly difficult to keep Magda's mind on work, with *this* man in the vicinity.

'Miss Forester?' His voice was soft, slowly hypnotic.

'Goodness, no! *I'm* Magda Llewellyn.'

The model pouted provocatively, as though he should have been instantly aware of her identity, her eyes never leaving his face, as one thin, bejewelled hand indicated Cinnabar.

'*That* is Miss Forester.'

He advanced and Cinnabar felt ridiculously apprehensive, as a large, well-manicured hand was extended in her direction.

'Miss Forester! Marlowe Hirakawa at your service.'

Her slender hand entirely lost in his, Cinnabar attempted to meet his bright gaze squarely and was furious to find herself blushing. Filled with an odd kind of panic, for which she was entirely unable to account, all her usual conversational openings mysteriously evaporated, and she said the first thing that came into her head.

'You don't look a bit Japanese.'

A smile crinkled the smooth, bronzed texture of his face.

'And you don't look a bit like my idea of a photographer!'

In his turn, he was appraising her ... the slender, lissom body, the square face ... serious for the moment ... its honey-gold skin lightly freckled about the nose, her dark bronze hair a close, wavy cap about her well-shaped head. Finally he looked directly into the blue-grey eyes, valiantly endeavouring to meet his.

'And am I not your idea of a model?'

Magda, accustomed to holding all available male attention, inserted herself between them, smiling up into his face, her bright moist mouth a moue of entirely false self-deprecation.

Marlowe Hirakawa's lazy, intelligent eyes swept Magda from head to foot, his whole mouth twisting into an amused, appreciative smile.

'Miss Llewellyn,' he said gravely, 'you are *exactly* my idea of a model.'

Predictably, Magda preened, one thin hand reaching out in an insincere admonitory pat of his bare, muscular arm.

'Flatterer! I think I'm beginning to enjoy Japan,' she purred.

'Mr Hirakawa!' Cinnabar interrupted desperately. If they were ever to get down to business, she must break up this mutual admiration society. 'Could we possibly see our hotel accommodation? We've been travelling a long time and. . . .'

'Of course! How inconsiderate of me.' He opened the door to the outer office and immediately the bespectacled secretary was there, bowing, his narrow eyes lifted enquiringly to his employer's face. 'Be so good as to escort Miss Llewellyn and Miss Forester to their apartment.'

He turned to Magda.

'We have our own hotel immediately adjoining this complex. It seemed simpler to have you close at hand. I hope you will find everything to your satisfaction.'

'Oh, I'm sure we shall ... if *you've* arranged it.' Magda took the opportunity of this brief parting for another light caress of the strong arm. 'I'm so glad you won't be too far away, Mr Hirakawa. A girl likes to feel protected in a strange city.'

As Magda followed the secretary out into the corridor, Marlowe Hirakawa laid a detaining hand on Cinnabar's arm, the warmth of his long fingers producing an extraordinarily disturbing effect upon her nerves.

'Perhaps, when you've freshened up, you'd come back here,

Miss Forester? There are certain details of your visit to be discussed.'

His slow smile was packed with compelling male charm, which she found strangely irritating. It was the smile of a man, she felt sure, who was accustomed to women concurring with his every demand.

'I imagine you are the business woman of this outfit,' he continued, 'Miss Llewellyn being purely for decorative purposes?'

Which meant, Cinnabar thought crossly, as she hurried after Magda, that Marlowe Hirakawa did not find *her* in the least decorative. The knowledge was oddly depressing; after all, why should she care what this man thought of her; and she should not be surprised by it. She was quite accustomed to her apparent invisibility, so far as men were concerned, whenever Magda was around.

The rooms allocated to them, in the adjoining hotel, were spacious, and although the décor was attractively Oriental, the whole apartment was equipped with every imaginable modern convenience; telephone, radio, television, and an unusual refinement: each girl was provided with a brand new toothbrush and toothpaste.

The smiling, diminutive maid indicated bedside slippers, wrapped in a paper band to indicate that they were clean and unused. Dressing gowns too were provided for the use of each guest; and in her faultless but lisping English, the maid informed them that laundry and dry cleaning facilities were available in the hotel.

Cinnabar showered quickly and changed into a soft, swinging skirt and T-shirt in matching shades of cinnamon, substituting a pair of sling-back sandals for her suede loafers. Marlowe Hirakawa's remark about Magda's decorative appearance had annoyed her disproportionately and she felt an urge to demonstrate that she too could appear both poised and feminine, as well as efficient.

As she made her way back to his office, she mused on the enigma of Hirokawa-San, as his secretary had dubbed him. His name would seem to indicate Japanese nationality, and yet he was completely unlike any Oriental she had ever encountered, with his fine European facial structure and imposing size.

The secretary rose and bowed her to a seat.

'Hirokawa-San now engaged. You wait, please?'

Cinnabar nodded and relaxed in the chair indicated, hoping that she would not have to wait too long. Though they had eaten on the plane, she felt hungry and tired too, ready for an early night in what had looked to be an extremely comfortable bed.

'I won't have to wait long, will I?' she asked after a while.

The secretary looked up from his work, his bland smile again in evidence.

'Yes.'

'Oh!'

Cinnabar was rather taken aback by such frankness, and the more she considered it, the more annoyed she became. Why had Marlowe Hirakawa asked her to come back to his office, if he hadn't the time to see her? She cleared her throat and the secretary looked up, immediately attentive.

'Do you know if Mr Hirokawa will be much longer?'

'Oh yes.'

That decided it. Cinnabar rose and marched towards the outer door, her voice icy with the effort of keeping her temper on a tight rein.

'Perhaps you'd let me know when Mr Hirokawa is free, and I'll come back then.'

Swiftly the secretary interposed himself between Cinnabar and the door, his manner apologetic, his fixed smile belying the worried lines between his narrow eyes.

'Please, Forester-San, you wait?'

'I'm sorry,' Cinnabar said firmly, 'but you must realise I have no intention of sitting here indefinitely, twiddling my thumbs.'

'Yes.'

The little man looked even more worried.

Cinnabar was just wondering if she should physically remove him from her path, when the inner door opened and Marlowe Hirakawa emerged, preceded by the daintiest, prettiest creature she had ever seen . . . a young Japanese girl, about five foot tall, her tiny stature accentuated by the giant proportions of her companion. The girl's magnolia complexion was lit by a radiant smile and the expression on Marlowe Hirokawa's face, as he wished her 'sayonara,' was one of great affection.

Cinnabar reflected with grim satisfaction that at least

Madga would find herself with plenty of local competition, which might be salutary for her conceit if not for her temper. Most probably this stunning-looking man was drawn more to Oriental girls than to European good looks, living as he did in Japan.

'Come in, Miss Forester,' he invited.

'Oh, thank you very much!' she said with sarcastic emphasis, as she followed him into his office.

Since their last encounter, he had found time to change into immaculately tailored evening wear, which accentuated his good looks far more effectively than the casual attire of an hour earlier. His well defined eyebrows had shot up at her tone and he closed the door firmly.

'Something is not to your satisfaction?' he asked.

'Your secretary's manner, for one thing,' Cinnabar told him coldly, 'and your assumption that I'm prepared to wait around for you indefinitely.'

He ignored the latter part of her remark, a frown marring his forehead.

'Watawabe-San has been impolite?'

'Not impolite exactly,' she admitted. 'I would call it ... obstructive.'

She recounted her frustrating conversation with the secretary, and was surprised and resentful when the broad shoulders began to shake with silent laughter.

'I don't find it at all amusing,' she snapped. 'I'm tired and hungry, and then to be told that I must await your pleasure, no matter how long you choose to be ...'

'Wait, please!' It was a command, though uttered politely. 'I assure you, poor Watawabe meant no discourtesy. It was merely a misunderstanding.'

'I thought his English seemed quite competent,' Cinnabar said coldly, totally unconvinced by such a lame excuse.

'But perhaps your own understanding of the Oriental mind is at fault,' Marlowe Hirakawa suggested gently. 'You see, you asked him a negative question. "I won't have to wait much longer, will I?" To the logical mind of the Oriental, the answer is "yes, you won't have to wait long." Do you understand?'

'I'm beginning to,' Cinnabar said slowly.

'Then you added to poor Watawabe's problem by asking if he knew just how long I would be. To admit that he did not know would be to lose face. Therefore he replied once more in the affirmative.'

Despite her fatigue, Cinnabar's ready sense of humour came to her aid, her smile lighting the blue-grey eyes and giving an enchanting curve to her soft lips.

'I can foresee pitfalls ahead,' she remarked.

Marlowe Hirakawa nodded.

'Which is why we must consider very seriously your plans for the next few weeks. Unfortunately, it will not be possible for me to accompany you on every occasion ...'

'I never expected ... or wanted you to,' Cinnabar interrupted swiftly.

She couldn't think of a more disastrous eventuality. There would be no sense at all to be got out of Magda, with such an attractive man as a companion; and she had even greater reservations, now that she had met this man, about allowing him too much involvement in her itinerary. This was no smoothly courteous Oriental, to be politely dissuaded from interfering. She judged Marlowe Hirakawa as being a man difficult to deflect once his purpose was determined.

'Which is why,' he continued smoothly, as if there had been no interruption, 'I've arranged a part-time guide for you, for those occasions when I'm too engaged in business. You noticed the young lady who left my office just now?'

Cinnabar nodded. It had been impossible not to notice the graceful Japanese girl who, despite her Western dress, had emanated the timeless, fragile femininity of the Oriental woman.

'Her name is Michiko. You will find her a delightful person.'

He paused, his expression thoughtful, and Cinnabar wondered, with an odd sensation which she could not define, if he was reflecting on the charms of the delightful Michiko.

At least it was a relief to find that she would have a young, malleable girl to deal with, someone who was unlikely to have strong views on artistic composition.

'On the subject of names,' Marlowe continued. 'It would be as well for you to know a little of the Japanese custom of address. It's a little confusing to the Western mind, but the suffix "San" after a surname can indicate Mr, Mrs, or Miss. But there'll be no need for formality with Michiko. It will be quite in order for you to address her by her first name.

Similarly, I hope you and Miss Llewellyn will call me Marlowe?'

Cinnabar's mischievous smile glinted for an instant.

'Hirokawa-San *is* rather a mouthful, but I don't know that it would be correct to address you by your first name?'

'Most certainly,' he assured her. He hesitated, then: 'It will not have escaped your observant eye that I'm not Japanese. Therefore I think we may dispense with Japanese formality.'

He smiled his slow charming smile, and Cinnabar was annoyed to find herself reacting, albeit reluctantly, to the impact of that charm. Whatever was the matter with her? Even Gary did not have this strange effect upon her ... could not charm her out of ill-humour so effortlessly.

'But I believe you complained of being hungry?' Marlowe consulted his watch. 'I should be honoured if you would dine with me. We can continue our discussion over our meal.'

'And ... and Magda?' Cinnabar suggested diffidently, imagining the model's vituperative chagrin if she were not included in the invitation.

'Naturally Miss Llewellyn too,' he agreed. 'I'll send her a message, to meet us in the hotel foyer.'

Naturally Miss Llewellyn was invited, Cinnabar thought, embarrassed to think that he might have received the wrong impression, that she was angling for an intimate dinner à deux.

But she was aware too of a slight feeling of disappointment; though why on earth she should have supposed that Marlowe Hirakawa desired only her company, she could not imagine. A connoisseur of all that was beautiful, he would hardly look twice at pleasantly ordinary Cinnabar Forester, when he could feast those lazy, intelligent eyes on Magda's more sophisticated charms; and what did she care anyway? she asked herself sternly. She was not Magda, to wish for a monopoly of his attention; and besides, she had a boy-friend back home ... though sometimes, in view of their long and frequent separations, it was difficult to remember the fact.

Cinnabar could tell at once from Magda's petulant expression, hastily disguised, when she saw the young photographer's companion, that the model resented her exclusion from their brief conference.

As Marlowe Hirakawa ushered Cinnabar into the hotel foyer, it was impossible to overlook Magda, whose striking appearance was drawing curious glances from passers-by. To a casual observer, her pose might look ingenuously unstudied, naturally graceful, but Cinnabar, who knew the other girl of old, was not deceived.

In the centre of the spacious, well-lit entrance, a large cherry tree, in the full splendour of new blossom, towered almost to the ceiling, a magnificent feat of ingenuity on someone's part; and it was underneath this tree that Magda had arranged herself, her brittle-thin model's body draped becomingly in an evening dress of soft silk which echoed the pink of the delicate blossoms, her cloudy dark hair making a soft frame for the face which had set off countless numbers of Lamonde creations.

Cinnabar was immediately aware of the contrast between Magda's elegance and her own casual clothes. Crossly she thought that she could have worn something more formal, had she known they were to dine with Marlowe himself.

The model glided towards them, possessing herself of Marlowe Hirakawa's arm; something Cinnabar would never have presumed to do with a man she had only just met. The other girl made it quite apparent, by her manner and conversational monopoly of the big man, that she considered Cinnabar's presence an unwelcome encumbrance.

Like their suite, the dining room was a pleasing combination of West and East, the furnishings Western, the décor Oriental; while one end wall was entirely composed of glass, through which a floodlit waterfall could be seen, cascading from the rocks and greenery of a hillside garden, into a pebbly pool.

'Would you like Western food, or would you care to sample a traditional Japanese dish?' asked Marlowe, accepting the morocco-bound menu from a hovering waiter.

While Cinnabar hesitated, torn between inclination and her innate courtesy, Magda had no such scruples.

'I never eat foreign concoctions ... give me Western food every time,' she said decidedly. 'I'll have a salad.'

Her choice, Cinnabar knew, was dictated by her unwavering concern for her figure and complexion, which took priority over every other consideration.

'Miss Forester?'

'W—won't you call me Cinnabar?' she suggested hesitantly, 'if we're to call you Marlowe ...'

He inclined his dark head.

'Very well . . . Cinnabar. And now, what will you have to eat?'

'I think I'll have salad too,' she said diffidently. 'I'll eat Western, for tonight . . . but only because it might not be wise to try unfamiliar foods on top of a long journey. That's if . . . if *you* don't mind?'

'Why should I mind?' he said goodhumouredly. 'As I told you, strictly speaking, I'm not Japanese, so you're not offending my patriotic susceptibilities.'

'Then why do you have a Japanese name?' Magda asked bluntly.

Cinnabar had been longing to put the same question, but had refrained, intending to wait until she knew Marlowe Hirakawa a little better before putting such a personal question. But Magda, of course, had no such finesse. Whatever she wanted, she went directly for it.

Marlowe did not seem put out by Magda's frank curiosity.

'My great-grandfather, Minamoto Hirakawa, was Japanese,' he explained. 'He had two children . . . a son and a daughter. The daughter was my grandmother, Uneme. Uneme married Owen Williams and their son, Lawrence, was my father.'

'But that means your name should be Williams,' Magda pointed out triumphantly, smiling with pleasure at her own perspicacity.

Oh, full marks, Magda, Cinnabar thought. Surprising how vivacious and intelligent the model could appear when it suited her.

'That is correct,' Marlowe agreed. 'But my story is not quite finished. Ichiro Hirakawa, my grandmother's brother, had one son, Yuji. My Uncle Yuji's wife died in childbirth and as he was a comparatively old man by then, with no son to succeed him, he invited me to join him at Messrs Hirakawa . . . on the condition that I took the family surname.'

'And you didn't mind?' Cinnabar said wonderingly.

Marlowe shrugged those incredibly broad shoulders.

'It was a small sacrifice to make, to please my uncle; and since both my own parents were dead, there was no one to be offended when I dropped the name of Williams.'

Nor was it too much of a sacrifice to make, in order to become sole heir to a wealthy Japanese business man,

Cinnabar thought with unwonted cynicism, seeing the same thought reflected in Magda's acquisitive dark eyes. The same thought, but a different reaction. Cinnabar felt faintly disgusted at the thought of such self-interest. But if Marlowe had searched for a month to find words to secure Magda's interest, he could not have chosen better.

The model, at twenty-seven, was five years older than Cinnabar and had often expressed her intention, in Cinnabar's hearing, of marrying a rich man some day.

'After all,' Cinnabar had heard her say on one occasion, 'I suppose there'll come a time when I'll have to give up modelling.'

And Cinnabar guessed that there must be moments when Magda dreaded and feared the decline of her appearance, her stock in trade. Of late, Magda's almost frenetic pursuit of every man with whom she came into contact seemed to indicate that, for the model, time was running out; and indeed, if one looked closely, the first faint lines of hardness were already beginning to mar that flawless complexion.

'Have you always lived in Japan?' Magda persisted.

Cinnabar listened eagerly for his answer. Despite her embarrassment at Magda's frank curiosity, she found herself as eager as the model to learn more of Marlowe's background.

'No, from the age of ten, until I left university, I was educated in England, and it was then, when I returned to Japan to visit my uncle, that he asked me to join him . . . to learn the import and export trade, particularly that side of it which deals in objets d'art. Hence my dealings with your employer, Mr Lamonde.'

Apparently deciding that he had indulged their curiosity sufficiently, he began his meal. He was, Cinnabar noticed, eating Western food, though whether from courtesy to Magda and herself or from personal preference, she could not decide.

Over coffee he reverted to the subject of their itinerary.

'I see that Mr Lamonde suggests that the first series of photographs be taken in Tokyo itself?'

Cinnabar nodded.

'Mr Lamonde said you would be able to provide me with darkroom facilities, so that the developed photographs can be sent off to him in batches, as they're completed.'

'So you develop your own photographs too?' His tone was admiring.

'Such a tedious, uninspiring occupation, I always think,' Magda drawled.

She was becoming restless; the mechanics of their assignment, Cinnabar's talents, were of no interest to her; all that concerned her was the clothes that she would be wearing each day, and sensing her discontent, Marlowe turned his attention to the model, his consummate tact drawing more sparkling conversation from her in five minutes than Cinnabar had elicited in twenty-four hours.

A silent witness to Magda's attempts to charm Marlowe Hirakawa, Cinnabar found herself with plenty of opportunity to assess the man with whom they would both be so closely associated in the weeks to come. Somewhat unwillingly, she found herself drawn by his powerful, compelling personality, and, not fooled by his slow charm, she sensed beneath the lazy insouciance, a tremendous vitality ... an inner energy. She had to admit that he was the most attractive man she had ever met, and the admission worried her.

It wasn't surprising, she thought, that Magda, with her predeliction for male company, had capitulated to his undoubted sexual charisma. What did surprise her was the knowledge that he could well be a danger to her own peace of mind. The prospect of seeing him almost daily for four months filled her with a kind of excited dread, mingled with a pang of guilt at this admitted disloyalty to the absent Gary.

Cinnabar often reflected a trifle wistfully that she had never been madly in love ... at least, not in love as contemporary romances described it. There had been transitory friendships with men, affectionate while they lasted, but never the earth-shattering revelation of mutual passion and desire which she had gathered from her reading that real love should be. Yet about that she had reservations, for, she told herself, she would not want a solely physical relationship; for her, love would have to be prompted by intellect and reason also ... based on something far deeper than superficial sensuality, and which could only be stirred by a very special kind of man.

She had assumed, since she was quite willing to marry him some day, that Gary Reid was that man ... that physical attraction would follow automatically upon liking and respect. Now she felt uncertain, and being a normally level-headed girl, she disliked this uncertainty where her deepest feelings were concerned.

It was an effort to change the direction of her thoughts, to remind herself that she was here to work, that her association with Marlowe Hirakawa would be an impersonal, businesslike one, on his part as well as on hers.

She must not allow the effect of his magnetism to sway her brain, to dispel the common sense on which she prided herself.

Besides ... with wry humour she applied the final damper to wild imaginings ... she was in no danger of having to resist temptation. She had only to watch Marlowe's all too evident absorption in Magda to realise that he would never give *her* more than a cursory glance. Judging by his interest in the model and having met the delicately lovely Michiko, it was pretty clear to Cinnabar that it took a very rare type of woman to measure up to his standards of beauty.

It was the sudden realisation that Marlowe's hazel eyes were meeting hers questioningly, that he had become aware of her intent stare, which finally recalled Cinnabar's dreaming thoughts.

'I'm afraid we've been neglecting Miss Forester.'

Magda's sensual lips curled slightly.

'Yes, poor Cinnabar must be very bored. She's not the least bit interested in clothes ... only in taking pictures of them.'

Her dark eyes swept scornfully over Cinnabar's simple skirt and top, giving point to her comment.

Cinnabar could resent the spitefulness of the remark, but in all honesty, she could not deny its truth. Hitherto, she had tended to dress for comfort rather than fashion and she had certainly never employed the tactics she had observed in other women ... Magda in particular ... of wearing clothes which revealed rather than concealed her femininity.

Marlowe made no comment. Cinnabar did not really expect him to, but a small compliment, to take the edge off Magda's remark, a word or two to reassure her that she did not look a complete mess would have been nice, she thought wistfully.

Instead he rose, suggesting that they take their coffee into the lounge, an apartment adjacent to the dining room, which also had a magnificent view of the floodlit gardens.

When Cinnabar commented enthusiastically, he nodded.

'Japanese gardens are unique. I would suggest that their

almost stark simplicity would make a very good foil for some of the clothes you want to photograph.'

Cinnabar stiffened. So, insidiously, it was beginning, the suggestion of interference.

'I'm afraid that's something only I can decide,' she told him, her tone repressively brusque. 'Compositions as seen through the camera lens are very much a personal thing to the photographer.'

'But surely,' he sounded puzzled, 'you want to set off Mr Lamonde's designs to the best possible advantage.'

'Naturally!' Her full lips tightened ominously, 'and I have my own ideas about how to do so. I might add that I've never received any complaint from him about the quality of my work.'

'Cinnabar is so self-confident,' Magda drawled. 'Really, it almost amounts to obstinacy. Such an unfeminine trait, if I may · say so, dear.' She looked meltingly at Marlowe. 'Personally, I always like to rely upon a man's advice . . . much wiser, and so much safer.'

The effort of keeping her temper with the two of them was becoming a strain, and Cinnabar rose, waving aside the waiter's offer of a second cup of coffee.

'I'm tired,' she said abruptly. 'I think I'll go up now.'

Magda rose languidly.

'Me too. After all, I must get my beauty sleep, mustn't I?'

She's hoping Marlowe will say she doesn't need it, Cinnabar thought, and was ashamed of the gleeful pleasure she felt when he did not make the anticipated response.

Instead he turned to Cinnabar.

'I'm sorry to hear you're so tired. I was hoping you could give me a few more minutes of your time. We haven't really finished discussing the arrangements for your tour.'

'I don't see the necessity for any further discussion,' Cinnabar told him, her usually generous mouth set mulishly.

She feared that any further conversation on the subject might entail more ideas from him, which she would be forced to discount.

'Oh, I'm sure we can spare Marlowe a little longer,' Magda began, about to reseat herself.

But to Cinnabar's surprise and reluctant admiration, Marlowe dealt smoothly with Magda's ploy; for it was all too obvious to Cinnabar that the model did not want her to be left alone with Marlowe a second time.

'As you so rightly said, Miss Llewellyn ... Magda ...' he corrected himself, 'it's essential that you have adequate rest. After all, it's you who'll have the strain of standing before a camera all day. Cinnabar has no such problem.'

What about standing behind it, in the heat of the day, trying to get Magda to fall in with my ideas? Cinnabar thought resentfully.

'In other words, Magda,' she said lightly, with no attempt to hide the chagrin she felt, 'it doesn't matter to Mr Hirakawa if *I* don't get any beauty sleep.'

But with a tact Cinnabar had to applaud, despite her reluctance to concede anything to Marlowe Hirakawa, he coaxed Magda towards the lift, and the model was actually smiling as the doors hid her from view.

'Now!' Marlowe turned towards Cinnabar and there was something in his manner that made her flinch. 'Perhaps *we* can have a little serious conversation.'

'I told you, I don't really see any necessity for further discussion tonight.'

'No? But I do. You see, Miss Cinnabar Forester, I think you owe me some explanations.'

CHAPTER TWO

CINNABAR stared at him, genuinely bewildered. His tone was so hostile.

Marlowe looked around the rapidly filling lounge.

'We can't talk here. Come with me.' One hand under her elbow, he began propelling her towards the door.

'Where are we going?' In vain, she tried to free her arm from his steely grip.

'To my apartment.'

'We most certainly are not!'

Cinnabar attempted to stop in the middle of the hotel foyer, to make her protest. No way was she going to be alone with this disturbing man. Besides, what made him think he had the right to order her about in this way?

But Marlowe had not slackened his grip, nor slowed his pace, and she was forced to keep moving or fall.

'For heaven's sake! What's this all about?' she demanded irritably, as they entered the Hirokawa building, the night security man bowing to Marlowe as they crossed to the lifts.

'That's what I'm expecting you to tell me,' he said grimly, as the lift moved smoothly upwards.

Marlowe's private apartment was on the floor directly above the offices, and as he unlocked the outer door, Cinnabar made one last attempt at remonstration.

'I don't see why we have to come up here to talk.'

'Don't you?'

His tone was still terse, as he thrust her into the small entrance hall and from there into a luxuriously appointed living room.

'Sit down!' he said curtly, gesturing towards a leather-upholstered armchair.

'I prefer to stand, since I won't be staying long.' Cinnabar tilted her chin defiantly.

'Suit yourself! Drink?' He moved towards a well supplied cocktail cabinet.

'No, thank you. I don't drink.'

'Coffee, then?'

'Nothing for me. I told you, I'm not stopping. Could we just get to the point of this . . . this interview . . . so that I can leave. At the risk of sounding repetitious, I *am* extremely tired.'

'You'll excuse me, while I make coffee for myself.'

It was an order, not an apology, and as Marlowe moved into the kitchenette, Cinnabar glared at his broad back view. She felt tempted to walk out of the flat and return to the hotel; but she had an idea she wouldn't be allowed to reach the lift, much less her room.

Forgetting her refusal, she sank wearily into the chair Marlowe had indicated and studied her surroundings.

The living room was a tasteful blend of beiges, russets, fawns and golds. Full-length russet curtains, as yet undrawn, framed a view of the night sky and the room with its wall-to-wall beige wool carpet was uncluttered and spacious; the only furniture consisting of two armchairs and a three-seater settee in cream leather. There was no overhead lighting; instead, two standard lamps of modern design cast a subdued aura around the seating area.

Cinnabar wondered that a connoisseur of objets d'art should have so little ornamentation in his apartment, but the only non-functional item in the room was a reproduction of a Hokusai painting, representing a distant view of Mount Fuji, threatened by the curve of a gigantic wave, as it fell in foam, shaped like dragons' claws.

It seemed that Marlowe Hirakawa, whatever his business interests, was a man with little use in his personal life for non-essentials.

With a little frisson of fear, she wondered what he wanted of her. Explanations, he had said, but explanations of what? And why the sudden change in his manner from suave courtesy to almost angry hostility?

She was not left in doubt for very long.

Surprisingly swiftly, Marlowe reappeared, carrying a tray with a coffee pot, cream jug and two cups, which he set down on a low table at Cinnabar's side.

'I said nothing for me,' she reminded him sharply.

He shrugged. 'I thought you might have changed your mind.'

'I never change my mind.'

He raised an ironic brow. 'Never? Not about anything?'

'Anything . . . or anyone,' she added rashly.

'Ah yes . . .' His brow darkened ominously. 'Now we come to it.'

He was still standing by her chair and she had to tilt her head at an almost impossible angle, in order to meet his eyes.

'For goodness' sake, sit down,' she said irritably. 'You're giving me a crick in my neck.'

His lowering expression indicated a strong desire to inflict pain on her in a far more vulnerable place, but he moved away, settling his great length on to the settee.

'Tell me, Miss Forester, why do you find it necessary to be so rude . . . and obstructive?'

She arched delicate brows at him. 'I wasn't aware that I was being either.'

'Come off it!' He was scornful. 'You've been edgy and hostile from the first moment we met . . . and every suggestion I've made, regarding your work here, you've blocked. Why?'

'Because I don't *want* any interference with my work.' She blurted out the words. 'I have my own ideas . . . plenty of them. I'm a good photographer, and . . .'

'And you're a stranger here.' He interrupted her impassioned flow of words. 'A stranger *and a woman*.' He stressed the final words and by so doing, inflamed Cinnabar still more.

'A woman! The way men say that! It . . . it makes me furious. I'm as good a photographer as any man . . . even Gary has to admit . . .'

'Gary?'

'My fiancé.'

What on earth had compelled her to utter such a falsehood? she wondered, amazed at her own almost unthinking claim. It was almost, she thought, as though she felt the need of the protection such a status conferred . . . but that was ridiculous, wasn't it?

'So there is a fiancé?' Marlowe said thoughtfully. 'I don't see any ring on your finger. And he's obviously not very concerned for your welfare if he lets you go racketing around the world on your own.'

'We haven't had time to choose a ring yet,' Cinnabar improvised defensively. 'Just recently our assignments have overlapped, and anyway, Gary accepts that I'm perfectly capable of looking after myself . . . he knows I wouldn't *allow* him to interfere in my way of life.'

'Not a happy basis for marriage, I should have thought,' Marlowe murmured.

'That's the sort of remark I'd expect from a man like you.'

'A man like me?' There was a warning in his tone, in the restless shifting of his large frame on the settee. 'And just what sort of man *am* I?'

'A chauvinistic pig!' she retorted. 'And to make it worse, you're probably steeped in Oriental tradition, where the little woman is seen but not heard and defers to her husband in everything.'

There was such a long silence that she thought he was not going to reply to her taunt.

'You are right in your assumption that I dislike unfeminine women.'

She had to restrain herself from flinching visibly. His considered, reflective words were more hurtful than if he had ranted at her. Daily comparing herself unfavourably with other girls, especially models like Magda, Cinnabar was unduly sensitive to such a remark.

'Plenty of men have found me feminine enough.'

Her hurt sounded in her voice and he gave a short, sarcastic laugh.

'You can't have it both ways, Cinnabar. You can't protest your rights to complete equality with men and still expect the consideration and courtesy extended to those women who don't deny their sex, their . . .'

'I *don't* deny my sex!' she contradicted him, 'but nor do I flaunt it. I suppose your idea of a woman is all exposed flesh and fluttering eyelashes, like . . . like Magda.'

It did not strike her as inconsistent that one moment she had accused him of having Oriental standards and the next of a standard more acceptable to Western men.

Marlowe was nodding, as though she had just confirmed something.

'I had an idea, somehow, that you were jealous of your friend.'

'Friend! Friend?' Cinnabar heard her own hysteria and deliberately lowered her voice. 'She's no friend of mine. I can't stand her—and believe me, the feeling is mutual.'

'I'm not surprised,' Marlowe commented drily, 'if you show your hostility as openly as you've done to me.'

Cinnabar opened her mouth, then shut it again. What was the use? He wouldn't understand.

'In any case,' Marlowe continued, 'we seem to have wandered from the point. I can see that you might possibly dislike Miss Llewellyn . . . and your motives are obvious; women are often jealous of each other. But I fail to appreciate your reasons for disliking me, on so short an acquaintance.'

'Will you get it into your head,' Cinnabar said savagely, 'I am *not* jealous of Magda. I merely dislike her.' Her tone became sarcastic. 'I believe that *men* do *occasionally* dislike each other . . . and that you don't consider that a purely feminine failing? As to disliking *you* . . .' She paused.

'Yes?'

'It . . . it's not dislike exactly. I . . .'

How true, she thought. It was partly the fact that she *could* like this man rather too much which made it necessary for her to keep up her guard, even to the point of appearing hostile . . . that and the fact that her professional pride forbade deferrring to his advice.

'Well?'

He was certainly persistent. Why should it matter to him whether she liked him or not . . . but he obviously didn't intend to let the matter rest, until he had the whole story.

'All right, I'll tell you. Something Mr Lamonde said gave me the impression that you might try to . . . to . . . well, run this whole operation, and I meant what I said. I'm used to choosing my own settings, composing my own photographs, and . . . and there is one other thing . . .'

His face was expressionless.

'Please don't spare me any of the details.'

Cinnabar drew a deep breath. All right, then, he'd asked for it. He'd probably think she was every kind of bitch, but . . .

'I won't get any sense or any work out of Magda, with you tagging on. You must have seen for yourself how she reacts to a man's presence.'

She leant back in her chair, both physically and mentally exhausted. There, she'd told him everything . . . well, almost everything. Let him make what he liked of it. She was just too tired to care any more.

After some moments had passed without a sound from Marlowe, she opened her eyes, surprised to see him pacing the room, his movements surprisingly silent for so large a man. His return journey brought him to her chair, where he stood, looking down at her, his hazel eyes unfathomable.

'I thought I told you before . . . don't tower over me like that!'
She was nervous, but in no mood to conciliate him.

'And don't you tell me what I can or can't do in my own apartment,' he returned.

'It's your own fault,' Cinnabar told him, with a faint resurgence of spirit. 'You shouldn't have forced me to come here.'

'It seems to me that there are a lot of things I shouldn't have done . . . was a fool to do.' His controlled voice did not quite disguise the banked fires of anger. 'Things which, in your opinion, I suppose, come under the heading of interference. It seems I should not have offered you comfortable accommodation, arranged your itinerary, but above all, offered you my protection in a large, busy city, which is not without its dangers to two women alone.'

'What city is?'

She shrugged, as though uncaring. But his words had made her acutely conscious of base ingratitude. Belatedly, she decided to make amends.

'Mr Hirokawa . . . believe me, I'm *not* ungrateful for any of the things you mention. I'm sure you meant well. It . . . it's just that . . . that I . . .'

'That you're a stubborn, overly self-confident little hothead?'

The words were insulting, but the tone was not, and his hazel eyes were laughing at her again . . . a marked improvement on their earlier cold implacability.

She breathed an imperceptible sigh of relief. He was prepared to accept her token apology and, always honest with herself at least, she knew his description of her was an apt one. A faint smile curled the corners of her own generous mouth and she was lost as an irrepressible giggle escaped her.

'At least you have a redeeming sense of humour,' Marlowe commented.

'Believe me,' she said drily, 'I need it, in this job . . . especially around the Magdas of this world.'

'Ah, yes.' The frown had returned. 'You seem to have a considerable hang-up where your friend Magda is concerned . . . though I can't think why.'

'Can't you?' Cinnabar's tone was ironic. 'It seemed to me that you gave her a pretty thorough appraisal. Don't tell me you were completely unaware of her "feminine attributes".'

'You're a girl of very strange contradictions, Cinnabar

Forester,' Marlowe said slowly. He perched on the arm of her chair, his thigh brushing against her arm, causing an involuntary recoil on her part, which did not escape his notice. 'Yes,' he murmured, 'very strange indeed.'

'I don't know what you're talking about,' said Cinnabar. His nearness made her feel oddly tense and restless, somehow threatened, and she made a move to stand up. 'You've heard all you wanted to hear, so . . .'

A strong hand restrained her.

'Maybe I have and maybe I haven't, but *you* certainly haven't heard everything *I* have to say.'

'Look!' Cinnabar was rapidly becoming exasperated. 'I've told you I'm sorry if I sounded rude, but I've explained that . . . and that I'm *not* ungrateful, but . . .'

'Forget that . . . forget the accommodation, your precious itinerary. I don't intend to make another suggestion in that direction, now that I know the response I'm likely to receive. But there *is* something else I'd like to suggest.'

She looked at him, only mildly curious, only aware of an intense longing for sleep, so that it was a shock when he suddenly yanked her out of the chair, sliding easily from the arm into the place she had occupied and deftly re-settling her on his knee.

'Wh—what . . . what the hell do you think you're doing? How dare you? Let go of me!'

Angrily she wrestled with him, trying to loosen his hold upon her, to escape the disturbing proximity he was forcing upon her. Clenched fists pounding his shoulders and chest, she repeated her protest.

'Take your hands off me . . . you . . . you've no right . . . let me go!'

He ignored her words, her struggles, easily holding her captive, with one large hand, while the other imprisoned her stubborn little chin.

'I suggest that you stop looking upon yourself as some kind of second-class woman.'

'A . . . a what?'

In her surprise at his words, Cinnabar forgot to struggle and as a result found herself being held very firmly against Marlowe's broad chest, her breathing apparently quite suspended, judging by the extreme dizziness she was experiencing.

'A second-class woman,' he repeated. 'You know, despite your claim to be engaged, I doubt very much that you've ever really been in love ... mainly because you have absolutely no self-confidence in your own powers of attraction, exhibited by women who love and know themselves to be loved. Hence this need to be the aggressive career girl ... plus your attempts to denigrate the very lovely Miss Llewellyn.'

Blue-grey eyes glared into hazel ones, so close ... dangerously close, as she strove to repudiate his suggestion.

'I'm very much in love with my fiancé ... and I may be aggressive, but only with men of your type ... and I *do* have self-confidence in myself ... in *every* way.' It wasn't true, but she wasn't about to admit it to him. 'Now will you please let go of me. I don't need your comments or advice ... and as I *am* engaged to be married, I certainly don't have to prove my powers of attraction to anyone ... and certainly not to you!'

'Oh, you're right there ... so very right.'

There was a subtle menace in the inflection of his voice, and some sixth sense warned her of his intentions, seconds before his mouth took hers in a kiss of frightening intensity, making her blood pulse urgently, even while she fought him, her fists once more pounding his shoulders, attempting to thrust him away, vainly attempting to kick his shins.

But he continued his relentless onslaught, until slowly her struggling stilled and she lay quiescent, unresisting in his arms, stunned and bewildered by the totally inexplicable effect he was having on her.

Once he had overcome her resistance, his kissing gentled, became teasing, exciting; his hands, released from the necessity of holding her captive, began to wander restlessly, heightening her palpitating awareness of him, and, her mental faculties drugged by the sensations he was arousing in her, she gave way to a sudden frenzy of response, her lips softening in welcome to his exploration, running her fingers through the crisp dark brown hair, exploring the muscularity of his neck, running a caressing finger around the inner rim of his ear, feeling him shudder responsively.

His mouth abandoned hers to run down the taut column of her throat, burying his lips in the gentle hollows at its base.

Cinnabar pressed against him, lost to all thoughts of past and future, only the present moment having any meaning ...

any reality. Only as his hand began to seek the gap between her T-shirt and skirt did a danger signal sound in her brain, recalling her bemused senses. She pulled away.

'Please . . . no, that . . . that's enough. Let me go!'

He regarded her flushed face, the blue-grey eyes still misty with arousal, then moved abruptly, depositing her on her feet.

'Yes,' he said curtly, 'I think perhaps you're right. That *is* enough. Enough to prove to me . . .'

Irritatingly, he stopped, leaving her wondering just what he felt he had proved. Mingled pride and a searing shame at her own unaccountable behaviour prevented her from enquiring . . . the answer might be unbearably insulting.

'The coffee's cold,' Marlowe announced. 'I'll make some more.'

'Please, not for me. I . . . I'd rather go . . .' she began.

But he was already out of sight, moving swiftly for such a large man, and looking in dismay at her wristwatch, Cinnabar felt reluctant to make her own way back to the hotel . . . even though it was only next door. Despite her protestations of self-confidence, even she felt a little nervous about emerging into the streets of Tokyo at two a.m.

Sighing, she sat down on the settee, reluctant to return to the chair still warm with the impress of Marlowe's body. Her thoughts inward turned, she could not deny the overpowering effect of his masculinity upon her, and shame once more engulfed her, as she remembered how easily he had mastered her, overcome her resistance, even succeeding in inducing a response.

What on earth would Gary think if he could see her now, alone in the small hours of the morning, in the apartment of a man whom she had only met for the first time today . . . and who had just been making love to her in a very comprehensive and disturbing fashion.

In an excess of guilt she closed her eyes, trying to visualise Gary's face . . thin, fresh-complexioned, pale blue eyes, sandy-blond hair. But it was no use. Time and again another face superimposed itself . . . square of feature and of jaw, dark-haired, hazel-eyed . . .

Cinnabar woke with a start. Surely she had not slept for long? But the early morning light, shafting in through the still open curtains, and a glance at her watch, confirmed her worst fears.

Moreover, she was stretched full length on the settee, a cushion beneath her head, a light blanket covering her; and she blushed to think whose hands must have performed these offices for her, the intent eyes that must have studied her sleeping countenance.

'My coffee seems destined to be wasted.' The sound of an amused voice brought her head up, bronze curls dishevelled, face rosy with sleep. 'Perhaps we could actually drink *this* brew, before anything else intervenes?'

She struggled into an upright position, noticing for the first time the tray he carried . . . noticing something else . . .

Obviously Marlowe Hirakawa had not been long awake himself . . . just long enough to shower and make coffee. For his dark hair was still damp and there was still a slight sheen to the muscular legs, revealed by the almost indecently brief towelling robe which was all he appeared to be wearing.

Cinnabar felt herself colouring and hastily averted her eyes from the disturbing sight.

'No . . . no, thank you. I must get over to the hotel. Magda will be wondering what on earth's become of me.'

'And hazarding a pretty shrewd guess, I shouldn't wonder.'

Unmoved by her protest, he was pouring the coffee as he spoke. He held out a cup towards her and with a sigh of resignation, she accepted it, taking the utmost care to avoid contact with his fingers.

The coffee tasted unexpectedly good and almost she relaxed . . . almost, because Marlow's next words reminded her of an unpleasant hurdle yet to be faced.

'How do you think Magda will react when she learns you spent the night with me?' He sounded lazily curious.

'Mad as a hatter and green with envy,' was her unthinking response, then: 'Oh, but I haven't . . . I mean . . . I didn't . . . not in that way . . .'

'But Magda won't know that.' His hazel eyes were teasing her.

'I shall tell her . . . you can tell her . . .'

He shook his dark head, laughing openly at her now.

'She won't believe you . . . and I shan't be so ungallant as to deny it.'

Cinnabar crashed her cup down on to the tray, with scant regard for its fragility.

'You're the most horrible, unscrupulous man I've ever met!

Is this your way of getting your own back because I won't let you interfere in my work? Are you deliberately setting out to embarrass me, or . . .' her eyes narrowed, 'or is this some subtle form of blackmail? Because if you think that after this I'll have to let you order me about, you couldn't be more mistaken!'

His mouth tightened, but he maintained his air of amusement.

'You really *are* a child, aren't you, and with an ungovernable temper to match . . . or is that the hair?'

He moved in on her, one hand raised to touch the bronze curls that feathered about her head.

'Cinnabar . . . that means "red", doesn't it? A very apt name. A lucky choice?'

'I was born with a lot of hair . . . red hair,' Cinnabar said.

She stood mesmerised, wanting, yet unable to move away from that hypnotic caress upon her hair.

'It's like a chrysanthemum,' he said, winding a strand around his forefinger, 'an exotic, curling bronze chrysanthemum.'

As she stood transfixed, eyes wide, gazing up at him, his mood seemed to change abruptly and he moved away from her, towards a door, which she assumed must lead to his bedroom.

'You'd better get back to your suite, freshen up and have a breakfast. We've a long day ahead of us.'

'We?' she queried suspiciously.

'Yes. Oh, didn't I tell you? Michiko doesn't work on a Saturday. She goes home at weekends. So I thought I'd give myself the pleasure of escorting you and Miss Llewellyn around Tokyo.'

'And where the hell do you think *you've* been all night?'

Standing in the middle of their shared sitting room, hands on slim hips, Magda regarded Cinnabar accusingly.

'As if I couldn't guess!'

'No need to ask, then, is there?' Cinnabar said lightly, making her way towards her own bedroom.

Swift as a snake, Magda intercepted her.

'Oh no, you don't! Not until you've told me exactly how you inveigled your way into Marlowe Hirakawa's bed. You of all people!'

Her appraisal of Cinnabar's rumpled appearance was scornful.

'Magda, you have a mind like a sewer,' Cinnabar said calmly, 'and you attribute actions to other people, just because you'd act that way yourself. Now, if you don't mind, I'd like to shower and change.'

'Oh, but I do mind.' Magda barred Cinnabar's attempted evasion of her. 'This conversation isn't over. You know darned well I've taken a fancy to Marlowe. He's the sort of man I've been looking for all my life. He's got everything a girl could ask for.'

'Including an expectation of his uncle's fortune?' Cinnabar asked cynically.

'So what?' Magda drawled. 'I've never made any secret of the fact that I intend to marry a rich man.' Her dark eyes became vicious. 'But one word from you to Marlowe about my plans . . . any attempt to queer my pitch, and I'll see that Gary gets to hear about last night's little escapade!'

'There *was* no escapade,' Cinnabar said wearily. 'I just fell asleep on his settee, and . . .'

'Pull the other one,' Magda scoffed. 'I'm no naïve girl to be put off like that. What were you doing in his apartment in the first place?'

It was obviously useless to attempt to tell Magda the truth. She judged everyone by her own standards, and given the opportunity, Cinnabar knew that the model would have had no qualms about sharing Marlowe Hirakawa's bed. But in any case, Cinnabar did not feel inclined to placate the older girl.

As tall as the model, Cinnabar, though slender, was more robust. She thrust Magda away from the bedroom door.

'What I do is my business. I'm not answerable to you.'

She slammed the door in the other girl's face. But the door could not shut out Magda's shrill threat.

'Maybe not . . . but it *is* Gary Reid's business, and I'll make it mine to see that he hears about it, if you don't lay off Marlowe Hirakawa!'

If the closed door could not keep out Magda's voice, neither could it keep unpleasant thoughts at bay.

Cinnabar sank down on the side of her bed . . . a bed which so obviously had not been used. What a fool she'd been to allow herself to fall asleep in Marlowe's apartment ... and what a fool to behave as she had. What on earth had possessed her, to let him kiss and caress her like that ... but even worse, to return his embraces with such fervour. Believing her to be engaged, he must think her the cheapest type of girl ... added to which he already thought her a shrew and a bitch, for her outspoken condemnation of Magda.

Oh, damn Magda, who now had a very handy weapon to use against her; and she had to spend a whole day in the model's company ... and even worse, in Marlowe's ... trying to get some decent shots of Vyvyan's day-wear.

Well, sitting here brooding wouldn't get her very far, she decided. Best to get the day started; the sooner it was begun, the sooner it would be over, and at least if she kept busy it would take her mind off her own foolishness and Magda's threats. She could only hope that by the time they returned to England, the model would have forgotten her fit of pique.

Quickly she showered and flipped through her wardrobe for something to wear. Though it scarcely mattered what she wore, she thought. All eyes would be on Magda, not on the girl *behind* the camera.

Finally she selected T-shirt and slacks in toning shades of blue, as being most suitable for a working day, the contrasting colour pointing up the vivid tones of her hair. The minimum of make-up and a brush dragged through her rebellious curls and she was ready. Now all that remained was to sort out the half dozen or so outfits that they must take with them on the day's photographic session.

Fortunately the Oriental collection was made up in the lightest of fabrics, for Cinnabar knew she would have to carry the specially constructed hanging case, as well as her own equipment. Magda always resolutely refused to carry anything.

'I'm a top model, not a beast of burden,' was her standard excuse.

Though what that makes me ... Cinnabar mused bitterly.

Magda's expression was still brooding, as Cinnabar rejoined her in their shared sitting room, and the younger girl feared that she had not heard the last of the model's petulant abuse.

They did not speak as the lift descended and Cinnabar actually found herself contemplating Marlowe's company with relief. At least Magda would be forced to behave in a reasonably civilised manner; she wouldn't want to show herself up in front of the man on whom she had fixed her predatory sights.

Marlowe was waiting for them in the foyer, his manner as formal and matter-of-fact as if the incidents of the previous night had not occurred, and Cinnabar relaxed slightly, even able to raise a smile at Magda's disgusted expression, when the model found she was expected to walk to the first site.

'Only as far as the Imperial Palace grounds,' Marlowe told her soothingly.

He looked at Cinnabar, weighed down with photographic equipment and the light but awkward portable wardrobe.

'Here, let me carry something.'

Without waiting for her assent, he took possession of the heavy camera, leaving her with only the bag containing spare film and flash-bulbs.

'I imagine this is Magda's?' He passed the weatherproof container to the speechless model, then strode out into the street, motioning to them to follow.

Cinnabar was forced to lag behind for a few seconds, in order to regain her gravity. The sight of Magda, dealt two crushing blows to her dignity in as many minutes, was almost too much for her composure and she knew the model would never forgive any signs of her amusement.

'Of course, you mustn't look upon Tokyo as being typical of the whole of Japan,' Marlowe told them, as they struggled to keep up with his brisk pace and long strides. 'It's become very Westernised. To see the true spirit of Japan one must go farther afield. Though you *will* find many ancient customs preserved, even in Tokyo.'

Used to more cosmopolitan cities, Cinnabar found it strange that almost everyone around her should have black hair, their eyes brown or even darker. Skin colours ranged from ivory to brown amongst the men, while women and children had delicate pink in their cheeks.

It was, as Marlowe had promised, only a short walk to the Imperial Palace, and when they reached the parklike grounds, set as a huge, irregular oval in the heart of the city, it seemed to Cinnabar like a peaceful oasis, set apart from the jangle of urban life. The park, with roads and pathways curving through its lawns, was dominated by the palace, whose walls were made of enormous blocks of stone ... all of different shapes, yet used so superbly that they rose smoothly without flaw, curving upwards.

Moat-encircled, the massive stone ramparts towered above them, crowned with gnarled and twisted pine trees, and a short walk across an area of crunching gravel brought them to the Nijubashi, the arched, double, ceremonial bridge, spanning the deep moat, on which drifted aristocratically gliding swans and the more briskly moving ducks.

'The pines were planted as young trees,' Marlowe explained, observing Cinnabar's fascinated gaze, 'and twisted into position by a system of wires and stakes, while the branches were being trained. Unfortunately,' he added, 'we can't go inside the Palace itself, but I imagine you can find something here to photograph?'

Cinnabar nodded, already engrossed in light calculations, angles and colour filters.

'Put on the peacock blue with the sprays of cherry blossom,' she told Magda abstractedly, as she peered through the view-finder at the bridge, visualising the fragile model draped against its solidity.

A sudden audible breath from Marlowe drew Cinnabar's attention and she looked around to discover the cause of his exclamation.

Magda, accustomed to posing when and where it was demanded of her, was equally uninhibited about the lack of changing facilities. Without turning a hair, she had discarded the button-through summer dress in which she had started out and stood revealed now in the briefest of undies, unconcernedly searching in the case for the selected garment.

A swift glance at Marlowe's face told Cinnabar that he was poised between fascination and disapproval, and she waited to see which would take precedence. However, after one riveted moment, he turned aside, with a would-be casual air, and as Magda was now dressed, Cinnabar became involved once more in her work.

There was one thing in Magda's favour, Cinnabar thought ... although she could be awkward when it suited her, and was easily distracted by a man's presence ... when she *did* choose to work, she showed her professionalism and adopted the various stances required of her with very little direction from Cinnabar, so that the necessary photographs could be very quickly taken.

'Now against that pine tree ... over there ... put the apple green on for this one,' Cinnabar directed.

Marlowe, she mused wryly, must be getting used to the uninhibited company in which he found himself, or he was beginning to enjoy the sight of Magda's scantily clad body ... for he did not look away this time.

Against her will, Cinnabar had to admit that Magda made an appealing subject; this time entwined around the gnarled trunk of the pine, her slender arms and hands apparently engaged in caressing its aged bark. In the delicate green silk, she looked like a wood nymph and at this distance, Cinnabar knew, the lines of hardness in the lovely face would be softened and erased.

The young photographer could not help being acutely aware of Marlowe Hirakawa's keen hazel eyes, watching her every movement, appraising her professional handling of the camera, as she took shot after shot, noting her instinctive knowledge, which even surprised her sometimes, of the way in which a dress would show to its best advantage.

As she completed her studies of the green silk and told Magda to take a break, she expected Marlowe to join the model, a move which Magda's eloquent dark eyes all too openly invited. Instead he lingered restively at Cinnabar's side.

'Do you intend to photograph all of today's designs here?'

'No.'

A line of concentration puckered Cinnabar's smooth brow as she carefully packed the camera into its carrying case, trying to make this task a block to her reaction to the tall figure standing so near to her. After last night, she was not going to allow her normally cool head to be swayed by his physical attractions.

'I'd really like to find a temple of some sort for the next item,' she told him. 'It was Vyvyan's suggestion, and although he leaves me a pretty free hand, I think it's a good idea.'

'No problem!' Marlowe told her. 'There's a place I think you'll both rather enjoy, on the other side of the city ... in the Asakusa district. It will mean taking a taxi, though ... for Magda's sake.'

Cinnabar looked at him sharply, to see if he was joking, but he seemed to be perfectly straight-faced. Prepared to share a goodnatured chuckle with him over Magda's distaste for walking, she found herself instead experiencing extreme irritation that his concern should be only for the model's welfare.

'I find walking in cities pretty tiring myself, you know!' she told him snappishly; then was mortified, as her shrewish tone resulted in him moving away to talk to Magda.

Cinnabar had expected difficulty in finding a taxi, it being her experience of large cities that these vehicles were at their most elusive when most urgently required. But Marlowe seemed neither to anticipate nor to experience any problem in this respect; and soon they were all three seated in a taxi, careering through the city traffic, in what she now realised was the normal procedure of these vehicles, as the driver cornered crazily, cutting in on other traffic, overtaking and making turns, without any apparent indication of change of direction.

Crowded trams swayed past, filled with twice as many people as could be thought possible, some dangerously strap-hanging. Underground and overhead railways engulfed or disgorged the populace; errand boys, seemingly unconcerned by their peril, darted here and there on fragile-looking bicycles; and in and out of all this hazardous traffic swung their taxi.

Several times Cinnabar was flung hard against the muscular body of the man seated between herself and Magda, and she looked in vain for some hand-hold which would prevent this unwanted and disturbingly intimate contact.

It did not improve her mood to realise that he was amusedly aware of her discomfort, and she wondered, a little tremulously, if *he* had given any further thought to the incident in his apartment. Probably not. To him, most likely, it had been a trivial incident, with nothing about it particularly memorable. In all probability, he was quite accustomed to women succumbing to his personal charms.

If only she could stop thinking about it herself! But the warmth of his thigh, pressed against hers in the confines of the taxi, was no aid to oblivion, even though she tried desperately to concentrate her thoughts on her work . . . on Gary . . . on anything at all so long as it was not the daunting masculinity of Marlowe Hirakawa.

'I thought we'd have a meal before going any further,'

Marlowe suggested, consulting the expensive watch which banded his powerful wrist.

Magda acclaimed the idea with enthusiasm, but Cinnabar was annoyed. She preferred to complete a day's schedule before eating, finding that both she and her model tended to be lethargic after a meal eaten at midday.

'No, thank you,' she said firmly.

But to her chagrin, her wishes were overruled, and she sat back in the seat, seething with frustrated anger.

As she had foreseen, the presence of Marlowe Hirakawa was proving very disruptive to her work in more ways than one.

He, of course, seemed totally unaware of her dark mood, responding, with what Cinnabar considered to be totally unnecessary attentiveness, to Magda's vivacious conversation, most of which seemed to consist of questions of a personal nature.

Magda weighing up her prospects, Cinnabar thought cynically, as the model, more subtle than usual in her approach, elicited all the information she required about Marlowe's private lifestyle.

The apartment in the Hirokawa building was not, apparently, his main residence.

'Just a pied-à-terre handy for the office,' he replied to Magda's query. 'I have a private house near Kyoto. But I only go there occasionally, at weekends mostly, and at holiday times.'

To her query as to whether he ever travelled abroad, the answer was in the affirmative.

'London and Paris mainly, but sometimes I have to go to New York.'

Cinnabar knew only too well what Magda was thinking . . . that the model was visualising herself as the wife of a rich business man, accompanying him on his jetting to and fro around the world. She could almost hear Magda's mental computer adding up the benefits which would accrue to her from such a liaison.

Their taxi pulled up outside a small, exclusive-looking restaurant. The nearside pavement being on Cinnabar's side of the vehicle, she was the first to alight and was thus treated to the spectacle of Marlowe handing Magda out.

Typically, Magda made the most of her opportunities,

allowing her thin hand to rest in his a little longer than was necessary. Never anything but graceful and sure-footed, she even contrived to stumble a little, so that Marlowe was forced to place a protective arm about her waist.

Cinnabar turned away in disgust from the sight of Magda making a play for Marlowe Hirakawa. To see this eminently attractive man taken in by the charming façade to Magda's shallow character was an irritating experience. Maybe, she thought, it wouldn't have bothered her so much if it had not been for last night ... after the weak way in which she had succumbed to the magnetism of his masculinity. I believe you're jealous, my girl, she told herself.

Yet immediately on the heels of this thought came the instinctive denial of Marlowe's attraction for her. She had been tired last night, she excused herself, and overwrought, in no condition to think clearly and she had been taken by surprise. After all, she was only human, subject to occasional weaknesses, and he had taken advantage of such a moment ... a typically male act.

Of course she wasn't jealous of Magda; she had no need to vie with the model for Marlowe's attentions; she had a boy-friend of her own ... a reminder which seemed to have become increasingly and worryingly necessary in the last twenty hours or so, since she had encountered the handsome Managing Director of Messrs. Hirakawa.

Almost as soon as they had taken their seats, they were presented with hot face towels with which to refresh face and hands, before eating, a custom of which Cinnabar thoroughly approved, though she noticed Magda was very careful not to disturb the immaculate matt finish of her complexion.

The model was looking around, in vain, for a menu.

'There's no need for one,' Marlowe explained. 'This is a Sukiyaki restaurant. Therefore one eats Sukiyaki.'

'You mean we have no choice?' Magda exclaimed.

Obviously Marlowe had forgotten Magda's preference for Western foods and salads in particular, and her mask of charm almost slipped at the realisation.

He nodded.

'In the West, people go to a restaurant and then choose their meal. In Japan, all good restaurants serve only one type of food. Therefore one decides what to eat and chooses one's restaurant accordingly.'

Cinnabar made no comment, though secretly she thought he had acted rather high-handedly in not consulting them beforehand as to their preferences, and she would have dearly liked to say so; but Vyvyan Lamonde had ordered her to co-operate with this man and one did not lightly disregard Vyvyan's commands. Besides, this was a small point . . . but just let him try interfering with her work!

Covertly studying Marlowe's arrogant but handsome profile, she sighed. The next few months looked like being a period of continual conflict between loyalty and her inclinations . . . loyalty to her employer and . . . unexpectedly . . . to her boy-friend. She wasn't sure which was going to be the harder trial of strength.

The ingredients of their meal were cooked before them, at the table, in an iron pot over a gas burner, and Marlowe indicated to the girls that they should choose from the pot, using the chopsticks provided.

Like Magda, Cinnabar was a little apprehensive at trying the unknown dish, but it turned out, gastronomically speaking, to be a very pleasant experience and in other respects rather amusing, as she noticed Magda, the languid and fastidious, the conservative eater of salads, struggling with the chopsticks.

Fortunately for Cinnabar, she had used them before, in Chinese restaurants in London, otherwise the operation could have been as frustrating and embarrassing for her as it was for Magda. The basic ingredients of Sukiyaki turned out to be thin slices of tender beef, mixed chopped vegetables, Tofu—a bean curd—and Shirataki—thin potato noodles, all simmered in a mixture of soy sauce. The waitress handed each of them a small bowl, containing a raw egg, into which they dipped the food just before eating. The meal was completed by separate bowls of rice, and by the time they had finished eating, Cinnabar felt more like falling asleep than resuming work, especially as Marlowe had insisted they drink saké with their meal.

Seated in another taxi, finally on their way to the temple site recommended by Marlowe, Cinnabar, unaccustomed to drinking intoxicants of any kind, became aware that saké had other effects besides the soporific feelings she had experienced in the restaurant.

To make their journey more comfortable, Marlowe had

spread out his arms, one around each girl, and the warm pressure of his thigh, the steady thud of his heartbeat furthering the effects of the wine upon her senses, Cinnabar found herself actually trembling, and was humiliatingly aware that Marlowe could not possibly fail to notice her agitation, nor to rightly attribute its cause.

Mingled with the fear of betraying herself was the almost irresistible longing to press herself closer to him, to rest her coppery curls against that comforting breadth of shoulder, and she wondered tremulously what would have happened if Magda had not made a restrictive third in the taxi.

Would she have been weak enough to give in to her impulse, and what would his reaction have been to such a move on her part? Would he have responded . . . drawn her closer . . . kissed her?

These imaginings caused such intolerable sensations within her that it was a relief when the taxi drew up at the entrance to the Kannon Temple, chosen by Marlowe as their destination.

CHAPTER THREE

IF Marlowe *had* been aware of the effect on her of their proximity, it was forgotten as soon as they reached their destination.

Retrieving the two girls' impedimenta from the taxi, he led the way up a broad, imposing avenue, lined with decorated, open shop-fronts, displaying sticks of incense, charms, amulets and other religious souvenirs.

'Tradition has it that the incense burnt here has curative powers,' he told Cinnabar, as she gazed about her, the world of haute couture temporarily forgotten in the fascination she felt at the colourful sight, so that she wanted to snap away with her camera like any tourist.

Not so Magda.

'Cinnabar, do let's get on with this and get it over. I can't think why we had to come *here*,' she complained sotto voce for Cinnabar's ears only. The crowds had become denser, the nearer their approach to the temple. 'You know how I hate being jostled!'

'We're here because Vyvyan wanted the white and gold gown and the saffron robe photographed against a temple background,' Cinnabar reminded her.

Both of these designs were based on the priestly robes of the Orient. But Vyvyan's interpretation, as set off by Magda, would bear little relation to their religious inspiration, Cinnabar reflected with some amusement.

'This temple is dedicated to the Goddess Kannon,' Marlowe said, 'or, as the Chinese call her, Kuan Yin, Goddess of Mercy.'

To Cinnabar's surprise, the temple grounds were invaded by other forms of commercialism, besides the vendors of religious souvenirs. Numerous showmen and quacks plied their trade; tough-looking men in judo uniforms gave displays of strength . . . snapping a brick in half, or pushing a clenched fist through two-inch-thick planks of hardwood, while itinerant beggar priests played the Shakuhachi, an archaic type of bamboo flute.

'I presume you'd like Magda to pose in the temple precinct

itself?' Marlowe suggested.

'Of course,' Cinnabar replied shortly, hoping he was not trying to take command again. At least, she thought, it was far easier to deny his attraction for her, when his suggestions seemed to threaten her independent spirit.

But without any further comment he led them under a high concrete monumental arch, up to a great bronze door, lavishly embossed with stylised chrysanthemums, each of which bore sixteen petals.

As Cinnabar paused with an involuntary exclamation of admiration, Marlowe said:

'I expect you know that the chrysanthemum has a great deal of significance for the Japanese. It's a symbol of the Emperor, of the sun . . . and of artistry. This door could be a possible background for one of your photographs?'

Cinnabar longed to disagree, to reiterate her statement that she chose her own subjects, but the setting was so right, she could not afford to waste the opportunity for the sake of a spurt of sheer contrariness.

Fortunately, she thought, the thronging crowds would not have to be scandalised by the prospect of Magda changing. The robes, as visualised by Vyvyan, though glamorous, were voluminous enough to be donned over her own light summer dress, and Cinnabar pictured the model first in the white and gold gown, with one of the great chrysanthemums framing her face, giving the effect of a halo around the head of a mediaeval saint.

Then she had Magda pose in profile, first left, then right, leaning slightly backwards, one thin hand raised as though tracing the outlines of the petals.

Her shots completed, she turned to find Marlowe watching her, a speculative expression on his handsome face, and as she made to stow away her gear, he stopped her abruptly, a restraining hand on her arm.

'You're on the wrong end of that camera,' he commented.

She bristled immediately, taking his remark as a reflection on her abilities.

'I most certainly am not!'

He brushed aside her pique.

'Don't be so touchy—I'm not casting aspersions on your technical skills. Look, will you trust me with your camera . . . just for one shot!'

'I don't need any more of this particular scene,' she began argumentatively.

'No, not of Magda,' he agreed impatiently, 'but I want to photograph you.'

'Me?' she exclaimed in surprise. 'I'm no model!'

'A pity,' he observed. 'Magda!' He turned to the model, who had been observing their altercation with ill-concealed impatience, 'I wonder if you would be kind enough to help Cinnabar put that gown on?'

'What on earth for?'

Even though his tone had been courteous, conciliating, her reply was petulant. Obviously Magda did not relish Cinnabar being in the limelight and for once Cinnabar agreed with her.

'This is ridiculous . . .' she began.

'Just this once . . . don't argue,' Marlowe told her.

Seeing that a curious crowd, sensing an interesting situation, had begun to gather, she decided to let him have his way with the minimum of fuss . . . besides, it was rather flattering that he should want to photograph her. Taking the white and gold garment from Magda's reluctant hand, she pulled it over her head.

Cut for Magda's ultra-thin model's figure, the outfit clung to Cinnabar's more ample curves, and she was acutely aware that Marlowe's hazel eyes were concentrated on her through the view-finder, as he waved her into position with one large, commanding hand.

The pose he wanted was similar to the first that she had demanded of Magda, with the chrysanthemum haloing her head, and she was suddenly, poignantly reminded of his words earlier that morning, when he had likened her closely curling hair to the petals of that flower . . . a flower which he had just reminded them was of great significance to the Japanese; and despite the influence of his European ancestors on his appearance, she supposed one should not forget his Oriental heritage. Was that the only reason for his fascination with her hair?

The camera restored to her, they moved on into the gaudily decorated temple, gleaming in black lacquer and gold and containing several large cases, holding sacred images. Enormous paper lanterns illuminated a painted ceiling of writhing dragons and once again Cinnabar wished she were not solely a fashion photographer. There was a wealth of beautiful subjects in Japan to excite the discerning eye.

The worshippers of the goddess stood facing the altar, at a rail separating the public portion from the sanctuary proper, tugging the cord of a clapper bell, which Marlowe explained attracted the attention of the deity. Then, after silent prayer, coins were thrown into a slotted opening in a huge collection box. Other folk burned incense sticks in the holders provided, women lifting tiny children so that they could stretch their hands into the fumes, while old ladies did likewise, rubbing arthritic hands in the ascending plumes of smoke.

Somehow it seemed inconsiderate . . . sacrilegious . . . to use a camera flash in this aura of sanctity, and Cinnabar murmured to Marlowe that she would continue her work in the grounds surrounding the temple.

'Why not wait then, until we go to Kyoto?' he suggested. 'There are fifteen hundred temples and two hundred shrines there to choose from, in and around the old capital.'

But Cinnabar had brooked enough interference for one day and stubbornly insisted on trailing her companions around the extensive grounds of the temple, with a jaded Magda becoming more and more fretful in her complaints.

Finally, tired and somewhat dispirited herself, Cinnabar had to admit that she could not find anything to inspire her next shot.

To her surprised relief, Marlowe refrained from the obvious comment that he had told her so, and with the minimum of fuss and the maximum of efficiency, soon had the two girls in a taxi and on the way back to their hotel.

'Don't be too cast down,' he advised Cinnabar, as he paid off the driver. 'Today was only the first of many, and Japan is rich in beautiful sights.'

'It's not Japan,' she said, uncharacteristically despairing. 'It's me. Somehow I couldn't work up my usual enthusiasm. I . . .'

'That's understandable.' His tone was soothing. 'You only arrived yesterday, after a long, trying journey. You're probably still experiencing jet-lag . . . and then you had a late night . . .'

'Very late!'

Magda's light tinkling laugh, with its malicious implication, jarred on Cinnabar's already jangling nerves.

'Well, I shan't make that mistake again,' she snapped, referring not only to her late night and knowing that Marlowe Hirakawa was quite aware of her dual meaning ... that she would never succumb to his seductive masculinity again.

She swept into the hotel, purposely leaving Magda to make their farewells. Let the other girl have her opportunity to hold Marlowe's attention. It didn't matter to her.

But she was not to escape so easily.

'Haven't you forgotten something?'

Furiously, Cinnabar snatched the expensive photographic equipment from him ... equipment which was usually her first concern. What on earth was the matter with her? she wondered. She had flown long distances before, been tired, but never before had it affected her work, or her temper, to this extent.

She hurried towards the lift, but, irritatingly, Marlowe kept pace with her.

'I've equipped a darkroom for you. I believe the idea is that you should send off each film as soon as it's been processed?'

Cinnabar nodded, annoyed with herself that she had needed to be reminded of this fact.

'Then after dinner I'll show you what I've arranged,' he offered, as the two girls waited for the lift.

Again she merely nodded her acknowledgment of his offer.

'Does that invitation include me?' Magda looked up at him, her dark eyes and pouting mouth coquettish.

The model's blatant cajoling was rewarded by the slow, melting smile that was an essential part of his charm.

'I hope, of course, that you will *both* join me for dinner, but I don't think the more mundane aspects of photography really appeal to you, Magda, do they?'

Magda could scarcely deny the fact, in view of earlier remarks she had made, but, with her usual aplomb, she attempted to make the best of the situation.

'I'm sure you can think of *something* to interest me, while Cinnabar dabbles with her boring old chemicals?'

The prolongation of their discussion had necessitated Marlowe's stepping into the lift with them. Gravely he looked down into the flawless features artlessly uplifted to his.

'I shall make it my very first consideration,' he assured her.

The lift stopped and Cinnabar was thankful to step out, making no effort to hide the curl of her lip. So she was to be relegated to the darkroom for a working evening, was she, while Marlowe entertained Magda, who no doubt would make the most of her opportunities!

Would his entertainment take the same form as last night's provision for *her*? she wondered, the thought causing her an unaccountable pang.

Magda, with no ties at home, or inhibitions to hold her back, would certainly make a more responsive and co-operative guest. Tonight, no doubt, it would be Magda's bed which remained undisturbed, but the younger girl felt that it was unlikely that Magda would be so unsophisticated as to fall asleep on a settee in the apartment of an attractive man.

Feeling thoroughly out of sorts, a mood she attributed to fatigue and her failure to complete that day's schedule, she was tempted to order a light snack in her room and excuse herself from viewing the darkroom facilities until the next day. After all, a few hours wouldn't make that much difference, she reasoned.

But, once she was refreshed by a shower, her normally optimistic and cheerful nature reasserted itself. The shots she *had* taken today were good, instinctively she knew that, and she was suddenly eager to see them, and . . . she had to admit it . . . to see the photograph Marlowe had taken of her, to see just what he had visualised when he had asked her to pose for him. Would he be pleased with the results?

As to dinner, suddenly she discovered she *was* hungry after all, and the prospect of the dining room with its attractive décor was more appealing than eating alone, imagining Magda flirting with Marlowe.

And now we're coming to your true motives, she reproached herself. You don't like the idea of Magda spending an entire evening with him. You're jealous of her . . . and you've no business to be. What about Gary?

Well, what about Gary? a rebellious inner voice argued. Despite the swift invention, prompted by pique, she was not really engaged . . . and besides, having dinner with a man, in the company of another woman, scarcely constituted disloyalty. Nor did viewing the facilities which he had provided in order to make her job easier. So why this uneasiness?

She did not have to seek far for the answer. Normally she was dedicated to her work, putting it before everything else.

But tonight, rather than spend her evening tamely working in the darkroom, she wanted to be the one being entertained by Marlowe ... this despite her determination not to give way to the effect he had upon her. It was really just as well, she mused, that Magda *was* to be the recipient of his attentions, if her resolution could be so easily overthrown.

Nevertheless, she dressed carefully for dinner. She was not going to be shown up tonight by the sophisticated model.

The strappy dress, with its pleated bra top and flowing, knee-length, pleated skirt in a vivid petrol blue, emphasised the colour of her hair and deliberately she arranged the curly, bronze-red fronds to duplicate the swirl of a chrysanthemum's petals, unable to quell the hope that Marlowe would notice and comment on it again.

She had just picked up a light shawl, for the evenings tended to be cool, when Magda tapped impatiently on her bedroom door.

'Do hurry, Cinnabar. We mustn't keep Marlowe waiting. If you're not ready, I can go on ahead.'

'Sorry to disappoint you.' Cinnabar stepped out into their communal sitting room, 'but I *am* ready.'

She had felt quite pleased with her own appearance, until she saw Magda's choice for the evening, a daring outfit, purchased at cost from an earlier collection ... Vyvyan's Turkish period. The brief jacket and harem trousers were almost indecent in their transparency. Only Magda could wear Vyvyan's more extreme flights of fancy and get away with it; and on the model, even the expensive fur she carried would not look incongruous worn with the bizarre outfit.

Cinnabar sighed inwardly. She might have known it was impossible to compete with the other girl. After all, Magda's looks had got her into every glossy magazine from London to New York. What chance did *she* have of outshining the girl whose face and figure had launched a thousand new fashions?

Magda might have fears that her career as a model was approaching its decline, but Cinnabar had not seen any evidence of any waning in her powers to attract men; and Marlowe Hirakawa had made no secret of the fact that he thought the older girl attractive.

Both girls were surprised to find that Marlowe was not alone when they rejoined him in the foyer. As he rose to greet them, his companion rose too, a tall, rather lanky young man, with closely cropped hair and horn-rimmed glasses which emphasised the glint in his eyes as he took in Magda's bizarre but striking appearance.

'Magda, Cinnabar, I'd like you to meet a business associate of mine, Hank Schuster.'

Hank, it transpired, was a wealthy young American, in Japan on a buying trip for his firm in New York.

'I come over two or three times a year,' he explained to the two girls, after the introductions had been made and they had all taken their seats in the dining room. 'I spend the first two or three days on business and then allow myself a week for making whoopee.'

Cinnabar took an instant liking to the fresh-faced, uncomplicated young man, and Magda, she reflected wryly, who could recognise a wealthy man at a hundred yards, was sparing no efforts to charm Hank Schuster.

Dinner was a pleasant meal, the presence of an extra man doing much to dispel the tension Cinnabar still felt in Marlowe's presence; the conversation centred on the reason for the two girls' presence in Japan, and Hank was flatteringly impressed by Magda's internationally known name.

Over coffee, Magda turned to Marlowe, laying one thin, predatory hand on the sleeve of his immaculate dinner jacket.

'Well, darling,' she purred, 'have you thought of a way of entertaining a poor hardworking girl for the evening?'

Though the endearment was common enough in the circles Magda frequented, Cinnabar cringed inwardly at the familiarity, though Marlowe himself seemed unperturbed.

'Indeed I have.'

His tone was polite, but his hazel eyes were enigmatic, as they glanced from one girl to the other. Then he turned to his American associate.

'Hank, I made a promise to this young lady,' he indicated Magda, 'which, unfortunately, I'm unable to fulfil myself.'

'Oh, but Marlowe . . .' Magda began to protest.

'Needless to say, it's a great disappointment to me,' he continued smoothly, patting the scarlet-tipped fingers which still rested on his forearm, 'but another commitment has intervened; and I'm sure Hank here would be delighted to show you Tokyo by night.'

Magda's expression was crestfallen and to Cinnabar at least, it was obvious that an evening on the town was not at all what the model had in mind. She had no doubt that a cosy evening à deux in Marlowe's flat would have been more to the other girl's taste.

But having expressed a wish to be amused, Magda could scarcely refuse to accompany Hank, especially in view of that young man's delighted acceptance of the situation, and she hid her chagrin well, turning the full battery of her smiles upon him.

Eagerly, Hank rose from his chair.

'Say, this is swell, Miss Llewellyn! Shall we be on our way? I can think of a thousand things I'd love to show you.'

'Save some for another evening, Hank,' Marlowe advised.

Cinnabar looked at him sharply. What made Marlowe think there would be other occasions; and why should he be so complacent about handing over the lovely model to his friend, when it was obvious that Magda was all too ready to throw herself at his own handsome head?

Magda rose too, her graceful shrug accepting the inevitable, and Cinnabar could guess at her thoughts. After all, one wealthy man was as good as another, and while Hank Schuster might not have the devastating looks of Marlowe Hirakawa, he was a personable young man, making no secret of his awed admiration for Magda. The model would not be averse to having two strings to her bow.

With the couple's departure, Cinnabar set down her coffee cup, anxious not to be alone with Marlowe any longer than necessary.

'I'll take the opportunity of having an early night, since you're going to be busy.' Then she did not know whether to be disappointed or relieved by his reply.

'No need for you to rush off yet; put your wrap on and come with me.'

One thing Cinnabar had learnt in her short acquaintance with Marlowe was the futility of argument. With unwonted meekness, she flung the shawl around her shoulders and allowed him to steer her through the foyer.

But when they reached the pavement, she was disconcerted to be ushered into the waiting limousine which had met them at the airport on the evening of their arrival.

'Where are you taking me?' she protested. 'I thought you were going to show me my darkroom, that you had another appointment . . .'

Her voice trailed away, as she met that enigmatic gaze in the dim light of the car's interior. Before answering her question, he leant forward and spoke in rapid Japanese to the chauffeur. His reply when it came was not at all what she had expected.

'I said I'd promised an evening of entertainment to a hardworking girl. That hardworking girl is you ... or don't you agree that you've earned that title today?'

'Yes, but what about Magda? I thought ... she thought ...'

'I promised Magda that I would make her evening's entertainment my first consideration ... and I did. As soon as I reached my flat, I telephoned Schuster and invited him over.' He chuckled reminiscently. 'Hank didn't need his arm twisting to escort a glamorous model around town!'

Bewilderment mingled with elation. Had Marlowe really gone to these devious lengths to take her, Cinnabar, out for the evening? But why? Was it because he sensed her attraction to him, was flattered by it, because of last night's seemingly ready capitulation to his lovemaking? Was he hoping for a repetition? If so, he was making an error of judgment. Didn't he realise that he'd be on to a far surer thing with Magda ... that last night had been an uncharacteristic lapse on her own part and certainly not to be repeated?

No, why should he recognise any such thing? He scarcely knew her, any more than she knew him; and was she so certain that her lapse would *not* be repeated? she wondered with a quiver of apprehension. If he were to take her in his arms and kiss her, wouldn't she respond in much the same way? No, she told herself again, that was something which must not be allowed to recur ... even to allow herself to think of it was dangerous.

Hastily she thought to divert her thoughts.

'But what about the darkroom ... the developing ... I really ought to be ...'

Lazily he slid an arm around her shoulders, not seeking to diminish the distance between them, but reducing her nevertheless to an inability to continue.

'Be honest, Cinnabar, which would you rather be doing right at this moment ... slaving over a tray of developing chemicals, or seeing more of Tokyo?'

Honesty won the day. Somewhat breathlessly, she replied:

'Seeing Tokyo, of course. But I do have to develop that film. Magda may ask to see them, and I . . .'

'Relax,' he urged her, and this time, despite an attempt on her part at resistance, he did pull her closer. 'There'll still be time to use the darkroom when we get back. I'll help you, if you like. I'm a pretty good amateur photographer and I know what I'm about.'

He might know what he was about when it came to developing photographs, Cinnabar thought uneasily, but was he equally aware of what he was doing to her . . . his arm about her, his fingers playing with a strand of the hair that he had likened to a chrysanthemum?

'Wh—where exactly are we going?'

It was an effort to speak coherently. The effect his nearness was having on her made her throat feel constricted, obstructed by a pounding heart, which, unaccountably, seemed to have changed its anatomical position.

'Have you heard of Sumo wrestling?'

Cinnabar nodded.

'Yes . . . aren't the wrestlers enormously fat?'

'Mmm. To train for the ring, a man needs to be abnormally tall and big to begin with. But they have to eat huge meals to put on more flesh. Anyway, I thought you might find a contest amusing. Certainly it will be a complete contrast to photographing dainty females.'

Magda was certainly dainty, Cinnabar thought resentfully, but did he have to sound quite so admiring? If he admired her so much, why hadn't he taken *her* to the wrestling? Aware that she was more generously proportioned than Magda, Cinnabar did not realise that her rounded, feminine curves were more attractive to some men than the rail-thin angularity of the model.

The Sumo Stadium was a vast, impressive place and Cinnabar looked about her with the keen eye of the photographer, as Marlowe ushered her to their seats.

Over the ring, where the contests were to take place, was suspended a magnificent canopy, hung with huge tassels of coloured silk. The square, raised arena itself was built of clay, with no side ropes as in a boxing ring, the only demarcation being a thick, raised rope of straw, formed into a circle and embedded in the clay.

Soon after they had taken their seats, the stadium lights

went down, only the arena being spotlighted, and a procession of figures approached, led by the referee in pointed black hat and gorgeous gown of brocade, the costume of a Shogun. In his hand he carried an ovoid fan, with which, Marlowe explained, he would direct the wrestlers and indicate the eventual winner.

Then came the wrestlers themselves, barefoot giants, black hair in oiled topknots, their bodies nearly naked, but for the Mawashi or waistband worn around their great stomachs, treading with dignity down the centre aisle.

Marlowe pointed out the reigning champion, as he paraded the ring, arms outspread, displaying himself to the admiring crowds.

'See how he claps his hands?' he murmured, his breath warm against Cinnabar's cheek. 'It's the traditional way of attracting the attention of the gods. Then he stamps his feet ... see ... symbolically crushing evil spirits.'

As Cinnabar watched, determined to ignore the distraction of Marlowe's nearness, the wrestlers performed strange limbering up exercises, raising first one leg sideways and then the other. Their buttocks were huge, their stomachs vast, their chests almost womanly.

An official, with a curiously high-pitched voice, announced the names of the first contestants. Then each wrestler entered the ring, taking a handful of salt from a tub and throwing it before him.

'It's a ritual ... to purify the ring,' Marlowe explained. 'The Japanese have purification rituals for every occasion.'

The first two contestants got down on their haunches, facing each other, only a few feet apart, bracing themselves with clenched fists, glaring at each other like fighting cocks, as they pounded the clay surface of the arena.

'This is a very important moment,' Marlowe said quietly. 'Unless they rise to grapple with each other at exactly the same moment, the referee will disallow the bout. They are also disqualified if they use closed fists, kick, hairpull or hit below the belt. Forearm smashes, eye gouging or ear and nose pulling are also forbidden.'

Cinnabar stole a sideways glance at his handsome profile, a little piqued to see him so concentrated upon the bout in progress. Would his concentration have been so great if Magda had been his companion?

Sensing her eyes on him, he turned with that slow smile which always seemed to melt her bones when she encountered it.

'Watch the fight, Cinnabar . . . the night is young yet!'

Quickly she turned away, flushing with embarrassed annoyance at the implication in his words. He really believed she was so eager for his attentions that she couldn't concentrate on the entertainment before her. Well, she'd show him . . . she wouldn't look at him, or say another word, all evening! Ostentatiously, she moved farther away from him on the padded bench seat, as the battle before her began in earnest, the opponents springing at each other with an agility she would never have dreamt possible.

One wrestler thrust the other backwards and the sight of the straining, quivering mounds of flesh . . . two flabby, monstrous men, with huge stomachs and legs like elephants trying to hurl each other out of the small ring, crouching, manoeuvring for position . . . was exciting, but at the same time extremely comical. Then they were feinting, side-stepping, pushing, shoving, hooking their legs around each other, until finally one man grabbed the back of his opponent's girdle and whirling him round, sent him headlong out of the ring.

Contest followed contest, each bout only lasting a few seconds. It was a slow-moving, even painful spectacle, but Cinnabar noticed that the mostly Japanese audience were completely involved and enthusiastic over the performance.

'Surely they must hurt each other,' she murmured, after one particularly dramatic victory, her resolution forgotten in her awed concern.

'They're trained to fall correctly . . . broken bones are rare,' Marlowe reassured her, 'and if one of the wrestlers suffers a nosebleed, the bout is stopped immediately, to preserve the purity of the ring.'

An idea was forming in Cinnabar's fertile brain, which rarely forgot her profession for long.

'One of the items in the Oriental collection is a judo-style suit,' she told Marlowe. 'Is there any chance of getting one of these men to pose with Magda? What a splendid foil a real wrestler would make!'

Marlowe agreed immediately.

'I'm sure any one of them would be delighted. Sumo has a

huge following and the most successful wrestlers are national celebrities well accustomed to being photographed. After the contest,' he promised, 'we'll have a chat with some of them.'

He was as good as his word, and they left the stadium with the promise of a photographic session the day after next, with Mosaburo Ishibashi, one of the country's foremost exponents of Sumo. Mosaburo had expressed his sense of the honour done him at being chosen to pose with a famous English model.

The elation Cinnabar felt lasted until the limousine pulled into the underground car park of the Hirakawa building and Marlowe guided her towards the lifts; and, instead of street level, he selected the button which she knew would bring them to his apartment.

'I . . . I planned to have an early night . . .' she began.

'Of course,' he agreed, 'and so you shall, but isn't there still a little matter of some developing to be done?'

'But the film is in my room.'

'On the contrary, I had one of the hotel staff bring your equipment over while we were out. You'll find it waiting for you.'

He was trying to organise her again, she thought crossly, as he unlocked the outer door and indicated that she should precede him into his apartment.

'Is the darkroom here, then?'

'No, but after watching all that physical exertion, I feel in need of a drink. Coffee for you?'

'I'd much rather get on with some work,' she demurred. Her memories of her previous visit to Marlowe's flat were still all too vivid and the last thing she wanted was a repetition of its outcome. Or was it? she asked herself. As his hand closed about her elbow, propelling her into the familiar sitting room, she felt the now all too predictable response to his touch and knew that if it were not for Gary's existence, she would have no protest to make at this opportunity of being alone with Marlowe Hirakawa . . . no objection whatsoever to his taking her into his arms.

Was it possible to be in love with two men at once? Common sense told her it was not. You couldn't divide your loyalties.

While Marlowe rattled cups in the kitchen, she examined her confused emotions. She hadn't actually promised to marry

Gary, though tacitly she had assumed that some day she would. She had even believed herself to be sufficiently fond of him to do so. But now she was beginning to doubt that emotion. Certainly she had never felt this mingled anticipation and dread at the thought of being alone with Gary, never felt this almost wanton pull of the senses, the feeling of breathlessness at his nearness, of knees that refused their support.

But was this love either ... or a mere physical attraction? She, who had always been so level-headed where men were concerned, so sure of herself, confident of her own judgment, was now as uncertain as an adolescent on her first date.

'Why don't you relax?' asked Marlowe, as he returned with the coffee, to find her perched tensely on the extreme edge of the settee. 'I don't bite, you know.'

The cup rattled in its saucer, as she accepted the coffee from him, and he seated himself beside her and removed the cup from her now nerveless hands, returning it to the tray.

'What is it, Cinnabar? What are you afraid of?'

Unable to meet his eyes Cinnabar clasped her hands tightly in her lap, desperately trying to still their trembling. This was ridiculous. She had never behaved in this way before in her whole life. She shouldn't have allowed him to override her better judgment, to bring her up here, knowing as she did the effect it would have upon her; and she must leave at once. She would tell him she was too tired tonight to develop photographs ... that she would not do justice to her work.

She turned to face him, but at the look of amused understanding in his hazel eyes, the words stuck in her throat, colour flooding her cheeks.

'Don't be afraid of me, little chrysanthemum,' he murmured, reaching out for her, and somehow it seemed the most natural thing in the world to go into his arms and nestle against the broad chest, while his gentleness stilled her trembling.

After a while she began to wonder if he would make love to her and knew that in spite of her fear, her resolutions, she wanted him to ... knew intuitively that he was moved by her nearness, but after a few moments he put her from him, gently but firmly, and handed her the coffee cup once more.

'Drink up,' he commanded, 'and then we'll see how those films turn out.'

For a moment she felt forlorn, but then rational thought reasserted itself, as she told herself severely that she should be grateful for his self-restraint.

They took the lift to the apartment directly above Marlowe's.

'I've fitted out the spare bedroom for you,' he said. 'I think I've remembered everything, but if you're short of any materials you must let me know.'

As they passed through the central living area, Cinnabar could not help noticing how different the décor was from Marlowe's almost spartan living accommodation.

Walls and ceilings were of palest pink, sofa and carpet in a deep peach, ruched curtains in stripes of pale pink and green. There was no overhead lighting; instead it came from a couple of table lamps and elaborate floral wall lights, the effect subdued and romantic. Surely, she thought, this was a woman's room. What woman did Marlowe know, who would permit him such easy access to her apartment?

But she was not allowed to linger, Marlowe apparently being eager for her to survey his handiwork; and he had been very efficient, she realised, as she looked around the compact room, where everything was arranged for maximum efficiency and economy of movement.

He had spoken the truth when he had claimed to know what he was doing. So many people imagined that a darkroom was just that ... a gloomy place, painted black. But Marlowe was obviously aware that a light tone, such as white or cream, was most suitable, making the most of the illumination within the room. It was a darkroom only in the sense that it was not lit with ordinary white light, but with light of a colour to which film was not sensitive ... red, green or brown, depending upon the materials to be used.

'Your case with the exposed film is over there,' he told her. 'Now, if you're sure you have everything you want, I have a couple of telephone calls to make, then I'll come back to see how you're getting on.'

'I thought you were supposed to be helping me,' she said, surprised at her own eagerness for his help. Normally she preferred to do her own processing.

But he regarded her quizzically, his hazel eyes mischievous.

'I have a feeling that if I remained here with you, other things besides film might develop?'

Cinnabar caught her breath in a gasp of dismay. He sounded so self-confident. Where's your pride, Cinnabar Forester? she asked herself. Are you going to let him think you're as bad as Magda, that you've no powers of resistance . . . or worse, that you're a flirt? She forced herself to speak coldly.

'You flatter yourself. I'm a professional photographer. Nothing distracts me from my work.'

'Nothing?'

He had been about to leave, but now he moved back into the close confines of the darkroom, making its desirable compactness seem claustrophically inadequate. Why hadn't she let well alone, kept quiet . . . let him go? Now he had taken her words as a challenge, probably thought she was being flirtatious, provocative.

As he moved in on her, she retreated, until her spine was pressed against the hard rim of the porcelain sink and he was so close that she could feel the warmth emanating from his hard, muscular body. Though she was tall herself, she had to look up at him, and was disconcerted to recognise the hazy warmth of desire in his eyes.

She swallowed convulsively. 'Marlowe, I . . .'

'Don't worry, Cinnabar.' He reached out and wound one bright curl around his finger, seemingly fascinated by its colour and tenacity. 'I'm not going to kiss you . . . yet. I have a feeling that once I begin, I may not be able to stop . . . and we both have work to do.'

He moved away, pausing in the door to add:

'But I'll be back!'

CHAPTER FOUR

AND how was she supposed to concentrate on her work with that thought in her mind? Cinnabar brooded crossly, as she set out the chemicals she needed. The thought of what might happen later, when Marlowe did return, was making her hands shake, and she needed a cool head and steady hands for this job.

But after a while, as her hands performed accustomed tasks and she became absorbed, excited as always at seeing the results of her photography, she was able to banish Marlowe to a distant corner of her mind where, resolutely, she kept him throughout the delicate operation.

She could find no fault with his arrangements. There was a long narrow work bench, the 'dry' bench, for making prints and enlargements and a 'wet' bench for developing, fixing and washing, ending in a sink fitted with a plug and cold water tap. All the essential equipment was readily to hand ... thermometer, dishes, measures, washing tanks, developing and accelerating agents, forceps and drying racks.

With the prints hung up to dry there was nothing more she could do for the time being, and still Marlowe had not returned.

She looked at her watch ... almost midnight. Should she go in search of him, or make her way back alone to her hotel room?

Somehow she was reluctant to do this without bidding him goodnight. Yet to go to his apartment would make her seem over-eager for his company. She would give him a few more moments.

Closing the door of the darkroom behind her, she wandered around the apartment. In layout, it was very similiar to Marlowe's, but the décor certainly did not indicate masculine occupation ... in fact, she decided, it was distinctly feminine.

Curiosity prompted her to explore the second bedroom. This showed unmistakable signs of female habitation and when, rather guiltily, she slid back the doors of the built-in wardrobes her supposition was confirmed, for they were filled with row upon row of dainty clothes, some Western style, but some Oriental ... in particular the kimonos in a range of bright jewel colours.

The several apartments in the Hirakawa building were provided, she knew, for the convenience of senior executives, such as Marlowe himself. But in a male-orientated world, was it likely that a woman would hold such a position? Since the room was so obviously occupied by a woman, she supposed it must be so.

The gentle purr of the lift ascending brought her swiftly back into the living room. Marlowe must not think she had been prying. She sat down and began flicking through a glossy fashion magazine, looking up casually, as he entered the apartment.

'I've just finished,' she told him.

'I'm sorry ... my calls took longer than I expected. How did the films turn out?' He moved towards the darkroom.

'Quite well. They're drying at present ... perhaps you should look at them tomorrow?'

He shook his head.

'No time tomorrow. I shall be out of town for a couple of days.'

Following him into the darkroom, Cinnabar was aware of a decided lowering of her spirits. Of course, she should have realised that Marlowe, the business man, would have other commitments. He could scarcely be expected to give all his time to escorting herself and Magda ... and indeed he had warned her of this fact, had arranged a guide for them. At the time, she had been relieved to find that he would not be constantly at her elbow, overseeing her work, but that had been before the onset of this insidious attraction she felt towards him.

Sternly she reminded herself that, in the event, it would be as well not to be constantly in his company; and she made up her mind that she would write to Gary tonight. Her letter would not reach him for several weeks, until his return from Spain, but it would ease her conscience and perhaps recall her to a sense of loyalty.

Marlowe was examining with interest the results of her work.

'They really are excellent, particularly this ... and this. ...'
He had picked on two shots, which Cinnabar herself thought

outshone the rest, but although he studied it intently, he made no comment about his photograph of herself. 'I wonder if I might have copies of . . . of some of them?'

So he wanted some photographs of Magda, did he? Well, it wasn't surprising. As she had anticipated, the distance and the filters she had used had softened and disguised a certain hardness in the model's regular features, and in Vyvyan's dreamy, flattering creations she looked very, very beautiful . . . enough to turn any man's head.

'I'll make you some copies when I have my next developing session,' she said wearily. 'But now, if you'll excuse me, I'm rather tired.'

'Must you go so soon? I'll be away for a day or two, you know. I thought a little supper, before . . .'

'No!' she said sharply. She was not going back to his flat again. He had more than supper in mind, she felt sure. Well, if he admired Magda so much, he could invite the model up for an intimate meal with all the trimmings!

'As you wish.' Marlowe sounded disappointed. 'Then I suppose we must say goodnight?'

'Yes. Goodnight,' she said hastily, moving towards the door.

'With a little more feeling than that, surely,' he suggested, interposing himself between her and her route to escape.

'I . . . I don't know what you mean.'

But she did. She didn't need the gleam in his eyes, the softening of those firmly moulded lips to translate his meaning.

'Come here, Cinnabar,' he urged, but he did not wait for her to complete the negative shake of her head, taking the initiative himself and putting his arms about her.

It was enough, she thought, ashamed of her own weakness, to overcome her token resistance, as meekly she surrendered her lips to his possession, trembling as his mouth covered hers, as he shaped her body with his warm, strong hands, slowly, sensuously. Strange flutterings coursed through her and she reached up to wind her fingers in the crispness of his hair, the wild compulsion he evoked in her making her curve fiercely against him, as she gave in to the tide of feeling sweeping her . . . everything . . . her work, Magda, Gary . . . all forgotten, her world condensed to this . . . Marlowe's arms about her, his deepening kisses, the hard thrust of his

muscular body against hers reducing her to a clinging
yielding, a wish to give him everything that he might demand
of her.

It was he who drew away first, his breathing uneven,
leaving her clamouring awakened senses unfulfilled.

'I think that's enough.' He sounded almost stern. 'I think
I'd better see you back to your hotel.'

She wanted to cry out, to ask him why . . . knowing that his
arousal had been as deep as her own. How could he terminate
his lovemaking so abruptly, with nothing to soften the painful
shock of his sudden retreat from her? But she did not have to
ask; he gave her the answer, unsolicited.

'I find it very hard to remember that you're engaged to be
married, when you don't even wear a ring.'

He was having difficulty restoring his voice to its normal
even level, and for a moment Cinnabar thrilled to the
realisation of her effect on him.

But then the implication of his words dawned on her,
reminding her of her invention . . . a spur-of-the-moment
fabrication, intended to salve her pride. She could scarcely
deny it now, without becoming involved in awkward
explanations.

'I . . . I told you, we're going to choose one, the first chance
we get.'

She felt perilously close to tears, the pain of unappeased
desire still tormenting her, ashamed of her longing for him to
hold her again. She knew that if he did so, the pulsating
tension that still stretched between them might not be so
easily denied again.

With an effort of willpower, she opened the door.

'I . . . I can find my own way back to the hotel room,' she
told him, very aware of him in the close confines of the slowly
descending lift.

'I'll see you safely to your room,' Marlowe said firmly.

She wished that, just for once, he would not be so
punctilious. It was prolonging her torture, for she still had an
almost ungovernable desire to fling herself back into his arms;
and she mustn't . . . she mustn't. Knowing of Gary's existence,
believing her to be engaged, he must already despise her,
thinking her behaviour cheap, promiscuous even.

On the way up to her room, she sought desperately for a
topic of conversation to deflect her thoughts from the

remembered expression in Marlowe's eyes, the relaxing of his firm mouth as it had come down upon hers.

'D—doesn't the occupier of that apartment mind my using one of the rooms as a darkroom?'

'Not a bit. She's only too pleased,' he reassured her, 'and she'll be very interested in your work. Besides, Michiko is a delightful girl, always ready to help anyone.'

So the apartment just above his was occupied by Michiko, the Japanese girl she had seen leaving his office ... her future guide. If Michiko was one of his girl-friends, as Cinnabar suspected, it was a very convenient arrangement, unless ...

'Does Michiko work for Messrs Hirakawa?'

'Good heavens, no!' He seemed amused by the idea. 'She's a student ... she just uses the apartment in term-time.'

'But it really belongs to you?'

'To Messrs Hirakawa.'

But Marlowe virtually was Messrs Hirakawa ... or would be some day, after his uncle's death. Michiko must mean quite a lot to Marlowe, if he was prepared to let her occupy such a luxurious flat. Students in Japan, she knew, were notoriously poor, taking other employment to subsidise their studies. True, Marlowe had said that Michiko often acted as a guide in her spare time, but that would scarcely support her at college and pay the rent of the apartment Cinnabar had just seen.

The thought crossed her mind, filling her with sudden revulsion ... if Michiko was Marlowe's girl-friend, perhaps even his mistress, it was despicable of him to make love to another girl ... and in Michiko's flat too!

They were at the door of the suite Cinnabar shared with Magda, and she turned to face him, her manner cool, though polite.

'Thank you for your help these past two days. I hope you enjoy your business trip.'

'Thank *you*,' he said gravely. 'You've made duty a pleasure. I shall look forward to my return ... and many similar occasions.'

'Oh, that won't be necessary,' she told him, endeavouring to make her voice sound hard and businesslike. 'By then, with Michiko's help, I'm sure we shall be able to find our way around quite well. Goodbye.'

'Cinnabar?' He sounded puzzled, one hand restraining her,

as she fumbled to insert the key in the lock. 'Why the sudden change? A moment or two ago you were so friendly . . .'

'Too friendly . . . as you reminded me,' she snapped. 'I have a fiancé back home. See that you don't forget the fact again, because I don't intend to!'

She succeeded in opening the door and shaking off his hand went in, slamming the door behind her.

Her brief show of bravado seemed to have exhausted all her strength for the moment, and she leant against the inside of the door, aware that she was holding her breath, wondering if he would knock on the door, or if he had accepted his congé.

It seemed an interminable time before she heard the lift descending and knew that he had gone.

Wearily she made her way to her own room, thankful that Magda was not back yet to quiz her on her evening's activities. It would have been difficult to hide the extreme depression she felt, and she shuddered to think of Magda's reaction if she ever discovered the way in which she had been duped. Thank goodness Marlowe had insisted that she develop the films, even though this had led to her shameless surrender to his kisses. At least she could tell Magda a partial truth . . . that she had been working in the darkroom this evening.

But what was she to do about this irresistible appeal Marlowe had for her? Only two or three days of her projected stay in Japan had expired and already she suspected her feelings for him had advanced beyond reclamation. How much more disastrous another few weeks could be; and there was no future in such a relationship. Even if she were to break with Gary, it was obvious that Marlowe had other fish to fry, that he was only amusing himself with her.

He had made it evident by his unstinted admiration of Magda that he liked beautiful women . . . he had his Japanese girl-friend installed on his very doorstep, and heaven only knew how many more lovelies he numbered amongst his acquaintance, made love to when circumstances permitted. A man of his looks and position could have almost any woman he desired.

She would have to be firm with herself . . . and with him. No more outings à deux, no more evening visits to his flat. She would enlist Michiko's help at her developing sessions in the apartment above and make sure that the girl was always present when Marlowe was around. She owed this precaution to her own pride . . . and to Gary. It did not strike her as odd that consideration for him should come second.

This reminded her, she had resolved to write to Gary before she went to bed . . . better begin as she meant to go on. She moved over to the desk provided by the hotel and equipped with embossed stationery for the use of guests.

But the letter was destined not to be written.

Cinnabar picked up the telegram which had evidently arrived in her absence.

'Spanish assignment completed ahead of schedule. Taking a few days holiday and joining you in Tokyo. Expect me Tuesday. All my love. Gary.'

The contents of the telegram came as a shock to Cinnabar, but upon reflection, she decided that Gary's presence in Japan, though unexpected, would be a good thing.

For surely, as soon as she saw him, this temporary madness which seemed to have afflicted her would vanish. It was several weeks since she had last seen Gary . . . no wonder she found it difficult to visualise his face, his voice. But in two days' time, he would be here and everything would be all right. Her topsy-turvy world would be restored to the normality she preferred.

She was glad now that Marlowe was going away the next day. It would give her a breathing space in which to get him into perspective before Gary arrived; so that she would be able to greet him with unreserved pleasure . . . and with no feelings of guilt to mar their reunion.

If he asked her again to marry him, she might even accept. Perhaps they might even choose the ring, here in Tokyo. Then Marlowe would not have the excuse that he had forgotten she was committed elsewhere . . . and she needn't actually *get* married . . . not for ages.

But in the meantime, there were two days to be filled, days which loomed curiously empty.

It was as well that she was not depending on Magda for company, for, as she discovered next morning, the model had already made her plans for the Sunday. It was the only day on which, by tacit agreement, they did not work, and Magda, she told Cinnabar, intended to spend her free time with Hank Schuster.

That young man was in for a shock, Cinnabar thought,

with a feeling of sympathy for his eventual disillusionment. Should Marlowe ever decide to turn the full battery of his charm upon Magda once more, the more homely American would find himself discarded with dizzying swiftness. Rich Hank might be, but Marlowe Hirakawa was both wealthy and irresistibly attractive.

Of course, Cinnabar told herself, she was not vain enough to believe that Marlowe really preferred *her* company to Magda's. Tonight had been some strange whim on his part, possibly to indicate to the overly self-confident model that he and not she was the hunter. But in any case, with Gary's arrival she would no longer be available and Marlowe would naturally turn his attentions to the model ... perhaps even with relief. There would be no timid trepidation from Magda, when and if he attempted to make love to her.

Entertaining herself on a Sunday presented no problem, as she had discovered that the big department stores stayed open all day. There, she knew, one could browse for hours, finding all one's needs under one roof.

It was not far from the business area to the glittering shopping district, where well-stocked displays tempted the window-shopper ... displays of transistors, cultured pearls, Oriental carpets ... even the latest Parisian fashions.

Some speciality shops displayed nothing but paper and silk fans, some elaborately painted in the 'Chinese' style. Chemists' shops seemed overflowing with drugs, lozenges and every kind of medicament.

Cinnabar resolved that she would return another day to investigate these smaller shops, but today her sights were set on the mammoth department stores.

She was not disappointed, as she explored floor after floor of the Depato she had chosen, seeing all the normal wares to be found in its Western counterparts; but it was the specialised displays which drew her most, such as the Kimono Department ... a riot of colour, the design of the beautiful garments reflecting the seasons. Cherry blossom hung next to azalea and wistaria, iris by morning glory and lotus blossom ... and, representing autumn, golden chrysanthemums and maple leaves.

Patterns were large and bold ... giant sprays of blossom, dark on light colours, or white on dazzling scarlet; flying birds of many-hued plumage spread their wings against gold and scarlet clouds.

Cinnabar succumbed to the temptation of a pale yellow kimono, ablaze with bronze chrysanthemums, and it was only after she had paid for the garment that she realised the subconscious motivation behind her purchase. Hair like a bronze chrysanthemum, he'd said.

She shrugged. Well, it was too late now. The salesgirl would think her most odd if she said she'd changed her mind, after the length of time she had spent in admiring it, and the painstaking fashion in which it had been parcelled up . . . the wrapping a work of art in itself.

In any case, there was no chance of Marlowe seeing her in it, so he wouldn't get the wrong idea. It would be worn only in private, for she knew that to Oriental eyes, the sight of a Westerner aping their apparel in public would be to invite derision, discreetly hidden, but nonetheless real.

Upon the roof of the enormous building was a recreational area, providing a playground for children, with merry-go-rounds and a big wheel; and for adult customers a restaurant, with a garden area, containing magnificent specimens of bonsai in tubs and hundreds of bamboo cages, filled with colourful, twittering birds.

After a leisurely coffee, Cinnabar visited the fine arts department, admiring the exquisite lacquer-ware, shimmering cloisonné, ivory and beautiful stoneware and porcelain . . . very tempting, but all priced beyond her means. Here too was the venue for cultural exhibitions of art, Ikebana and Japanese calligraphy.

Yet despite the fascination of shopping in Tokyo, Cinnabar was not sorry when her day of freedom was over. It was possible, she discovered for the first time, and with some surprise, to feel lonely, even in a crowd.

Magda was not in to dinner and Cinnabar, deciding on an early night, was on the verge of sleep when she heard the other girl come in.

Predictably, after a hectic weekend and two late nights, Magda showed a sullen, Monday-morning face, when they met at breakfast, and her mood was not improved, when she learnt of the arrangements for a photographic session at the Sumo wrestlers' training school, where it had been arranged that they should meet Mosaburo Ishibashi.

'Why can't we take it easy today?' she complained.

'Because we have a schedule to keep to,' said Cinnabar, more patiently than she felt, knowing that the model's displeasure was, in part, due to Marlowe's absence.

Michiko, back from her weekend at home, joined them at breakfast, introducing herself, and was transparently eager to take up her duties as guide. It was she who arranged for the taxi to take them to their destination.

Cinnabar had not been keen to meet the younger girl again, suspecting what she did about her relationship with Marlowe, but against all expectation, she found herself liking Michiko. The Japanese girl was intelligent, bright and talkative, her English almost faultless, and in view of Magda's early morning taciturnity, Cinnabar found herself keeping up the conversation and enjoying the younger girl's lively company.

The only time Magda showed a spark of interest was when Marlowe's name was mentioned. After Michiko had chattered on for some time about him, the model roused herself sufficiently to remark rather acidly,

'You seem to think a great deal of *Mr Hirakawa.*'

Her formality, Cinnabar knew, was Magda's way of trying to give the young Japanese girl a set-down, with its implication that a hired guide had no business to be using her employer's first name. If only Magda knew!

But either Michiko did not perceive the snub, or blandly ignored it.

'Oh yes,' she declared, 'Marlowe is kindest, most generous, loving man. Noble also ... descended on grandmother's side from ancient order of Samurai, most honourable swordsmen. You like him too?'

She addressed her remark impartially, but Magda did not deign to reply and it was left to Cinnabar to mutter:

'Oh, yes ... yes, of course.'

Descended from a Samurai warrior, she thought. She knew that the Samurai class no longer existed, but that there were still many Samurai families who were proud of their ancestry. That would account for Marlowe's self-assurance, his arrogant carriage ... straight, unbending steel, like the swords of his ancestors.

'He has been very good for me,' Michiko said gravely. 'Has done many good turns ... nothing too much trouble for him.'

I bet! Cinnabar thought cynically. She had experienced his

good nature, his helpfulness, herself, and while they were probably quite genuine, he seemed to think he had the right to exact due payment for them. She wondered if he was as generous or helpful to his own sex as he appeared to be with any attractive woman who crossed his path. Not that she imagined for one moment that he included *her* in that category. In her case, his aim would be to preserve amicable relationships with a valuable customer ... Vyvyan Lamonde.

Michiko kept up her bright chatter, interspersed with a running commentary on their surroundings, as they drove to the training school just outside Tokyo. Here they were greeted by Ishibashi-San's trainer, who insisted on giving them a conducted tour and explaining to them some of the finer points of Sumo wrestling, with Michiko translating.

'Mosaburo Ishibashi now breakfasting,' she told Cinnabar.

As it was eleven o'clock, Cinnabar could not help expressing her surprise.

'Wrestlers rise at four a.m. for six hours' training before breakfast,' Michiko explained. 'Altogether, wrestlers train sixteen hours per day.'

They were conducted into the long dining hall, where men of all ages sat at wooden trestles, and even Magda discovered sufficient animation to gasp at the array of foods set out before them. Cinnabar had already learned from her visit to the stadium that to the Sumo wrestler, large quantities of food were of the utmost importance, but even so, her eyes widened as Michiko listed the contents of just one man's breakfast ... a dozen bowls of noodles, a generous helping of Chank-Wabe, a kind of boiled stew containing fish, pork, chicken and numerous types of vegetables.

'Sumo wrestler commence training at age fourteen,' Michiko interpreted, 'retire about thirty. Life too rigorous for older man. Many die young ... gout and diabetes.'

Cinnabar wasn't at all surprised to hear it, and wondered that any man should put his life at risk in this way.

Michiko, however, was most matter-of-fact.

'Sumo wrestler earn hundred and ten thousand pound a year ... most worth while.'

Breakfast over, they found Mosaburo Ishibashi very eager to pose for them, and at the sight of Cinnabar, a smile creased his fat face into a multitude of chins.

'Ah, little Miss again, who come stadium with Hirokawa-San!'

Unfortunately, his English was good enough for even Magda to understand.

'When was this?' she asked sharply.

Her question was directed at Cinnabar, but Mosaburo answered happily.

'Sat'day night . . . I meet then.'

This was an eventuality Cinnabar had not foreseen. She had been briefly introduced to the wrestling champion, but had not expected him to remember and comment upon the fact.

'So!'

Magda hissed the word from between clenched teeth, completely oblivious to everything and everybody around her, her glittering eyes on Cinnabar's tell-tale cheeks.

'Magda,' she said hastily, 'I can explain . . . but not here, not now.'

'Oh yes?' the other girl sneered, 'so that you have time to cook up a good story. What kind of fool do you take me for? Just how did you persuade Marlowe to ditch me?'

'It wasn't like that . . . really it wasn't. I had no idea he was going to . . .' A brilliant idea occurred to her. 'Besides, it was only a business trip, to arrange today's photographic session.'

The model's eyes narrowed.

'If you're going to tell lies, Cinnabar, make sure they tally. First you say you'd no idea he was bringing you here, then you say it was a business arrangement. I know darn well you don't let other people make your decisions for you. You *must* have known!'

Cinnabar was uncomfortably aware of their interested audience of wrestlers . . . and the Japanese girl, who she suspected was something more than just a close friend of Marlowe Hirakawa. Taken all round, the situation was very embarrassing.

'Look, Magda,' she tried again desperately, 'I'll tell you the whole story . . . the truth, I promise. But later. Don't make a scene here, please.' She tried an appeal to the girl's vanity. 'Remember, you're a very well known person.'

For a moment Magda hesitated and Cinnabar thought she was going to insist on an immediate showdown; then she seemed to realise that her public image was indeed suffering. With a visible effort she erased the lines of ill-temper from her face.

'Very well,' she said, her inflection still venomous. 'But it had better be a good explanation. I meant what I said about Gary Reid. If you're playing around behind his back, I'll see that he gets to hear of it!'

She would. Cinnabar had no doubt of it; and though Magda didn't realise it, with Gary's arrival imminent, her opportunity was close at hand. Somehow she must placate the model, persuade her not to say anything to Gary.

But now professionalism asserted itself. The photographic session must come first . . . the purpose of their visit.

Mosaburo Ishibashi was really entering into the spirit of the thing, she thought with delight a few moments later, as he presented a mighty leg for Magda to perch upon. Then he lifted the model above his head, her slender body in a limply graceful attitude, and finally he submitted to lying prone, Magda poised above him, one dainty foot on his enormous chest in an attitude of victory.

Cinnabar, kneeling, crouching, darting from side to side, taking shot after shot, was momentarily lost in the excitement of what she was doing, certain that the poses were superb and that Vyvyan would be wildly enthusiastic.

It was with a sense of anti-climax that she indicated that she was satisfied and began to pack up her equipment, knowing that the moment of reckoning with Magda could not be postponed much longer.

Promising Mosaburo that he should receive copies of the photographs in due course, they left the training school and found that the efficient Michiko had already procured another taxi for the return journey.

'You want to go somewhere else today?' the Japanese girl asked Cinnabar.

'No, thank you, Michiko. If it's not inconvenient to you, I'd like to come up to your apartment and develop these shots right away. I'm dying to get them off to my boss. I know he's going to be really pleased with them.'

Despite the Japanese girl's diverting chatter, the journey back to their hotel was fraught with tension. Magda, released from the necessity of concentrating on holding a pose, of adopting a charming expression for the camera, was obviously brooding again; and she barely waited for the door of their suite to close behind them before she turned on Cinnabar with an ominous:

'Well?'

Cinnabar told her the plain, unvarnished truth, ending with the words:

'It really *wasn't* my fault, Magda. He deceived me just as much as you. I really thought he was going to show me my darkroom and then go off to some business appointment.' She hesitated, then: 'It was all perfectly innocent on my part, so there really isn't any need to worry Gary.'

Magda chose to ignore the unpalatable fact that Marlowe had chosen Cinnabar's company in preference to hers.

'You could have refused to go along with his plans, once you found out what he was up to,' she said scornfully. 'But you didn't even try, did you? How it must have inflated your plain little ego, to think you'd scored over me! What other plans did he have for later, and how did you try to discourage him then? Did he kiss you, make love to you? Did you end up in his bed again, like that first night? You're a fast worker, Cinnabar Forester. I feel sorry for Gary Reid!'

Suddenly, true to her name and the promise of her fiery hair, Cinnabar saw red. It was obviously no use appealing to Magda's better nature; she just hadn't got one. She was furious with the model for her insinuations ... and with Marlowe, for getting her into this intolerable situation. Never before had she allowed the model to get under her skin like this, and she refused to be cowed by her now.

'I've told you before, Magda, what I do is no concern of yours. The trouble with you is that you're pea-green jealous. Well, you can keep your dirty little mind in exercise, wondering just how Marlowe and I did spend the rest of the evening, because even in your wildest imaginings you'll never come near the truth. And now, I've got work to do.'

Seizing the case containing the results of the morning's filming, she swept out and made her way over to Michiko's apartment.

On the way, the spurt of defiance, bred by anger, began to waver. Damn Magda Llewellyn and damn Marlowe, for giving the model a weapon to use against her. Hitherto, she had managed to steer clear of open conflict with the older girl. But Magda was unlikely to forgive or forget the blow her pride had received today ... nor to overlook Cinnabar's heated retort to her accusations; and tomorrow, though Magda did not know it yet, Gary would be here.

Cinnabar's problems were mounting ... her attraction to

Marlowe, despite her conviction that his affections were given elsewhere, Magda's suspicions, unfounded though they were ... the inevitable attempts she would have to make to convince Gary that there was nothing in the model's insinuations. And she had to make up her mind, too, just what to do about Gary. The whole situation seemed to be getting out of hand.

As Marlowe had predicted, Michiko was intensely interested in Cinnabar's work and begged to be allowed into the darkroom, to watch the film being developed.

Afterwards, when the last print had been hung up to dry, she pressed Cinnabar to stay for a meal. Cinnabar was glad to accept. She did not relish facing Magda again just yet. Perhaps by morning the model's rage would have cooled a little. She didn't really have much faith in this eventuality, but at least she could avoid another unpleasant flare up, so soon after the first.

Just to think, she groaned inwardly, she and Magda still had weeks to spend in each other's company!

Michiko was a splendid hostess; the meal she provided was tasteful, both to the palate and to the eye, the colourful lacquered dishes being set out on a tray of unstained wood, polished so that the grain stood out like the whorls of a human thumbprint. Cold savoury rice was garlanded with dark green seaweed, while other dishes contained brown bean cake, white leeks, hot fish soup and slices of pink and white raw fish. Cinnabar was a little doubtful about the latter, but found it extremely palatable.

They rounded off the meal with a further bowl of rice and green tea, relaxing afterwards in the peaceful atmosphere of the pink-hued sitting room. Unlike Marlowe's apartment, Michiko's was a treasure-house of knick-knacks ... fans, painted scrolls, jade figurines jostled each other for attention, and there was a particularly delightful collection of costume dolls from all over the world.

To one or two of Cinnabar's enquiries, Michiko replied: 'My papa give.' But mostly, and with particular reference to the dolls, the answer was simply: 'Present from Marlowe. He generous man.'

Cinnabar endeavoured to fight the unaccountable and sickening waves of jealousy, which increased with the enumeration of each treasured possession, for she really liked the slim, vivacious Japanese girl, able to see how a man of Marlowe's taste and refinement would be drawn to her delicate beauty. But at last she could stand it no longer, hearing Michiko's enthusiastic praise, seeing the affection in her brown, almond-shaped eyes; and on a plea of extreme fatigue and of a busy day to follow, she finally managed to take her leave.

There was no sign of Madga, and once again she heard the older girl come in very late. This time, the loud, drawling sound of her voice was interspersed with the quieter, deeper tones of a man's voice, and Cinnabar gathered that the model had been out with Hank Schuster and that he had accompanied her back to the suite.

The talking and laughing went on for some time and eventually Cinnabar fell asleep, not knowing what time Hank finally left.

'I suppose you're going to drag me round from pillar to post again today?' Magda enquired belligerently over breakfast.

All these late nights were beginning to tell on Magda, Cinnabar thought worriedly, studying the model's discontented face. If she wasn't careful she'd have to resort to a heavier make-up, to disguise the signs of dissipation from the camera.

Aloud she said:

'No, you can have an easier day, Magda. I thought we'd ask Michiko to take us to the nearest park today. Several of the designs will do very well in a simple, natural setting. I won't keep you very long ... I want to be back early myself.'

'Oh, why's that?' Magda asked suspiciously.

Cinnabar traced the pattern around the rim of her cup. She thinks Marlowe is expected back today, she thought. Well, there was no point in being secretive any longer about Gary's imminent arrival. Magda would find out soon enough.

'Gary will be here later,' she admitted. 'He has a few days' leave, so he's joining us.'

She met Magda's hard, dark eyes squarely and the model was the first to look away.

Cinnabar sighed. She knew she couldn't trust Magda. Somehow or other, the model would endeavour to make trouble for her with Gary. She would just have to hope that

Gary would accept her word, rather than Magda's. She wasn't ready for a showdown with him just yet.

As she had expected, the willing Michiko knew of a suitable park, only a short taxi ride away.

Cinnabar reflected, with scornful self-mockery, that Marlowe had made the original suggestion of a Japanese garden as a setting for Vyvyan's creations, and she, in her pigheaded shortsightedness, had snubbed him; and now here she was, about to follow his advice. She was just glad that he wasn't here to gloat about it. Though her feelings towards him had undergone a considerable change, she still did not intend to let any man make her decisions for her.

Magda, of course, had fault to find with Michiko's choice, a Japanese landscape garden, without a flower to be seen, only the azalea shrubs, which would blossom in June and the cherry trees which had now passed their springtime glory.

But there were plenty of other trees, shrubs and grasses, set against a soft blue Japanese sky; the lichen-mottled grey of the stones; dwarf pines; white gravel; coarse sands and tall stone lanterns in abundance.

'Call this a park?' Magda exclaimed scornfully, as she donned the first garment, a crêpe-de-chine dress with graceful, flowing lines, patterned in red and black on purest white.

'Japanese landscape gardens very beautiful ... symbolic.' Even the naturally courteous Michiko could not forbear jumping to the defence of her country's traditions. 'Something beautiful always hidden ... for visitor to discover.'

Michiko's claim was vindicated as they rounded a corner, coming upon a small pavilion temple, brooding over its own gilded reflection in a lily-patterned pond; and even Magda had no criticism to make as she took up her stance, clad this time in a peacock blue pants suit, which cleverly combined Western styling with an Oriental print.

'We'll do the happi coat here as well,' Cinnabar decided, as Magda swayed and postured and she darted from side to side, capturing the scene in swift, competent shots.

Michiko giggled as Magda donned the red, short-sleeved, blouse-like jacket, with its motifs of Japanese characters, worn with black, silky pants.

'What's the joke?' Cinnabar asked.

'In Japan, boy wear happi coat, for big festival, special occasion ... not girls,' Michiko explained.

'Ah well, this is a Western adaptation,' Cinnabar told her. 'In our country, anything goes, if you have the nerve to wear it.'

The park was a photographer's paradise. Of many acres, it also incorporated a rock garden and a moss garden, where little streams ran beneath trees and among the twisted roots of azalea bushes. Stepping stones rose from the moss, or were submerged in the green, cushioned slopes; and, at the very heart of the park, they discovered a lake, with more stepping stones, surrounded by stone lanterns and ... a cleverly contrived finishing effect ... an old boat, deliberately half submerged.

Cinnabar sighed happily as they left the serenity of the gardens. Once again she had some beautiful work to send off to Vyvyan.

Michiko was thrilled to hear that Cinnabar expected Gary that afternoon.

'Japan in spring very romantic place for lovers,' she enthused. 'You take time off work to be with boy-friend?'

'Heavens, no!' Cinnabar laughed. 'My boss would have a fit! He wants these photographs yesterday.'

'Please?' Michiko looked puzzled.

'I mean he's a very impatient man,' Cinnabar explained. 'But I expect Gary will come on location with us. He's a photographer too.'

'Ah, you have much in common,' Michiko said wisely. 'Marlowe say that very important between man and woman. Last longer than passion.'

If Marlowe and Michiko were intimate enough to discuss such things, it would seem that he and the lovely Japanese girl had the very compatibility she described. It was too easy, Cinnabar thought, to forget Marlowe's Japanese ancestry, albeit diluted by European blood; but quite possibly he had inherited many Oriental traits and traditions, sufficient to make him seek a partner with the same values.

She would have given much to know what the exact relationship was between Marlowe and Michiko. *Did* he look upon her as a prospective bride, or was she just one of a long line of girl-friends? Their tenancy of adjoining flats would seem to indicate quite a strong degree of intimacy. Surely the Japanese girl must be his current mistress.

Much as she longed to know, and friendly as Michiko was, there was a natural delicacy in Cinnabar, which precluded prying into the affairs of others. It really was none of her business, she reflected ... Marlowe's private life should be of no significance to her, but then why this sharp pain, like the thrust of a sword?

Since Michiko had told her of his ancestry, the thought of him was always coupled in her mind with the image of a sword ... the ancient implement of chivalry and honour, yet which could inflict grievous wounds.

Back at their hotel, Cinnabar enquired of the desk clerk whether Gary had arrived. But the smiling young man informed her that no Mr Reid had checked in as yet.

When she reached the suite she found Magda chatting animatedly on the telephone, and from her provocative manner, Cinnabar knew that it must be a man at the receiving end. As the other girl finished her conversation, Cinnabar announced that if anyone wanted her she wouldn't be long, that she was going to take a shower.

'Trying to make yourself beautiful for poor old Gary?' Magda taunted. 'Hypocrite!'

Cinnabar set her lips, refusing to be drawn into a slanging match.

''Fraid you'll have to wait your turn,' said Magda, moving swiftly towards their shared bathroom. 'Hank is picking me up in twenty minutes.'

Before Cinnabar could open her mouth to protest, the bathroom door had slammed shut and there followed the sound of running water.

Fuming, Cinnabar went into her bedroom. This, she vowed, was the very last time she was going to work on an assignment with Magda Llewellyn! The girl was completely self-centred, thoughtless and two-faced. So far she had managed to disguise her flawed character from the men she encountered, dazzling them by her physical beauty and veiling her insulting verbal thrusts at other women under a cloak of apparently disingenuous frankness.

Cinnabar felt sorry for the man Magda eventually married. Sooner or later he would be thoroughly disillusioned; it would be impossible even for Magda to maintain her façade in the necessarily closer proximity of marriage.

She sat listening to the sound of running water and hoping that she would have time to freshen up before Gary arrived ... that Magda would not use all the warm water.

Eventually the model relinquished the bathroom to Cinnabar's use, and though the water was now only lukewarm, she felt pleasantly refreshed after her shower.

She heard the sounds of Magda's departure and drew a breath of relief. At least she would be able to greet Gary without the model looking on. They would be able to relax and accustom themselves to being together again ... something which Cinnabar always found necessary after one of Gary's protracted absences.

She wound a large towel around her, sarong-wise, and using another, smaller towel, had just begun to dry her hair, when there was a knock on the outer door of the suite. Gary! She ran to open the door, flinging it wide.

'Hallo! Oh!'

She blushed furiously and, clutching at the bath towel, she retreated, before the amused, speculative gaze of Marlowe Hirakawa.

CHAPTER FIVE

HER instinctive retreat had been a mistake; she realised that immediately. She should have slammed the door in Marlowe's face. But instead he took advantage of her discomposure to enter the room, closing the door behind him, his enormous stature dwarfing his surroundings.

'After your abrupt farewell on Saturday night, I scarcely expected such a warm welcome,' he observed, as he circled her, his prowling gait reminiscent of some predatory animal, his eyes intent upon her unconventional attire.

'It wasn't!' she snapped, thoroughly disconcerted by his presence, the knowledge of the very inadequate protection afforded by her towel. 'Wasn't a warm welcome, I mean . . . at least, not for *you*.'

'Oh?' The well-shaped eyebrows quirked enquiringly, the hazel eyes were quizzical. 'Obviously your social life has expanded in my absence. Though I hardly expected *you* of all people to make such rapid strides in intimacy.'

'I . . . I wasn't expecting a man,' she stammered, her discomfort increasing by the moment, under the appraisal of those mocking eyes. 'I'm expecting Gary.'

His laugh was one of pure amusement.

'A scarcely flattering distinction! Am I to take it you don't find your fiancé sufficiently endowed with male attributes?'

Cinnabar stamped her foot, seriously imperilling the security of the bath towel.

'Don't try to twist my words! You know perfectly well what I mean. It's your fault if I didn't express myself clearly. You . . .' she faltered, 'you confuse me.'

'Do I, Cinnabar?' he said softly, ceasing his prowling inspection of her, which had brought him uncomfortably close. 'Do I? I wonder why?'

She knew, even if he didn't, she thought . . . standing there with flagrant sexual interest in his hazel eyes, as he watched her ineffectual struggles with the recalcitrant towel.

'You look as if you could use some help with that,' he suggested, moving in on her . . . reaching for her.

She panicked.

'No! No, thank you. Will you *please* go away? I . . . I have to get ready.'

Despite her protest, her instinctive movement backward, Marlowe had been too swift for her, his large hands even now deftly rearranging the folds of the towel, tucking the end in more securely, lingering over the task, his warm fingers brushing her skin . . . *was* it inadvertently?

'If this Gary has any red blood in him at all, I imagine he'll be quite satisfied with you as you are . . . especially if you give him the same welcome you accorded me.'

He stood looking down at her, his hands now enclosing her upper arms, gentle strength in the warm fingers, further imperilling her composure.

'I was *not* welcoming *you!*' She was finding it difficult to articulate. 'Don't be so . . . so obtuse!'

'Right at this moment,' he said softly, his hands moving up to caress her bare shoulders, rising creamy-white and still slightly damp above the enveloping towel, 'right at this moment, obtuseness is the last thing you could accuse me of. I assure you, I have all my senses very much about me. *All* of them,' he repeated insinuatingly; his hands, continuing to move in sensuous caress, encircled the slender column of her neck, thumbs stroking the sensitive hollows behind her ears.

Cinnabar was racked by a very strange sensation, which seemed to her to begin in the pit of her stomach and rise to the back of her throat, making her oddly breathless, so that it seemed vital to sigh deeply, her breasts rising and falling on the movement, drawing his eyes to their shape, ill-disguised beneath the damply clinging towel.

The sight seemed to snap the taut control he had so far exercised and, almost roughly, he pulled her against him. Though her brain told her she ought to resist, at his nearness all physical strength seemed to be sapped from her. With one strong hand clamped between her shoulder blades, he was moulding her to him, while his free hand strayed amongst the moist, curling tendrils of hair framing her flushed face.

'Like a chrysanthemum after a shower of rain,' he murmured huskily. He bent his dark head, inhaling the fragrance of the shampoo she had used, then his lips brushed her forehead, traced the line of her brows, sought out the delicate, fluttering eyelids, then moved over her cheeks, seeking the mouth she sought to avert from him.

'Cinnabar,' he breathed. 'Have you missed me?'

'Don't be ridiculous,' she said faintly.

She ought to move away, to repulse him, but she knew that if he released her now, she would fall, her knees felt so tremulous, her whole body limp and languorous.

'Why is it ridiculous?' he asked, his teeth tantalising the lobe of her ear.

Fists clenched against his broad chest, she leant back, trying to meet his eyes.

'Because ... because I hardly know you ... it's been less than a week. So why should I miss you?'

'Of course you hardly know me ... or I you. But I do know that you're very lovely, very desirable. Think of the pleasure we can have, getting to know each other better.'

He was certainly a fast worker! How many women had he said that to? She imagined that very few would have resisted his hypnotic, persuasive voice, his compelling good looks.

'Marlowe,' she insisted, 'you ... you have to stop this! It ... it isn't right ... you've no right ...'

But he ignored the words, stopping her protests with his mouth, and at the now familiar intoxication of his kiss, she relaxed against him once more, her brain totally incapable of waging war against the overwhelming demands of her body.

'Say it!' he demanded, lifting his mouth fractionally for an instant. 'Admit that you've missed me.'

Like one mesmerised, she murmured, 'I've missed you.'

The tightening of his grasp, his low triumphant laugh, released her from thrall and she began to struggle, qualifying the shaming admission he had wrung from her.

'Yes, I missed you, you conceited brute, but not for the reason you imagine. It was a relief *not* to have you around ... no one to interfere or boss me about. I've been able to please myself. If *that's* missing you, then yes, I certainly have!'

Marlowe released her so suddenly that she stumbled and she faced him defiantly, though her breathing was still erratic, her lips still tingling from his kisses. Lashing herself into a fury, because it was the only way she could fight off his insidious attraction for her, she continued her diatribe.

'And just because you own this hotel, it does't give you the right to walk in here any time you choose, to . . . to insult me like this . . .'

A short laughed answered her.

'Before you declare war, my dear, you should check that your ammunition is effective. The hotel does *not* belong to me. It belongs to my uncle. I did *not* just walk in. You opened the door to me; and how can it possibly be an insult to say that I find you very, very desirable?'

'It's an insult,' she flared at him, 'because I haven't given you the right to . . . to find me desirable, and certainly not to kiss me, to . . . to hold me like that. I've told you, I'm engaged to be married, and you insult me by thinking I'm the sort of girl who would behave like that, when . . . when I'm going to marry another man.'

'When *are* you getting married?' Marlowe asked curiously, ignoring the rest of her indictment.

'I . . . I don't know exactly . . . some time, when I'm . . . Oh, I don't *know* yet. And it's no business of yours anyhow.'

'This year, next year, some time, never,' he quoted softly. 'If you were really in love with this fiancé of yours, you'd be panting to be married, now, as soon as possible . . . not in some dim, unforeseeable and probably non-existent future.'

'It's not non-existent . . . it's not!' she said a trifle wildly, because he must not know that her engagement had never existed. The pretence had arisen in the first place out of pique, when he had accused her of lacking self-confidence in herself as a woman, and it had become even more necessary to maintain the fiction, to hide her growing vulnerability to him . . . now that she knew about his relationship with Michiko. 'I *am* going to get married. I *want* to get married!'

'Yes,' he said thoughtfully, 'I think you probably do . . . but not to this Gary chap.'

'What can *you* possibly know about it?' she asked scornfully.

His voice was husky, seductive.

'I know what my senses tell me . . . what I've learnt about you, when I've held you in my arms. Gary isn't the right man for you. It's obvious that he's never awakened you to a knowledge of what love is . . . can be.'

Cinnabar stared at him, knowing he was right. Gary had never made her feel . . . feel . . . well, the way she'd felt just now, pressed against Marlowe's hard body . . . aware of him in the way she had never been aware of any man before.

But then Gary was younger than this man, nearer her own age, less experienced. *That* was it, of course! The basis from which Marlowe asserted his knowledge of her ... his experience. How many women had he awakened to a knowledge of their own potential sensuality?

'I said you were like a chrysanthemum,' Marlowe said reflectively, 'but I was wrong.'

'Oh!' She felt a searing sense of disappointment. She had liked his imagery. It had made her feel different ... special.

'No.' He smiled, and it was a teasing smile, as if he sensed her chagrin. 'As yet you're only a tightly curled bud, needing the warmth of passion, the rain of joyful tears to open you, to mature you into glorious bloom. Then and only then will you really be a beautiful bronze chrysanthemum.'

His voice was soft, hynotic, drawing her towards him, step by step, without any physical effort on his part. She stood before him, totally bemused, gazing up into his eyes ... eyes as mesmeric as his voice, his slow smile, as he reached out for her.

'Cinnabar, I have to go away again tomorrow, to visit my uncle, but first I ...'

'There! What did I tell you, Gary?'

The door, insecurely closed after Marlowe's arrival, was flung open and on the threshold stood a smiling, triumphant Magda; and with her Gary, a Gary who stared at Cinnabar as though he did not believe the evidence of his own pale blue eyes ... eyes which were slowly hardening with contempt and condemnation.

'Gary!'

Cinnabar, the spell which held her broken, walked towards him. Meanwhile, Magda, quietly elated, had joined Marlowe, slipping her arm through his.

'I think we're rather de trop just at this moment, darling. Shall we leave these two lovebirds to their reunion?'

Marlowe made an impatient gesture, as if he were about to repudiate her suggestion, then, apparently thinking better of it, turned on his heel and strode from the room, Magda almost running to keep pace with him.

As the door slammed behind them, Cinnabar spoke again, controlling her voice with an effort. Why, oh, why had Gary to arrive at that precise moment?

'Gary, your telegram was such a surprise. But it's lovely to see you, I ...'

'Go and get dressed,' he interrupted her, the words issuing from between clenched teeth, 'or I won't be responsible for my actions. My God, to see you ... blatantly offering yourself to that man! It's enough to make me ...' He turned abruptly and stared out of the window, tension in the set of his head, in the clenched hands at his side.

'You're wrong, Gary,' she said quietly. 'It wasn't how it looked. We ...'

'Wasn't how it looked!' He turned on her, his pale blue eyes colder still with anger. 'Shall I *tell* you how it looked? It looked to me as if that ... that fellow had got further with you, Bar, in four or five days than I have in a couple of years!'

Gary always called her Bar, and she had never liked it.

'You've always been so ... so reserved with me, never let me ...' He spread his hands expressively. 'When I came in just now, I thought, *I've* never seen Bar like that ... glowing, warm, so ... so *abandoned*. And ... and that towel! Damn it, Bar, *will* you go and get some clothes on!'

Sighing, she turned to obey him. This had turned out worse than she had expected. Magda might almost have stage-managed that little scene with Marlowe, so well had it suited her purpose, her threat to cause trouble. But there was something that Magda could not possibly know, something which nullified her scheming.

A few minutes later, soberly clad in jeans and a blouse, severely buttoned up to the neck, Cinnabar re-entered the sitting room. Gary was exactly where she had left him, staring out of the window, but she had the idea that he saw nothing beyond the pictures in his brain ... pictures of her and Marlowe.

She drew a deep breath, then, with an attempt at lightness:

'Gary? I'm decent now.'

Slowly he turned to face her.

'Are you? Are you, Bar? I wonder.'

Suddenly she wanted to scream at him, 'Don't call me Bar! It's not my name.' But she steeled herself to remain calm.

'Gary, sit down, please.'

Grudgingly he complied.

'The man you saw,' she began, 'was Marlowe Hirakawa, managing director of ...'

'I know all that,' he said impatiently, 'Magda told me all about *him*.'

'Yes, she would! Gary, you *know* what Magda's like. She's earmarked Marlowe for herself, but she's got the idea that I . . .'

'I'm not surprised, after what I saw just now,' Gary interrupted, his face sulky, 'seeing him here with you, and you . . . well, half naked.'

'He took me by surprise. I was showering, getting ready for *you*. He knocked and I thought it *was* you. I opened the door, and . . . and the rest you know.'

'Do I? Do I?' he asked savagely. 'Just how long had he been up here? When I met Magda in the foyer, we talked for quite a while, and it was some time before she told me she'd seen this Hirakawa chap on his way up to your suite.'

'He *had* been here for a few minutes,' Cinnabar agreed, 'but I couldn't very well throw him out. I had to be civil. After all, his uncle does own the place, and . . .'

'A few minutes!' Gary derided. 'More like half an hour!'

'And what was so interesting about Magda's conversation to keep you talking for half an hour?' Cinnabar retaliated. She was tired of being conciliatory, of being put in the wrong. She had nothing for which to apologise. 'I bet she was filling you up with all kinds of lies and insinuations.' Her eyes narrowed. 'I bet Magda deliberately set this up, kept you, didn't let you come up until . . . until . . .'

'Until what?' His thin, fresh-complexioned face was twisted with scorn.

She shrugged fatalistically. Better to tell a partial truth than to deny what had been patently obvious.

'Until Marlowe was likely to be making a pass at me. You can believe it or not, just as you like. But I didn't encourage him, Gary. He doesn't *need* encouragement. He's so certain of his own irresistible charm. He . . . he's a philanderer.'

At the recollection that Marlowe only sought to add her to his list of conquests, despite her resolve to remain calm, her voice cracked on the last words.

'He . . . he's even got a mistress, a Japanese girl. She lives in the flat above him.' Involuntarily her lips quivered.

Though he misinterpreted the cause, the sight of her distress convinced Gary as nothing else had. Swiftly he moved towards her, taking her in his arms.

'I'm sorry, Bar,' he said penitently. 'You're right, I should have known better than to believe Magda. But all the same,

I'd like to sock that chap on the jaw . . . taking advantage of you like that. I wish now I'd . . .'

'I'm glad you didn't,' she told him, smiling a trifle shakily, at the thought of the slender Gary in conflict with the powerfully built Marlowe. 'He . . . he's so enormous . . . so tall, so strong. Sometimes he . . . he scares *me*.'

Gary immediately leapt to the wrong conclusion.

'There's no need to be scared now *I'm* here,' he said confidently. 'Tell you what, Bar. Let's get engaged, hmm? You know you're going to marry me some day. While I'm here we could buy the ring.'

Cinnabar experienced panic. A few hours ago she would have welcomed Gary's repeated offer of marriage, but now . . .

'Oh no, I don't think I . . .'

But Gary was insistent.

'I want the whole world to know you belong to me, Bar, and it will give this Hirakawa chap the hands-off sign too.'

Cinnabar doubted it, in view of Marlowe's expressed opinion of her relationship with Gary, but she couldn't tell Gary so. He had accepted the fact that she feared Marlowe, but he had wrongly interpreted the cause of that fear, thinking it stemmed from the other man's redoubtable size, her description of him as a philanderer.

What Gary couldn't realise was the *true* source of her emotion, her own vulnerability to Marlowe, the almost irresistible lure of his sexual charisma upon her senses.

With more pain than joy, she recalled his kisses, his husky voice declaring her unawakened state . . . wondered what he had been about to say when Magda and Gary had made their sudden entrance. With a sharp pang of desolation she remembered that he was going away again, to visit his uncle . . . but for how long?

Gary seemed happily complacent now, his suspicions allayed, and unwilling to hurt his feelings so soon after his arrival, Cinnabar was forced to endure his kisses, the increasing enthusiasm of his caresses, as she tried to simulate a response which she did not feel. Gary might be deceived by her efforts, but she felt absolutely nothing. His kisses were ordinary, exciting no reaction in her, and he seemed to think that their engagement was a settled fact, licensing him to dare familiarities she had never before permitted.

Gently but firmly she pushed him away from her. She would have to make up her mind what she was going to do about Gary ... and when.

'Not now, Gary, please. I want to talk to you. I've such a lot to tell you. I've had a pretty hectic schedule up to now and I'm glad you're here. I could use some help. So far I've been developing the films as I go along. There's some marvellous stuff ... Vyvyan will be in raptures!'

At first she was talking just for the sake of it, desperate to distract him, but as she spoke of her work, she became increasingly enthusiastic, and reluctantly Gary abandoned his attempts to make love to her.

'Though considering we haven't seen each other for weeks ...' he grumbled.

'Gary, why don't you come over to the darkroom,' she suggested hastily, 'and have a look at the work I've done. I'll be sending the first batch off to Vyvyan tomorrow. But I'd like you to see them first, to tell me what you think.'

'You've never wanted my opinion before, Bar,' Gary said sceptically, as they took the lift down to the foyer. 'In fact you've never welcomed any comment, unless it's been unqualified praise.'

'Am I *so* bigheaded?' she asked him lightly; but in reality she was rather horrified by this view of herself. Was that what Marlowe thought of her too?

It was evident that Gary was impressed by the size and obvious prosperity of the Hirakawa building. But then Gary was always impressed by wealth, a trait Cinnabar could not understand. A reasonable competence was desirable, but health and happiness, a career that was interesting for its own sake, was all she had ever demanded of life.

Michiko opened the door of her apartment. She had changed from Western dress into the comfortable informality of a kimono, the black silky material liberally sprinkled with varied pink spring flowers, accentuating the darkness of her upswept hair, deepening the brown of her almond-shaped eyes. Against the pink-hued sitting room, the tiny Japanese girl was a most attractive sight. Cinnabar knew, even before she heard Gary's indrawn breath, that, with his photographer's eye, he would be enchanted by the picture Michiko made.

The Japanese girl was quietly delighted to see them. Cinnabar had noticed that, despite her vivacious chatter, unlike many of her contemporaries, she had no tendency to constant giggling. Instead she had a bubbling zest for life, tempered by a grave, gentle wisdom.

Gary seemed restless, showing only a cursory interest in the darkroom and in the photographs already developed.

'They look fine to me. But you go ahead, Bar, and develop today's batch,' he advised. 'You don't really need me. Besides, I'm supposed to be on holiday. Tell you what,' he suggested casually, 'I could sit and talk to Michiko. Gosh, I'd love to take some photographs of her. Do you think she'd let me?'

Working alone, though her hands were busy, Cinnabar's brain was able to function independently. What an odd situation, she mused, one in which anyone else would be feeling jealous right now. Here was her boy-friend, only just arrived, after several weeks' separation, and instead of wanting to be with her, he was talking to another girl ... a very attractive one. Of course it was only professional interest ... his eye for a striking subject ... but most girls would feel a twinge of jealousy, no matter how implicit their trust.

Gary didn't stand a chance with Michiko, of course. What man would, with a girl who, if she was right, was mistress to just about the most sexually attractive man in existence? And that, Cinnabar admitted, was the true reason for her own lack of jealousy. What she had once felt for Gary had not been love, merely affectionate liking. Perhaps she had always realised that ... hence her reluctance to commit herself to an engagement.

She didn't care what Gary did, how attractive he might find the Japanese girl, because she herself wasn't in love with him. She was in love with Marlowe Hirakawa. She admitted it with no sense of surprise. It was as if she had always known.

She supposed the knowledge of her love for Marlowe must have been growing on her for several days ... perhaps even from the moment of their first encounter. But the dim light of perception, which had flickered on and off, with her fluctuating moods of attraction and resentment, had burst into full illumination tonight. Not when he had kissed her ... he had kissed her on other occasions, without giving rise to this blinding revelation.

No, it had been that moment when, with a voice full of amused tenderness, he had likened her to an unawakened bud, not yet ready to bloom; and she had known then, with absolute certainty, that she wanted *him* to be the one to nurture her emotional growth, to supply the warmth of passion, induce the joyful tears which would bring her into the full splendour of maturity, making her, in his imagery, an unfurled bronze chrysanthemum.

Nobody seemed to know how long Marlowe would be away this time, not even Michiko, and despite a full work schedule and the addition of Gary's company on their daily expeditions, the next week dragged for Cinnabar.

It was unbearable, not knowing when she would see Marlowe again. Now that Gary was here, believing him to be her fiancé, he might deliberately stay out of the way.

She had hoped too that Gary's presence might put Magda into a sweeter frame of mind, but this improvement had not transpired. True, he accompanied them each day, but he seemed quite content to leave model and photographer to get on with their work, while he conversed with Michiko.

They seemed to find a lot to talk about, Cinnabar thought, and there was much laughter from their direction. On one occasion, when Magda was in one of her particularly unco-operative moods, Cinnabar found herself actually envying Gary his freedom from responsibility and wishing that she too were just a holidaymaker in this delightful country. It was the first time she had felt any distaste for her chosen career.

The shots scheduled to be set in Tokyo were complete, with only the developing to be done, and Cinnabar knew that it was necessary now to go farther afield. Yet she was reluctant to leave the capital without having seen Marlowe just once more.

But the longer he stayed away, the more resentful she felt. It was illogical, of course. At the beginning of their acquaintance, she had make it known that she resented his supervision, so she had no right to any consideration from him . . . no right to expect his attendance on her. Nevertheless, resentment gradually turned to anger and stiffened into hurt pride, until she resolved not to hang around in Tokyo any longer.

'I'm going to finish off the developing tonight,' she told Gary and Magda one afternoon, as they returned to the hotel. 'Then tomorrow we can leave for Kyoto. Michiko,' she turned to the Japanese girl, 'you can telephone ahead? Arrange accommodation for us?'

'Yes,' the girl said doubtfully, 'but Marlowe . . . he . . .'

'Oh, bother Marlowe!' Cinnabar snapped. 'I have a schedule to keep to and I want to go to Kyoto tomorrow.'

Michiko looked as if she would have liked to protest further, but Cinnabar gave her no opportunity, as she gained the lift and went up to her room, to wash away the day's dust.

'I thought you were rather rude to poor little Michiko this afternoon,' Gary said reprovingly over dinner.

Michiko had not joined them for the meal and Cinnabar's query as to her whereabouts elicited this remark.

'Yes, I suppose I was.' Cinnabar was ashamed of her sharp manner with the pleasant younger girl. 'But I'll apologise tonight. I'm going up to her apartment to finish that developing. I'll post this batch off to Vyvyan when we get to Kyoto.'

'Michiko won't be in tonight,' Magda volunteered, and Cinnabar wondered at the spiteful edge to the model's drawling voice. 'She's going out with Gary,' Magda continued.

Cinnabar understood at once. The older girl was expecting her to be hurt by the news, and although she was not at all troubled, she looked at Gary for confirmation, surprised to see him looking extremely disconcerted and ill at ease.

'I knew you were going to be busy all evening, Bar,' he mumbled, 'so I thought it would be a good opportunity to take Michiko up on a offer she made me.'

'Oh, what's that?'

Cinnabar was genuinely interested, but Gary still looked a little wary, as he replied.

'She has a friend who's a geisha. I said I'd like to go to a geisha house ... take some photos. It ... it's strictly professional, you understand?'

'Sounds like a very good idea to me,' Cinnabar said cheerfully, knowing that she surprised both Magda and Gary by her calm reaction.

She rose from the table.

'I'll see you in the morning, then ... *early*; and that goes for you too, Magda!'

'How do we get to Kyoto?' Gary asked.

'By train, of course,' Cinnabar told him, and seeing Magda's outraged expression, hurried away before the other girl could give vent to her discontent.

Cinnabar found herself humming cheerfully as she worked. It seemed just possible that the problem of Gary was going to be solved for her. She was not deceived in the least by his claim that tonight's outing was purely for the purposes of photography. She knew that, right from their very first encounter, he had been fascinated by the delicate loveliness of the tiny Japanese girl; and, thrown together as they were on their daily outings, a firm friendship had sprung up between them.

Of course it wouldn't get him anywhere, she reflected, with a pang of sympathy for Gary's inevitable disappointment. Michiko belonged to Marlowe. But Gary couldn't say he hadn't been warned; even before they'd met, she had told him that Michiko was Marlowe's mistress.

Still, at least this situation might alter his determination to marry *her*; and while still able to use Gary as a cover-up for her pride, she would not have to make her pretended engagement a real one. It was a selfish attitude, she admitted, but a necessary one, if Marlowe was not to guess at her hopeless, foolish feelings for him. She could imagine his mocking expression, if he thought she had taken his flirtatious manner seriously.

She frowned slightly, as she noticed that some of her earlier negatives had been moved and put back in the wrong order. Perhaps Michiko, interested in her work, had been looking at them. Anxiously she studied the films for fingerprints or damage, but they seemed unharmed. The last batch finished and hung up to dry, she relaxed, straightening her aching back, and looked at her watch.

Good, it would be possible to get her packing done and have a reasonably early night, ready for the day ahead.

She wondered if Magda had gone out too. Today had been Hank Schuster's last in Tokyo; he was flying back to New York tomorrow. Would Magda genuinely miss him, or had he just been used? Knowing the model, Cinnabar thought it quite probable that she would immediately transfer her attentions back to Marlowe.

Did Magda know what she was up against? It was rather

strange that, while she had been downright offensive to Cinnabar over her supposed pursuit of Marlowe, Magda had never made any insinuations about the Japanese girl, even though she must be aware now of the conveniently adjoining apartments.

Frankly, Cinnabar was puzzled. It wasn't like Magda to miss a chance to denigrate or belittle any opposition.

The reliable little travelling alarm clock which accompanied her everywhere woke Cinnabar on cue.

She had ordered an early breakfast, to be served in their suite, and having showered and donned the clothes put ready the previous night, left her room, with the intention of checking up on Magda, who had a rooted objection to rising early.

But Magda was already immaculately dressed and groomed, and making inroads on the coffee pot.

'Good heavens!' Cinnabar exclaimed. 'What's got into you? Not that I'm complaining, mind. The sooner we get away the better. It's a fair distance to Kyoto.'

'Except that we're not going to Kyoto,' Magda announced calmly, helping herself to the single piece of toast which was all she permitted herself for breakfast.

'We most certainly *are*.'

Arrested in the act of pouring herself a coffee, Cinnabar looked suspiciously at Magda. What was the model up to now? She groaned inwardly. Surely Hank hadn't decided to extend his stay? Magda was quite capable of digging her heels in, if she had to choose between her work and a man.

'Sorry, but you're a bit out of date, *darling*!'

The 'darling', as applied to Cinnabar, bore not the remotest resemblance to its honeyed emphasis when addressed to a man.

'I don't know what you're talking about, Magda,' Cinnabar said irritably, 'and I don't know what devious little scheme you've been cooking up, but our schedule says we have to go to Kyoto and we are going there . . . today.'

'Not according to Marlowe,' the model rejoined smugly.

'Marlowe! Marlowe? What's it got to do with him? He's not even here, is . . . is he?' Cinnabar's confident tone faltered suddenly.

'Oh yes.' Magda stood up and wandered over to the room's full-length mirror, candidly assessing her own appearance and inspecting her already faultless make-up for any flaws which might have occurred in the last ten minutes. 'He came back very late . . . after you'd gone to bed. We made quite a night of it, Marlowe and I . . . . and *Gary and Michiko*.'

She put heavy emphasis on the final two names, and though she did not reveal it, Cinnabar felt the stab of jealousy she was intended to experience, thought not, as Magda intended, over Gary.

'Oh?' she said, with an air of forced nonchalance. 'Then how come you've managed to get up so early?'

'Because, my dear, Marlowe told us all to be ready. But we're not going anywhere near Kyoto. Marlowe says we're going to some place called Gifu.'

'Oh, he does, does he?'

Cinnabar forgot the faint frisson of excitement she had felt at the news of Marlowe's return. Instead, a wave of indignation swamped all sensations of pleasure. So he thought he could just walk back into their lives and start disrupting everything again. Right! She'd show Mr Marlowe Hirakawa. They'd soon see who was in charge of this assignment!

Tight-lipped, she threw down her napkin and made for the door, wrenching it open.

'Where are *you* going?' Magda enquired languidly.

Cinnabar turned.

'To see Mr High and Mighty Hirakawa, of course . . . to put him right about a few things.'

'Such as?'

Cinnabar started at the sound of that slow, lazy, all-too-familiar voice. She swung round to encounter its owner, who appeared to have materialised soundlessly in the doorway to the suite, his powerful physique and proud bearing emphasised by the impeccably tailored linen suit which streamlined his long body, making him seem taller and more imposing than ever.

For a brief second she was taken aback, but, her anger intensified at being taken by surprise, she snapped at him furiously.

'Such as arbitrarily cancelling *my* plans for the day . . . making other arrangements without even consulting me . . .'

She broke off, as a long arm shot out and dragged her into the hallway, Marlowe's other hand firmly shutting the apartment door on Magda's interested gaze.

'*When* I got back . . . late last night,' Marlowe informed her evenly, 'you were already in bed. Delighted as I should have been to hold a consultation there, I can't believe that *you* would have been equally pleased?'

A tremor coursed along her spine and she felt the insistent contractions deep in the pit of her stomach. He was back and already he was having his usual effect on her. But this time she was going to fight it . . . and him. He was not going to add *her* to his string of easy conquests!

'If I wasn't available,' she told him curtly, 'you should have waited. You've no right to change my itinerary. I'm going to Kyoto.'

'Then you'll be going alone,' he drawled, 'because the rest of your party is going with me.'

Cinnabar was incredulous, staggered at such unprecedented, high-handed behaviour.

'You can't *do* that! I need Magda. There are photographs to be taken . . . I . . .'

'Photographs which can quite easily wait another day or two.'

'No,' she denied. 'They can *not* wait. Vyvyan's instructions . . .'

'Mr Lamonde's instructions were that *I* should arrange and supervise your itinerary,' Marlowe reminded her, 'and I don't think your employer would deny you the opportunity of seeing Gifu . . . the spectacle it has to offer.'

'Gifu! Gifu!' Cinnabar realised he was still holding her arm and tried to wrench herself free from a contact that was like fire to her quivering nerves. 'That's all I've heard this morning! Well, *I* want to go to Kyoto, and . . .'

'If you go to Kyoto,' Marlowe said slowly and with emphasis, 'Gary Reid will photograph Magda at Gifu, and when the films reach London, *you* will not be able to claim the credit for them.'

'You . . . you wouldn't dare!' She stared at him. 'Even you wouldn't be so unscrupulous . . . and besides, Gary wouldn't . . .'

'Oh yes, he would. I happen to know that he has his own camera with him and that he's a very ambitious young man.'

'Gary wouldn't do anything to hurt *me*,' Cinnabar whispered. 'He . . . he's my boy-friend, and we . . .'

'Is he?' Marlowe enquired sardonically. 'Then why has he

spent all his free time this last week with Michiko? Scarcely
the action of an engaged man.' He lifted her left hand. 'Still
no ring, I see.'

She snatched it away, terrified by the pulsing heat that
engulfed her body at his slightest touch.

'I . . . I haven't seen one I like yet; and you're just taking
out your own jealousy on me.'

'My own jealousy? The hazel eyes widened interrogatively.

'Because Gary's made such a hit with your mistress,
you . . .'

'My what? My . . . Michiko?'

Marlowe gave her an odd glance, but apart from a
tightening of his lips there was no further reaction to her
challenge.

Furious at her own inability to penetrate that enigmatic
mask, Cinnabar was about to rush into further angry speech
when the door behind her was jerked open.

'Closed or open, I can hear every word,' Magda drawled,
'so I thought I might as well join in the fun.' Languishingly,
she looked up at Marlowe. 'Well, darling, what's it to be . . .
Kyoto or Gifu?'

'Gifu!' he said shortly, turning on his heel. Over his
shoulder he spoke briefly to the seething young photographer.
'And if you're coming with us, you'd better be ready in fifteen
minutes.'

They flew from Tokyo Airport to Nagoya and made their way
from Nagoya to Gifu by train . . . a train which, to Magda's
evident surprise and relief, was clean, fully air-conditioned
and comfortable.

'Travelling any distance by car is not always a luxury,'
Marlowe had said smoothly, in reply to Magda's slightly
petulant enquiry. 'Owing to frequent earth tremors, many
roads are in a bad condition.'

Since they had been in Japan, the girls had not experienced
any of these minor earthquakes, said to be quite a common
occurrence, and Cinnabar hoped fervently that they never
would. She was no coward, but the very idea of such natural
disasters made her go cold with fear.

She had not spoken to Marlowe throughout the journey,
deliberately sitting as far away from him as possible, and
though she was curious about their destination and the nature

of the spectacle Marlowe had hinted at, stubborn pride prevented her from questioning him.

It hadn't been strictly necessary that they should go to Kyoto today. Cinnabar could admit that to herself. She had made her plans in a fit of pique, intending to have left Tokyo before Marlowe returned. He had arranged this trip, she knew, entirely for the benefit of the House of Lamonde party, but in her determination not to be swayed by his disturbing presence ... to show her pleasure at his return ... she had greeted Marlowe's suggestions with hostility, and now she was paying the penalty for her ingratitude. Magda had contrived to sit with their host, and as Gary was engrossed in conversation with Michiko, Cinnabar sat alone, miserable and resentful and all too aware that she had only herself to blame.

There was no doubt that Marlowe brought out the worst in her. Basically, because she was so determined to demonstrate to him that he meant nothing in her life ... just because he had presumed to kiss her a few times and because he must not know how helplessly she had fallen in love with him.

She sighed irritably, remembering Vyvyan's strictures on co-operation. She would have had no difficulty in being civil or in co-operating with Marlowe Hirakawa, if he had lacked his undoubted charisma. But, she reminded herself, whatever his physical attraction, whatever her own feelings, he had a mistress and a nice cosy ménage in the same building as his own apartment; and it was incumbent on her to fall out of love with him as readily as she had fallen in love.

'Tell us some more about this cormorant fishing, Marlowe darling.'

Magda's words broke into Cinnabar's reverie and she pricked up her ears, glad of the distraction from her own thoughts. This was the first she had heard about cormorants ... or fishing. Too proud to ask him herself, she might glean a little information from the model's questioning of Marlowe.

But, frustratingly, Marlowe was shaking his head.

'No description of mine could match the actuality. I'm afraid you'll just have to wait and see!'

His charming smile took the edge from his refusal, a smile that was for Magda, and despite her resolution to root out her growing obsession with him, to stiffen her resentment against him, Cinnabar felt the old familiar pain gripping her heart, as the whimsical movement of his lips accentuated his disruptive attraction.

Accommodation had been arranged for the five of them at a Ryokan or inn, and as they descended from the taxi which had brought them from the railway station, they were greeted by a procession of smiling, bowing maids, sprinkling water on the path they must take to the door.

'The Japanese have a horror of dust,' Marlowe told Cinnabar, 'thus this courtesy extended to guests.'

It was the first time he had addressed her directly since they had left Tokyo that morning, and Cinnabar was tempted to ignore him, to show him that it didn't matter at all to her if he never spoke to her again.

But one sideways glance under her lashes at the strong face, with its heart-tugging good looks, the mouth twisting in humorous acknowledgment of her pique, and she was lost, words unnecessary, as her square, stubborn little face relaxed, albeit unwillingly, into her own enchanting smile.

'Going to forgive me for "managing" your life again?' Marlowe enquired, his hand imprisoning her elbow, as he guided her across the entrance courtyard, surfaced with fine gravel, raked in parallel lines. Not a scrap of litter marred its perfect surface.

'Here you will have an opportunity to see the more traditional side of Japanese life,' Marlowe continued, not waiting for her reply; and on a last fading shadow of chagrin, she reflected that he probably realised all too well how impossible it was for any woman to resist his compelling charm for very long . . . or to sustain antagonism against him. 'These inns are virtually unchanged since the time of the ancient Samurai,' he said, adding reassuringly, 'but they do have modern conveniences, such as electricity and running water.'

He was forced to stoop from his great height, to pass through a sliding latticework door, by which they gained the entrance porch. Here a smiling maid dropped to her knees before them and with hands placed before her on the matting, bowed, until her forehead touched the ground. This ceremony performed, she removed the visitors' shoes, replacing them with floppy, backless hotel slippers.

'They certainly believe in putting out the welcome mat,' Cinnabar observed, as the proprietress now appeared, with short, slightly pigeon-toed steps, to repeat the salutation of greeting. Then, with a clap of her hands, the woman summoned more maids, whose task it was to bring in the luggage.

In a shuffling procession, owing to the unaccustomed slippers, Marlowe's guests followed the proprietress to their rooms, passing along endless corridors, with squeaking wooden floors, polished to a high sheen by the traffic of hundreds of slippered feet.

Cinnabar's room was at the back of the Inn. From a small lobby she stepped up on to straw matting, the proprietress indicating that first she must remove her slippers, for no footwear must soil the golden straw of the tatami.

Left alone temporarily, while the others were conducted to similar apartments, Cinnabar took the opportunity to look around her. She was surrounded by incidences of the exquisite simplicity of Japanese design; furnishings and décor, though simple, were pleasing to her discerning eye. The low ceiling was of plain wood, while two walls were made of paper, mounted on rectangularly patterned frames of thin woodwork, in the form of sliding doors. A third wall had an alcove which contained only a simple flower arrangement and a decorated scroll, depicting a flashing fall of water, within which the shadow of a fish bravely attempted to leap the cataract.

In the centre of the floor was a black, lacquered table with massively carved stubby legs, less than knee-high, and in the corner a pile of silken cushions.

The fourth wall of the room was another papered lattice, which, Cinnabar discovered, slid open to reveal the garden. Just outside, a small stream gurgled busily around mossy rocks, cascaded over a tiny waterfall, then glided beneath a vermilion-painted bridge. Narrow paths of patterned stone meandered under old pines with twisted branches, while miniature azaleas edged a rock pool, the centre of which was occupied by a fountain, formed from green copper, representing a small, sinuous dragon.

Her attention was recalled to the interior by the entrance of a maid, carrying hot perfumed towels and a tray, on which stood a charming little ceramic teapot and a teabowl with a saucer of lacquered wood.

Seated on one of the silken cushions, sipping the traditional green tea, Cinnabar watched as the maid opened a paper-covered door in one wall, to reveal another, smaller room, containing a low, doll-sized dressing table, its tiny drawers at floor level, while a deep closet proved to contain bedding of padded quilts.

These facilities demonstrated, the maid closed the window panel and held out a thin kimono-like robe, indicating by gesture that Cinnabar should undress, and she recalled Michiko telling her that, on arrival at a Ryokan, tea was always followed by a hot bath. She was a little embarrassed at being helped to undress, but submitted to the girl's deft ministrations, after which the maid led the way across an inner courtyard to the bathhouse.

Michiko and Magda were there before her, and while Michiko seemed quite unselfconscious, it was obvious to Cinnabar that Magda was as uneasy as she at this custom of communal bathing.

'You do not mind?' Michiko enquired anxiously. 'It is possible to obtain private bath, but as Marlowe say show you all traditional activities. . . .'

Thank heavens the men didn't join in as well! Cinnabar thought, flushing from head to toe at the disturbing idea of sharing a bath with Marlowe.

It was the custom, apparently, to wash outside the bath, removing all traces of soap before stepping into extremely hot water. At first, the immersion was a shock to the system, taking the European girls' breath away, but it was immensely relaxing, Cinnabar decided, and refreshing, after their long journey.

Clad once more in their bath-kimonos, they were led back into the main building, where they were joined by the two men.

During their absence, a low, red-lacquered table in Marlowe's apartment had been set for dinner, covered with numerous dishes, each of a different colour and shape, the contents looking almost too beautiful to eat. When they had eaten, Marlowe suggested that, as it was no great distance, they should stroll down to the riverside.

'The spectacle we've come to witness doesn't begin until after dark.'

The Nagara river, the scene of the cormorant fishing they had come to see, ran through spectacular rocky gorges, and as they arrived the last sunlight of the day was spangling its waters. It seemed that the thing to do was to hire one of the boats, floored with tatami, and complete with a couple of boatmen, from which to view the proceedings.

Some of the boats were long, open-sided, with prows of unpainted wood, paper lanterns and bunting dangling from their canopied roofs, each vessel capable of holding thirty or more people.

'The fishing is only part of the spectacle,' Marlowe promised them, as he negotiated for the hire of two smaller boats, each suitable for only two or three people.

How it was managed, or whether it was even intentional, Cinnabar had no idea, but when they eventually pushed away from the river bank, she found herself sharing Marlowe's boat, while a visibly petulant Magda watched them from the boat she occupied with Gary and Michiko; and despite her resolutions to the contrary, Cinnabar could not suppress the shudder of excited apprehension, the sense of exaltation she felt at being once more alone with Marlowe Hirakawa.

'Cormorant fishing goes on almost every night from mid-May to mid-October,' he said, as he settled himself beside her, very close in the narrow confines of the boat. 'But tonight is a special occasion ... the opening night of the fishing season.'

The actual fishing grounds were farther downstream from the embarkation point, and as their boats moved soundlessly over the dark waters, seemingly isolated from that of their companions, Cinnabar was more than ever aware of the man at her side. She felt, rather than saw his face turned towards her, and as his arm slipped around her shoulders, drawing her closer, a frisson, half fear, half anticipation, ran through her, increasing the rapidity of her heartbeat, setting her blood racing faster than the waters beneath their craft.

'Are you still sorry we came to Gifu?' he murmured, his voice just a breathy movement against her temple.

'I ... I don't know.' The reply came tremulously. How could she possibly know if it was an experience to be welcomed or regretted, until it was over? At the moment, it held a suffocatingly exciting promise of pleasures to come ... but wouldn't it just result in more heartache? Much of this kind of situation, this proximity, enclosed in the enfolding intimacy of night, the silent boatmen no intrusion upon them ... and she would be falling even more irretrievably in love, less and less able to release herself from its insidious meshes.

'I think I can promise you an unforgettable experience,' Marlowe said softly.

As if she had not already experienced moments with him, which were likely to remain with her for the rest of her life ... moments of exquisite torture. Was it wise, she asked herself again, to add to their store?

She craned her neck, seeking a glimpse of the other boat, anything to break the thread of tension stretched intolerably between them.

'Where are the others ... Gary, Magda ... Michiko?'

'Never mind the others.' His tone was a trifle impatient. 'You have me.'

Oh, if only she had! If only she had the security of knowing that he was hers, now and for ever. The yearning sensations within her, induced by the thought, caused her, almost involuntarily, to press closer to his side, and she heard the breath catch in his throat, before a strong hand came up to twist and lift her chin, his mouth coming down on hers in possessive invasion.

CHAPTER SIX

THE impact of his exploring mouth on hers was remorselessly sensuous, making every nerve and pulse stir and flutter, so that the little sound that rose in her throat was half gladness, half protest at his fervour.

When he finally released her from the thrall his seeking lips had imposed upon her, his arms still held her fast, in an aura of mysteriously drowsy tenderness, her lips still moist and lingering from the sweetness of that hypnotic kiss.

'Is it really only a week since I last kissed you?' he murmured against the softly curling tendrils of her hair. 'It seems a lifetime, doesn't it?'

Cinnabar was silent, making no such admission, feeling a sudden dragging emptiness deeper than any superficial sensation. Marlowe's kisses, his words were insidiously seductive; he seemed always to have this power of making time stand still, making her forget the hour, the place and the truth, bound up in some mystical spell of his making.

But now reality was filtering back into her bemused consciousness, as she remembered their surroundings, their silent witnesses, the boatmen ... and somewhere, not far away, the others ... Gary, who Marlowe supposed to be her fiancé ... Michiko, Marlowe's endearing little Japanese mistress, whom it was impossible to dislike ... and Magda, with whom he was not at all averse to flirting, when opportunity offered; and yet *she* had still been fool enough to fall in love with this man, whose sexual sway over her always succeeded in making her forget his unattainable status ... worse, his unscrupulousness ... for no man of honour would make love to another man's fiancée; nor could she condone his behaviour in engaging in relationships with three different women at the same time.

'You're very quiet,' he observed now, his large, strong hands moving caressingly under the cover of the darkness that engulfed them.

'I was just wishing...' she had to force the words from between unnaturally stiffened lips, 'that you wouldn't take advantage of me every time we happen to be alone together. What sort of girl do you think I am?'

He sighed.

'A very attractive, desirable one, as I believe I've mentioned before.'

But his hands had stopped their mesmeric movements.

'You find *all* women attractive,' she snapped, made irritable by withdrawal symptoms from the very caresses she had condemned. 'There's Magda *and* Michiko that I know of. How many more?'

'As you say, all women have their attractions,' he said enigmatically.

'To you, maybe. Some men are more single-minded!'

'Like Gary Reid?' he said, 'who abandoned you for Michiko in the space of only a few hours?'

He had withdrawn his encompassing arm now and she felt increasingly bereft, but with a need to salvage her pride somehow.

'He has *not* abandoned me! His interest in her is merely professional, as . . . as a photographic study.'

'Really?' he drawled. 'That's not what Michiko tells me.'

So he and Michiko discussed her and Gary, did they? Laughed together, no doubt, over the foolish Europeans, each hopelessly infatuated with one of the pair who mocked them . . . only Marlowe did not know of *her* infatuation . . . must not know.

'Michiko is extremely concerned about this,' he continued, 'the fact that he's your fiancé. She's asked me if she should discourage his attentions.'

'And what did you . . .?'

'Look!'

As Marlowe spoke the gliding boat had turned a bend in the river, revealing the fishing grounds they had come to see, bright with the light of multi-coloured paper lanterns from dozens of other boats. Their craft had pulled alongside that occupied by the other members of their party and there was no further opportunity for private conversation, as Magda strove to gain Marlowe's attention.

But Cinnabar, moving farther away from the disturbing proximity of her companion, vowed that the first chance she had, she would remind Marlowe of his comment. She was very curious to know what reply he had returned to Michiko's question.

The lanterns of their two boats were being lit now, as were those of the other vessels drawn up in ranks on either side of the river, when around a bend appeared a large, flat-bottomed boat, resembling a floating pavilion, garlanded with flowers. The interior was lit with lanterns and in it stood ten attractive young women, clad in brightly coloured kimonos. These girls sang, danced and played their guitars, while four boatmen poled them up and down the long line of spectators.

Enchanted by the sound of their song, Cinnabar wished she could understand the content.

'What do the words mean?' she asked.

'First they praise the cormorant fishers and their home town of Gifu,' Marlowe told her. 'But then they say ... "Let us follow the fire of our love into the night, as the fisherman follows the fire in the bow of his ship in the dark ... and so find each other, as he finds fish in the waters of the flowing river." '

He leant towards her, speaking the words softly for her ears alone, and seemed to imbue them with such deep personal significance that she felt herself trembling.

'It ... it's almost like a love song,' she whispered, so tremulously that he had to bend his dark head even closer to hear her voice.

'It *is* a love song,' he agreed, 'a love song for lovers who hear it.'

His arm was about her once more and she had neither the will nor the desire to remove it. The boat with its attractive occupants was moving away now, their voices fading and for an instant there was silence, in which Cinnabar could hear only the river sounds and the tumultuous, panicky beating of her own heart.

It almost seemed as though Marlowe was deliberately trying to make her fall in love with him. It was cruel. Surely his European blood was strong enough for him to realise that she could never accept the presence of another woman in his life. But then it was the Chinese who had kept concubines, she recalled. Japanese men had only one wife ... but thought nothing of visiting geisha houses ... and even though she had heard that these girls were not as numerous these days, the men had probably adopted, with other Western ways, the more modern concept of the mistress.

Marlowe probably acted this way with every woman he met
. . . a sort of constant proof of his own masculine power.

She was glad when the short lull was over and more
distraction was offered, in the form of a magnificent firework
display, as now the fishermen appeared, great fires, like flags
of flame, dangling in iron baskets in the bow of each boat.

'The fires attract the fish to the boats,' Marlowe explained.
With his free hand, he pointed out the master cormorant
fisher, in his traditional dress . . . a kilt of heavy straw, blue-
black shirt-like garment and neckerchief knotted cap-like
around his head. 'Like the origin of his costume, this custom
is a thousand years old.'

There were other customs, even older, Cinnabar thought,
feeling the subtle, suggestive movement of his taut thigh
against her own, the light, teasing exploration of his fingers on
her ribcage, almost, but not quite moving up to the swell of
her breast, making her faint with the breathlessness of desire,
so that she was glad of the darkness hiding her flushed cheeks,
disguising his actions from the occupants of the other boat
nearby.

There were four men in each of the flat-bottomed fishing
vessels and perched on the forward gunwale, twelve
cormorants, each with a string tied around its neck and
gathered in the master fisherman's hand. In the middle of the
boat, an assistant controlled another half dozen birds, while
the two remaining men paddled the craft.

'Each bird wears a neck-band, so that it can swallow only a
portion of its catch.'

Marlowe seemed to find it necessary to point out this
information by closing his long fingers about Cinnabar's
neck, making a sweet restraint upon her own convulsive
swallowing.

'The rest of the catch must be given up to its master.'

Languidly, Cinnabar watched the birds as they moved,
darting, disappearing into the water, dyed by the reflection of
the fires. They were prisoners, she reflected . . . as she was at
this moment . . . imprisoned by the desires of her body, which,
overcoming her pride, kept her riveted to this man's side, for
as long as his fingers chose to continue their hypnotic caress
of her flesh.

'How . . . how do they train the birds?' she managed to say.
'They . . . they're wild, aren't they?'

She felt him nod.

'After capture, the cormorant's beak is bound, with a piece of wood stuck in it, and the beak pared so it can't peck its captor.'

'But that's cruel!' Cinnabar protested.

'Perhaps I'd better not tell you any more?' he suggested.

'Oh . . . oh yes, go on.'

Anything to distract her from the fondling movements of his hand, which were making her almost mindless.

'The bird is rendered temporarily sightless, by a thread stitched through the lower lid of each eye and tied on top of the head.'

This time her shudder was due to distaste and not to the sensations waxing and waning within her.

'Why couldn't they just use a blindfold?'

'Because the bird would only scratch it off. Shall I go on?'

'Yes.'

'The birds are bathed and powdered with plaster. When it dries, all their parasites fall off with the substance, and being relieved of these irritants makes the birds better tempered. Once they're calmer, the eyelid threads are loosed, one wing is cut and they're brought to Gifu. Here they're fed and petted and gradually come to accept the touch of their master . . . to accept that they belong to him.'

As Marlowe's touch was telling her that she belonged to him, Cinnabar thought. Only its message was false. She ought to be wishing for this evening to be over . . . these moments of dangerous intimacy ended. Yet, as the excited spectators applauded the splashing, darting birds, as catch after catch of silver fish was removed from their capacious beaks, Cinnabar knew that she could easily be content to remain here, spellbound, for ever.

But even as the wish took form, the first edge of a great moon began to climb above the clear line of the nearby hill, until it was so bright that it eclipsed even the fishermen's fires. Somehow, in Japan, the moon seemed twice as big and impressive as in any other country. Suddenly the sport was over and the boats turned for home.

Soon they would be back at the landing stage, reunited with the others and Cinnabar remembered that she had a question to ask Marlowe.

'You said earlier that Michiko asked your advice . . . about Gary,' she reminded him.

'Yes.'

'Well,' impatiently, 'what did you tell her?'

In the moonlight, he regarded her doubtfully.

'I wonder if you can take the truth?'

'I'd rather you told me the truth than. lies,' she retorted hotly.

He shrugged.

'Very well. I told her that I'm not too sure of that young man's motives, or of his character . . . but provided she remembers that she scarcely knows him as yet, *I* see no objection to their friendship.'

Cinnabar stopped in her tracks, eyes and mouth widening in shock. What sort of man with this, complacently to countenance his mistress's relationship with another man . . . and how dared he encourage her to steal another girl's fiancé? Well, anyway, he *thought* Gary was her fiancé, she amended.

'Satisfied?' Marlowe asked.

'Satisfied!' Cinnabar squeaked. 'Satisfied! No, I am *not*! That's just about the most outrageous, immoral thing I ever heard!'

Thrusting past him, she began to run up the uneven, sloping track from the river's edge, not heeding his call, anxious only to rejoin the others. She took no account of the rugged terrain, made slippery by the muddy feet of others, and her unwary flight resulted in a stumble. Unable to regain her balance, she fell, striking her head against a projecting rock and feeling an agonising pain in the hand she had thrust out to save herself.

The hospital room that morning could have been in any similar establishment anywhere in the world, but the faces of doctors and nurses were Oriental, their language unfamiliar, as Cinnabar mistily regained consciousness.

As she opened her eyes, began to focus, there was an approving smile and a pat on the arm from the nurse at her bedside, before the woman hurried away, leaving Cinnabar to assemble the fragmented, kaleidoscopic memories of the last few hours. Piece by piece, she reconstructed the previous evening, the spectacle of the fishing, Marlowe's tormenting lovemaking, her horror at his reply to her question . . . her flight . . . and her fall.

That was it. Experimentally, she wriggled her legs, then

attempted to lift her left hand to touch her head. The arm seemed curiousy heavy. Moving her head carefully—it still had a tendency to swim—she regarded the large plaster-encased object sharing her bed—her arm . . . her left arm, the arm which normally held the heavy weight of the camera. Cinnabar began to feel panicky. Using the right hand instead, she discovered the bandage around her forehead. So that explained the throbbing, muzzy headache.

Her panic increased. How badly hurt was she? What hospital was this? How long had she been unconscious? Where were the others? Where was Marlowe? It did not seem inconsistent to her that, above all others, she desperately needed the company, the reassurance of the man with whom she had quarrelled.

She tried to sit up, but her body did not seem capable as yet of obeying the signals from her mind. Weak tears of pain and fear began to trickle down her cheeks.

'Now, Forester-San, please not to get upset.' The nurse had returned, a nurse who, miraculously, spoke English.

'Here is a visitor for you . . . not to get upset now, or visitor sent away.'

'Marlowe!' His name came out on a broken little sob of relief. 'Thank goodness! I . . . I wanted you. What's happened? Where am I? I . . . I'm scared, and I hurt all over.'

Her sobs threatened to become uncontrolled and swiftly he bent to gather her close, muffling the sound against his broad chest.

'Hush now! Do you want to get me sent away?'

'No . . .' She fought for self-control. 'No, please don't leave me. I . . .'

'I'm *not* leaving you,' he said firmly, one large, gentle hand brushing the tears from her cheeks. 'With the doctor's permission I'm taking you home with me.'

'Home?'

'To my house in Kyoto.'

'Oh, but . . . I . . . I couldn't! I . . .'

'Why not?' he asked, his voice softly teasing. 'I thought you were desperate, only twenty-four hours ago, to go to Kyoto.'

'Yes . . . to take pictures, but . . . oh, Marlowe, my hand . . . the camera . . . I won't be able to hold it, will I?'

'I'm afraid not,' he said gravely.

Fearfully, blue-grey eyes stared into his.

'But my assignment . . . my job! I can't just . . .'

'All taken care of,' he soothed her. 'A cable is on its way to England, explaining the situation. Gary will be completing your assignment . . .'

'Oh!'

Fresh tears welled up. It was all over, this marvellous experience. She'd have to go home, never see Marlowe again. 'I was so enjoying Japan. This was the most wonderful opportunity I've ever had, and now everything is ruined, and . . . and it's all *your* fault . . . and I *hate* you!' Finding she was unable to fling herself from his arms, she turned her head away from him, her voice high and hysterical. 'If it hadn't been for you . . . your interference in . . . my . . . my work, and in my private life, this would never have happened, and I . . .' She trailed into incoherence.

'Listen, Cinnabar!' His voice was stern. 'Listen . . . if you don't want to get me thrown out of here, shut up and listen.'

'I *do* want you thrown out. I never want to see you again . . . and I won't listen, I *won't*!'

To her fury, a large hand was clamped over her mouth, restricting her breathing, cutting off all further sound, so that perforce she had to listen to his words.

'Let's get this straight. Everything is *not* ruined. Gary will complete the schedule, exactly as you would have done yourself . . . and provided Mr Lamonde agrees, you shall still have the credit.'

'*Gary* said that?' Cinnabar muttered indistinctly against his restraining palm. It didn't sound like the ambitious Gary Reid she knew.

Cautiously Marlowe removed his hand.

'Yes. *Now* are you going to listen to me, like a good girl?'

Mutely she nodded, her mind scarcely on what he was saying anyway. If Gary was going to complete the Oriental portfolio, her usefulness here was ended. She would have to return to England, never see Marlowe again . . . to sit idly at home during her convalescence, imagining the others carrying on without her . . . Gary with Michiko and . . . and Marlowe? With Magda, probably. The melancholy rose in her like nausea, constricting her throat.

'And you are coming to Kyoto with me.'

At last his words penetrated, and a ray of hope pierced the gloom of her thoughts. At least that meant she wasn't being

sent home immediately. But ... but she couldn't go home
with Marlowe, could she? It wasn't exactly the impropriety of
the suggestion ... though certainly that must be taken into
account ... it was the thought of the increased intimacy it
would involve ... more and more time being spent in his
company, with the inevitable results. It would be bad enough
to be sent back to England now, but to have to leave Japan
after actually seeing Marlowe's home, after being exposed to
more moments like those which had preceded her accident.
She shuddered; she could not ... she dared not.

But she was being given no choice.

'I'll have to leave you, just for a few minutes, while the
doctor makes his final examination. I have a hire car ready
outside.'

With these words he strode away, and contrarily, Cinnabar
felt a little spurt of gladness that she had not been given a
chance to press home her refusal.

Cinnabar looked around the bedroom. Except for the
Western-style bed, installed in deference to her incapacity, the
room was much like the one she should have occupied at the
Ryokan. Somehow she had not envisaged Marlowe's private
home as being so typically Japanese, equating him with the
setting in which she was accustomed to see him ... his
apartment in the Hirakawa building.

The house was one-storeyed, but large and rambling, and
Marlowe had told her that it had once been an inn, before its
purchase as a private dwelling, which accounted for its
similarity to the Ryokan at Gifu.

The doctor at the hospital had grudgingly approved her
removal from his care, enjoining upon Marlowe that she must
go straight back to bed, immediately they arrived in Kyoto.

'Miss Forester has had very nasty blow to head ...
concussion still possible. Suggest you ask local doctor to
keep eye on her,' he had said, using English for Cinnabar's
benefit.

Despite the cushioned comfort of the hired car, the journey
had been a tiring one and Cinnabar had made no protest
about the continuation of her invalid role. Held securely in
tne circle of Marlowe's arm, to protect her, so he said, from
the worst of the jolts, over roads sometimes rippled and
uneven due to earthquake activity, her hand and head had

ached too badly for her to be disturbed by his closeness; and, to her relief, he had made no attempts to further their intimacy, speaking very rarely, except in answer to her one remaining reservation.

'Marlowe, it . . . it's very kind of you to offer to put me up while I'm convalescent, but . . . but . . .'

It was difficult to express what was in her mind . . . her fear of the propriety, of the wisdom of being alone with him. But he seemed to be attuned to her thoughts.

'You won't be unchaperoned, if that's what's concerning you. Akoya will be there. She'll . . .'

'Akoya? Who's she? Another of your mistresses?'

A particularly violent jolt of the car sent agonising pain through her aching head and the ill-tempered words seemed to be uttered involuntarily.

His tone was repressive.

'You're a little too swift in your assumptions . . . your condemnation of others. Akoya is my uncle's housekeeper . . . and mine . . . when I'm at home.'

'You live with your uncle?' This was completely un-expected.

He nodded.

'But you'll see little of him. He's very frail and keeps mainly to his own room these days.'

Cinnabar was glad when their journey ended and the hired limousine pulled up at the black wooden gateway of Marlowe's home and he carried her up the white-flagged path, with its borders of deep green grass. The house and its grounds were completely enclosed, the walled garden smelling of moss and trees, the only sounds those of birds and crickets.

The beaming housekeeper met them in the doorway and after Marlowe had carried Cinnabar to the bedroom she was to occupy, took complete charge of her, undressing her and putting her to bed.

Akoya was short, elderly and plump, with a broad face, low cheekbones and a receding chin, and Cinnabar, grateful for the woman's gentle care, felt ashamed of her outburst in the car.

Like her room at the Ryokan, this bedroom was designed to give the effect of living close to nature, with a fine view of a small adjoining, enclosed garden, set on a slope, so that the whole panoramic effect was visible to the occupant, the only difference being that the sliding panels had been replaced by glass Western style picture windows.

Beyond the window a little stream flowed between miniaturised, ancient pines, dropped into a tiny lake, emerging to twist and turn through diminutive hills, vanishing finally into a small bamboo grove. An arched bridge curved over the stream and, at the top of its curve, appeared to be broken.

'Oh, what a shame!' involuntarily Cinnabar exclaimed aloud.

'What's a shame?'

She turned her head, wishing she had not moved so precipitately, as it swam, then cleared, allowing her startled gaze to refocus on the doorway, where Marlowe stood, his gigantic stature sightly stooped to allow his admission to her room.

'The . . . the bridge is broken,' she said, a trifle breathlessly, trying to hide her confusion at his sudden appearance.

She was probably more decently clad than when she had encountered him wrapped only in a bath towel, but she was burningly aware of the provocation of the filmy, almost transparent material of her nightdress, and hastily she adjusted the quilt, which was all that covered her.

Marlowe came to sit on the edge of the bed, increasing her discomfiture, but after one swift, appraising glance, which had not missed her attempt at concealing herself, his eyes seemed to be intent on the garden.

'The bridge isn't broken,' he told her. 'It's merely formed into a zig-zag. It's another old and rather delightful idea of our ancestors. Evil, the ancients said, is like a rhinoceros, always charging in straight lines. Thus, the designer breaks the line of his bridge, so that evil cannot cross, but falls over the edge, to drown in deep water in the middle.'

Cinnabar had the sensation that she too might drown in deep water, if she didn't keep her wits about her, as his hazel eyes left the prospect outside, returning to that which obviously interested him infinitely more . . . her square, mobile face, her blue-grey eyes enormous in her still pallid face.

A large brown hand covered hers, as it gripped the edge of the quilt, the knuckles white as she held on to this, her only barrier.

'How do you feel?' he asked.

'My head still hurts,' she confessed, 'and my hand.'

'Ah, yes, that reminds me.' He drew a piece of paper from his pocket. 'I've had an answer to the cable I sent last night. Mr Lamonde is quite agreeable to your staying on here as long as necessary ... and to Gary finishing the assignment. He states that he won't need either you or Gary until his new designs are completed.'

'That will mean a trip to India for someone,' Cinnabar said. 'I wonder which of us he'll send?'

With a sense of awe, she realised that she didn't care. A few weeks ago there would have been fierce competition between her and Gary for such an assignment. What on earth had happened to the stubborn career girl she had once been, determined to compete on equal terms with men and equally positive that one of them should not be allowed to dominate her life or interfere with her profession?

'I forgot to ask you,' Marlowe interrupted her musings. 'Is there anyone else I should have notified of your accident? Family? Or will Mr Lamonde ...?'

'No, there's no one,' she told him.

'No one at all?'

Cinnabar shook her head. 'My parents were killed in a road accident when I was a year old. I don't remember them. I was brought up by my grandmother; and I lived with her until I was seventeen. Then, when she died, I ...'

'No aunts, uncles, cousins?'

'Both my parents were only children,' she said simply, with no trace of self-pity.

'Poor little orphan girl,' he said softly, drawing her into his arms.

A week or so ago she would have fiercely resented his sympathy, feeling quite competent to manage her own life, as she had done for many years, but her injuries had undermined her usually indomitable spirit and she felt the hot tears pricking her eyelids as she buried her face in the comfort of his strong shoulder.

'So you only had your fiancé,' he continued thoughtfully, 'and now that he's defected ...'

'Which was entirely your fault,' she muttered, reminded of the cause of their recent contention. But she could not put as much indignation into her voice as she would have wished, since Gary now meant absolutely nothing to her.

But then Marlowe incensed her by agreeing with her.

'Of course it was my doing.' He sounded utterly complacent. 'I told you Gary Reid wasn't the man for you, even before I met him . . . and I was right.'

'You mean you deliberately set out to split us up?' she asked disbelievingly, drawing herself away from him.

'I didn't have to try that hard. One look at Michiko, apparently, and . . .' he shrugged, 'the rest you know.'

Curiously she stared at his handsome, untroubled face.

'I just don't understand you,' she said slowly, 'how you can be so . . .'

'You'll have plenty of opportunity in the next few weeks to learn more about me,' he said, his voice huskily insinuating. 'I'm looking forward to a much better understanding between us.'

'*A few weeks!* I shan't be here that long!'

'I'm afraid you will, you know.' Marlowe didn't sound particularly regretful. 'That's a nasty break you've got there. It will be some time before you can use that hand again.'

'But . . . but what am I going to *do* all that time? I can't just lie around here . . .'

'I shall personally see to it that you're kept fully occupied.'

Now what did he mean by that? There was an oddly enigmatic gleam in those hazel eyes and his mouth was twisted into the whimsical shape which, with him, was usually a prelude to sexual mockery.

She sought to divert him.

'But . . . but your work . . . Messrs. Hirakawa?'

'Can well manage without me for a week or so. My uncle, once I'd explained the circumstances, was quite willing for me to take some of my annual holiday.'

Just what *had* Marlowe told his uncle? Cinnabar wondered. How much *did* he tell his elderly relative about his private life? Did Yuji Hirakawa know of Michiko's existence, and would he approve of his nephew's torrid relationships with numerous members of the opposite sex?

'Once the bandage is removed from your head and the doctors have assured me there's no concussion, there are many interesting things in and around Kyoto which I'd like you to see.'

'But until then . . .?'

'Until then,' he murmured, 'we shall just have to find some enjoyable, but less strenuous occupation for you.'

'It . . . it will be a bit boring for you,' she said rather wildly, for she mistrusted the sparkle in his eyes, his unobtrusive edging towards her.

'I don't believe I shall find it at all boring . . . I've never experienced tedium in your company yet.' His face was grave, but the bright eyes were laughing at her.

'I'm here to convalesce, you know,' she said sharply, 'not for your amusement.'

Marlowe raised shapely brows.

'I thought we were discussing *my* amusing *you*.'

'I'm not amused by what you have in mind.' As he frowned, she added hastily: 'Don't think I'm not grateful for your hospitality. I am . . . very. I wouldn't have liked to go home on my own just at this moment, but I don't want you to get the wrong idea. I'm not . . . not . . .'

'Not in love with me?' he suggested softly. 'I wonder if we could change that state of affairs?'

Far from improving the situation, this conversation was only leading in the very direction she most wanted to avoid.

'No,' she snapped, 'you couldn't.'

'You'd object to my trying, I suppose?' He contrived to sound only mildly, academically interested, but Cinnabar was not deceived.

'I . . . I'd object very strongly.'

'What a pity,' he sighed. 'How *are* we going to fill these days until you're able to get out and about?'

'If you've only one idea on how to pass time with a woman, I feel sorry for you. There's more to life than . . . than physicality.'

'Much, much more,' he agreed, but his eyes, the sensual mobility of his mouth, as he studied her face, belied his words.

'I mean it,' she said desperately, trying to quell the storm brewing deep inside her, the thunder of her heart, the tension which was growing in the room, threatening to flash like forked lightning between them.

She had always prided herself on self-sufficiency, that her intellect was capable of controlling feeling, but since she had met Marlowe Hirakawa, many of her long-held tenets seemed to be crumbling, her strength of character dissolving into a melting desire to be mastered by him, to have the barriers she had erected about her ruthlessly flung aside, ignored.

'Why won't you give me a chance?' he asked abruptly.

'A . . . a chance?'

'To make you care.'

To make her care . . . if only he knew! She had to fight back the hysterical laughter, verging on tears, that threatened to engulf her. As if she needed any lessons in the art of falling in love with Marlowe Hirakawa! But it wasn't as if he really wanted . . . no, *needed* her love. To him this was just a flirtation, a holiday diversion. Perhaps . . . she almost choked on a laugh that was not mirthful . . . perhaps he thought it would take her mind off her pain. Well, it was true, wasn't it, that in inflicting a greater pain, you took the sufferer's mind off the lesser injury?

'If you're still hankering after your so-called fiancé, you might as well realise it now as later . . . you don't stand a chance, now that he's met Michiko.'

'Why, is *she* so completely irresistible?'

She meant irresistible to Marlowe, though she felt she already knew the answer to that, but he misunderstood.

'To Gary? Are you blind? Surely you can see he's completely infatuated with her?'

'Infatuation isn't necessarily love. He . . . he might come back to me. I mean, he's not likely to . . . to marry her, is he?'

Again she meant because of Marlowe's relationship with Michiko, but he misinterpreted her question.

'I agree he's unlikely to marry her . . . but would you really take him back? Have you so little pride?'

Cinnabar was swept by a wave of depression. So Marlowe wouldn't release Michiko to marry someone else. Perhaps she didn't want to be released, and who was *she* to condemn her for that? As to pride, did he but know it, it was the only thing she had to cling to at this moment.

'I see you would.' His tone was contemptuous. 'You'd be content to be what at heart you believe you are, a second-class woman, prepared to settle for second best. What a cold, clinical little soul you must have! I could have sworn there were warmer, hidden depths in you. Now I know I was mistaken.'

'I'm not cold. I'm *not*! You know nothing about me . . . because I don't choose to *let* you know. I'm not second-rate and nor will I settle for second-hand goods!'

'And you don't think Gary Reid is . . .'

'Blow Gary Reid! It's *you* I'm talking about. You're

decidedly second-hand, if not third and fourth. At least Gary has't had a whole train of girl-friends, or tried to make it with two or three at the same time, the way you do. Well, you're not going to add me to your list of conquests! Perhaps you've never met anyone like me before ... a career girl, with a few intellectual interests, instead of an idiotic female who just moons after anything in trousers. And if you think you're going to keep your hand in on me while Magda and Michiko are out of reach, you're very much mistaken!'

Marlowe stood up, his towering height oddly menacing in the low-ceilinged room. His square, determined face had lost its usual aspect of lazy good-humour and was now a cold, fixed mask. The casual timbre of his voice became one of controlled authority.

'That's not the first time you have made implications about Michiko ... implications which I strongly resent.'

'Nothing hurts more than the truth,' she taunted him.

'Will you be quiet! I neither intend to confirm nor to deny your assumptions. You're not entitled to any excuses or explanations from me. But you're right when you say I've never met anyone like you before. Your manner, your beliefs, your whole attitude is unnatural ...'

'Unnatural,' she jeered, 'because I didn't leap into bed with you at the first opportunity. You picked the wrong girl. Magda would have ...'

'I dislike cattiness in women, Cinnabar; and I have no intention of exposing myself any further to your insults, of listening to you ... lowering yourself in my estimation. I shall assume that you are *not* yourself, that this is a direct result of your injuries.'

He moved towards the door, and instantly her bravado collapsed.

'Wh—where are you going?'

'Back to Tokyo,' he said grimly.

'But ... but what about me?'

'What about you? You apparently have no desire for consideration from me. I shall ask my uncle to allow you to remain under his roof until you're fit to travel. From then on, since that's the way you want it, your life is your own concern. Goodbye, Cinnabar.'

CHAPTER SEVEN

CINNABAR stared disbelievingly at the sliding door, as it closed behind him; and at first incredulity predominated. He couldn't just go off . . . leave her here alone with two complete strangers.

But, as she discovered when Akoya came in later to settle her for the night, that was exactly what he had done.

'Hirakawa-San called back unexpectedly to Tokyo on business.'

With conviction came misery, acute depression at his desertion of her, so that she had to swallow the lump in her throat and blink furiously to hold back the threatening tears.

'Then I can't stay here, Akoya,' she said. 'It wouldn't be fair to you.'

'I am most happy to continue to look after Hirokawa-San's girl-friend,' the other replied placidly.

Perhaps she was used to Marlowe having female guests, Cinnabar reflected with the pang that always accompanied such thoughts.

'Besides, my master express great wish to meet you tomorrow,' Akoya continued. 'Very old man, not many visitor. You see him?'

'Yes . . . yes, of course,' Cinnabar agreed hastily. 'It's very kind of Mr Hirokawa to let me stay here. I should love to meet him.'

Her politely expressed enthusiasm had time overnight to cool into apprehension. She had no idea what to expect of the forthcoming interview. Was Yuji Hirokawa an old tyrant, controlling his firm and his nephew from his sickbed? Was his desire to see her really due only to his lonely life, or was he curious to know what type of girl Marlowe had brought home this time?

'Does Mr Hirokawa speak English?' Cinnabar asked nervously, as she followed Akoya along the polished corridors of the rambling old house.

'Oh yes. Speak all the same like European,' Akoya assured her proudly.

Cinnabar had expected to find Yuji Hirakawa in a quilted bed upon the tatami of his bedroom floor, but instead she discovered him sitting bolt upright in an uncompromisingly European chair.

Interpreting correctly her startled look, he explained, a wry smile creasing the taut skin of his ascetically structured face.

'My old bones are too stiff these days to be lowered on to cushions. I am less nuisance to myself and everyone else in this chair. Please excuse me if I do not rise?'

Yuji Hirokawa must be very old, she decided, studying the small, shrunken figure in the chair. But despite his years and frailty, he was immaculately clean and tidy in his cream house kimono, his aged features gentle and intelligent, his sunken eyes still alert.

'You are enjoying your stay in our country?'

'Oh yes, very much. Everyone has been so good to me . . . and *you* are very kind to offer hospitality to a complete stranger.'

'Any friend of Marlowe's welcome in this house,' he said courteously.

He indicated that she should take the chair close to his own and feeling his deep-set eyes scanning her with unexpected penetration, Cinnabar felt her colour rising.

'Marlowe has talked much of the two girls from England . . . the model and the photographer.'

She inclined her head in acknowledgment of his statement. She was not surprised to hear that Marlowe had told his uncle about Magda, but she was ridiculously glad that he had mentioned *her* too. She wondered what he had said about her.

'You are this product of the Western culture . . . a career woman, I believe?' Yuji Hirakawa asked. 'I have not been to the capital for many years, but I believe our Japanese girls are beginning to adopt these independent ways.' He sighed . . . rather heavily, Cinnabar thought.

Did the change in convention trouble him *so* much, here in this isolation and towards what must surely be the end of his life?

'Tell me,' he continued, 'and forgive my impertinence . . . much may be allowed so old a man, yes? Tell me, do *you* wish to pursue your career always? Is there no room in your life for marriage . . . a family?'

Once she could have answered this question in the

affirmative, being positive that she meant it . . . that her career came first . . . but now? All the same, she thought, not knowing what Marlowe might have told his uncle about her, she must tread warily. Best perhaps to be consistent in her story, in case Yuji Hirakawa was fully informed.

'I . . . I have a boy-friend . . . a fiancé.'

She said the word reluctantly. Somehow it felt worse, telling the white lie of convenience to this gentle old man who, she felt, would value integrity, than it had felt telling the same lie to Marlowe himself.

'And you will marry soon?'

'I . . . I'm not sure . . . not too soon.'

He shook his head. 'All this is very puzzling to me.'

'Surely that's because of the way you were brought up?' Cinnabar decided it was time to distract him from her affairs.

'Weren't marriages arranged in *your* youth, so that you didn't have to bother about whether you were really in love or not?'

'That is so,' he agreed, 'but Marlowe has long since persuaded me that this will not do for the present generation . . . that they demand freedom of choice.'

Did this mean that Yuji Hirakawa had tried to arrange his nephew's marriage? If so, the old man could scarcely approve of his nephew's lifestyle, even if he had tacitly accepted it.

Disconcertingly, Yuji returned to the latter part of her question.

'Love, as you so rightly said, was not an important prelude to marriage. Suitability of rank and temperament, astrological pairings, were far more important . . . and with the years came respect and affection. But your words imply that you have doubts about this "love"? Are you not then "in love" with your fiancé?'

Age had certainly not dulled this man's intellect, Cinnabar reflected; his insight was too acute for her liking.

'Perhaps I agree with you,' she said lightly, 'that liking and mutual interests are more important.'

He shook his head. 'I think not. I have heard that Western women are different . . . "passionate" is the word my nephew used, I think?'

To which of Marlowe's many women had he been referring? Cinnabar wondered drily.

'In the Western world, women also have equality with men,' she said.

'So I have heard. Tell me, Miss Forester, have you ever heard the advice which used to be given to the wife of a Samurai?'

Cinnabar shook her head, remembering as she did so that, according to Michiko, the Hirakawa family were of Samurai descent.

'The old law says: "Approach your husband as you would heaven itself ... be courteous, humble and conciliatory, never peevish and intractable, never rude and arrogant." '

Cinnabar suppressed a smile. Yuji Hirakawa would have a shock if he heard the way many Western women addressed their husbands ... even the way *she* spoke to Marlowe. Except that Marlowe was not her husband.

'Approach him as you would heaven itself!' She could not agree with the subservience the words expressed, but all the same, she knew that it would be heaven to be married to Marlowe Hirakawa.

'Your ancestors were Samurai, I believe?' she asked politely.

Perhaps this subject, appealing as it must to his family pride, would distract Yuji from the uncomfortable topic of marriage and woman's role therein, which was only reminding her painfully of things she could never have. For if she could not have Marlowe, she would have no one else. The prospect of the empty life this promised made her shudder.

As she had expected, Yuji nodded complacently.

'Some time perhaps I will show you ancient relics of those times, but I fear I become weary too easily these days.'

'Of course,' Cinnabar rose immediately. 'I'm sorry if I've tired you.'

He lifted one parchment-frail hand.

'Please ... I have enjoyed our talk. I hope you will do me the kindness to visit me each day? May I suggest that now you explore the surrounding countryside. It is quite safe to do so and here the countryside is most accessible ... not like Tokyo, where one must travel considerable distances to find open ground.'

Cinnabar reflected on her encounter with Marlowe's uncle and their conversation, as she followed his advice and found herself very soon well away from all signs of habitation, wandering a quiet, lonely path, which wound up a hillside ...

coming across lovely little wayside shrines, one actually sited beneath a sparkling waterfall.

She had been longing to explore Kyoto itself, but knew that much of the magic for her would have been in having Marlowe's company, his deep voice interpreting for her the customs and spectacles they witnessed.

Dully, she wondered if he intended to stay away for the whole period of her convalescence and whether she would see him again before she left for home.

Thus was established the pattern of the following days. In the mornings, Cinnabar visited Yuji Hirakawa and listened, as in his gentle, scholarly voice, he spoke of the ancient traditions of his country; and, on days when he felt well enough to move from his chair, conducted her around his house, showing her the art treasures he had lovingly amassed. Then, in the afternoons, she would continue her exploration of the immediate area, gradually feeling stronger, knowing that soon she would have no excuse to remain beneath the Hirakawa roof.

One morning, their conducted tour took them to Marlowe's suite of rooms, in a wing of the house which she had never entered before. It was almost like a separate dwelling, with its own courtyard dividing it from the main house.

Compared with the stark utility of Marlowe's apartment in Tokyo, his home was a treasure house, showing an exquisite taste and refinement which, Cinnabar felt, must be attributed to his Oriental heritage. Even the most insignificant corners of his rooms were thoughtfully arranged, with due regard to the harmonies of light and shade, space and shape.

Yuji pointed out delicately painted scrolls, interpreting their significance.

'The fresh, evergreen pine represents prosperity, the wading crane is a symbol of longevity.'

The collection over which Cinnabar spent most time was that of charming little Haniwa figurines, which, Yuji told her, commemorated a custom dating from the third century, when models of humans, animals, birds, etc., originally made of terra-cotta, were placed on the burial mounds of dead chieftains.

'These, of course, are not originals,' Yuji said. 'Such would be priceless treasures, for museums only. These are only good reproductions.'

The figures were lively and charming, but somehow the collection reminded Cinnabar of the dolls in Michiko's flat and of who had given them to her. Was Marlowe with Michiko now? Her heart ached suddenly at the thought.

It was the Tokonoma or recessed alcove of the inner bedroom which finally proved to be of most interest.

In Yuji's own room, the Tokonoma had been occupied by the traditional hanging scroll and a simple flower arrangement. But here the occupant had wavered slightly from convention. Here indeed was the scroll, its design showing chrysanthemums by a rocky stream ... curling bronze chrysanthemums. Cinnabar caught her breath at the memories the sight evoked. But there was no flower arrangement. Instead, to one side of the scroll, hung two swords.

'Every Samurai warrior carried two swords,' Yuji said softly, almost reverently. 'The long one, the Tachi, was used in combat. The short one, Wakizashi, was used to commit Seppuku ... more commonly referred to by Westerners as Harakiri.'

Cinnabar shuddered at the thought of such dedication, which could impel a man to destroy his own life for a matter of principle. She moved closer to examine the weapons, their blades elegantly proportioned and gracefully curved. The decorations on handguard and hilt were superbly executed in the most minute detail and ... her heart leapt treacherously once more at the sight, the design incorporated the sixteen-petalled chrysanthemum.

She turned to ask Yuji the significance of the combination, but he anticipated her question.

'The sword was thought to be the soul of the Samurai warrior, the symbol of his potency. Under the rule of the Shoguns, the population was divided into four classes ... at the top, the Samurai, below them the peasants, the artisans, and lowest of all, the merchants. Every man was required to post on his doorway the details of his hereditary status. One of our Hirakawa ancestors took as his symbol the combination of the chrysanthemum and the sword. It is a tradition we are proud to continue, for it was from Kyoto that the greatest Samurai leaders came.'

Yuji reached up and lifted down the Wakizashi sword, allowing Cinnabar to test the sharpness of its edge.

'Only a Samurai might regain his lost honour by ritual

suicide. Commoners were assumed to possess neither the courage nor the dignity for so painful an ordeal.'

Cinnabar only half heard his words. Out of the corner of her eye, she had seen a familiar sight . . . a familiar face. On a lacquered table lay a pile of photographs, and from the top of the pile Magda's face stared back at her. She recognised her own work and realised now who had disturbed the negatives in her darkroom at Michiko's apartment. She remembered Marlowe saying that he would like some copies. So why did he have to go behind her back to obtain what he wanted? If he wanted photographs of Magda Llewellyn so badly, then he was welcome to them! Disturbed by this discovery, she hastened their return to the main building.

Cinnabar had been at the Hirakawa home for three weeks when the old man's doctor pronounced her fit to travel.

'No further danger of concussion, no need I examine you any more.'

This should have been good news, but not to Cinnabar, who knew the time had come for her to leave. There was no necessity for her to stay any longer and she could not impose on Yuji Hirakawa's hospitality without good reason.

The old man looked thoughtful when she told him she must leave.

'Another two or three days will make no difference?' he asked. 'I have much enjoyed our discussions. To please *me*, stay a little longer?'

Put like that, Cinnabar could not refuse . . . had no real desire to do so. Of course it would make no difference in the end. Marlowe would not return while *she* was here, but even so, she saw Yuji's invitation as a reprieve, a pushing away of that final moment, when she must leave Japan and make her dread a reality . . . when she would put the whole world between herself and Marlowe.

The next afternoon it poured with rain and Cinnabar was at a loss for occupation, until Akoya came to her room with an invitation from Yuji.

'Hirakawa-San wish you to take tea with him.'

Yuji greeted her warmly.

'The wet season is upon us. I fear there will be no more walks for a while. But if you could bear to spend still more time with an old man . . .?' He paused interrogatively.

'I'd love to,' she said. She had conceived a very real affection for the gentle, scholarly Japanese and having no relatives of her own had almost come to look upon him as a surrogate uncle.

'This afternoon we show you ancient, traditional tea ceremony, Akoya and I. Mastery of this ceremony is a long and tedious one ... every word, action and gesture must be learnt by heart. It is one of the many stages in the education of a geisha.'

'But Akoya isn't a geisha girl, is she?'

Yuji smiled.

'Akoya is elder sister of my late wife. She trained as geisha, but when I was left alone, she retired from public life and came here as my housekeeper.'

Akoya's usually cheerful face was drawn into lines of solemn concentration, as she began the ceremony. The tea used was not like European tea, for there were no tea-leaves, only a form of powder.

As Cinnabar watched, Akoya boiled water over a charcoal fire, then the Matcha ... fine green powder ... was scooped up with a piece of bamboo into two ceramic bowls, the water being added with a ladle and the resulting mixture whipped to a bright green froth, using a whisk that in itself was an object of loveliness, delicately cut and splayed from a single piece of bamboo.

With a bow, Akoya handed one of the bowls to Yuji, the other to Cinnabar.

'We receive the teabowl in the left hand and bow in return,' Yuji explained, suiting the action to the words, and Cinnabar copied him. 'Now place your right hand underneath the bowl ... so ... and turn it around three times, admiring its design. Take three sips of tea, then set the bowl down.'

He watched her anxiously, as she tasted the brew, which was served without milk or sugar.

'The guest then compliments the host on the quality of the tea,' Yuji said, 'but most foreigners find it unpleasant.'

'I've tasted green tea before,' Cinnabar reassured him, 'at the Ryokan.'

'And?'

'It's ... it's not bad,' she said frankly, 'rather bitter, though. I suppose the trouble is that I'm not used to it. But I'm sure I could acquire the taste.'

Solemnly, Akoya passed her a plate of small cakes.

'These are O-Manju,' Yuji said, 'sweet bean cakes, made from rice powder, red beans and sugar. They are eaten to relieve the bitter taste of the tea.'

'Why all that performance over a cup of tea?' Cinnabar asked afterwards.

'The ceremony has a purpose,' Yuji replied. 'The ancients held that it taught the participants the virtue of poise, sincerity and courtesy; it induces tranquillity and contemplativeness. The whole procedure, you will have noticed, has taken us an hour, allowing for inspection and admiration of the utensils, especially the teabowl and the caddy, which should always be works of art in their own right.'

He chose that afternoon also to show her his own collection of Netsuke, the carved and decorated toggles which, he explained, had once been affixed by a cord to a purse, tobacco pouch or any object suspended from the waistband of traditional Japanese dress.

'See, they are carved from a variety of materials . . . wood, ivory, amber, metal, even porcelain.'

Reverently Cinnabar handled the dainty things, representing many subjects . . . animals, demons, gods, masks and flowers. It was as she sat fingering a tiny Netsuke, formed in the shape of a chrysanthemum, her mind, inevitably, on all that it now represented for her, that she heard Yuji give a small grunt of satisfaction.

She looked up, and following the direction of his gaze through the window, glazed Western style against the elements, to protect his frail old bones, she saw a sight which caused the blood to course frantically, dizzily in her veins, so that if she had not been seated, she must surely have fallen.

'Marlowe!'

She breathed the name, the Netsuke slipping through her fingers on to the table, as she watched his tall, strong figure, striding purposefully across the courtyard which separated his private wing from his uncle's home.

He was all too obviously on his way to Yuji's room, and Cinnabar rose, poised for flight. But Marlowe was moving too swiftly for her, so that she all but collided with him in the doorway.

Automatically his hand came out to steady her, and at the feel of that hand, whose touch she had sorely missed in the past weeks, the familiar waves of sensation engulfed her, flooding her face with colour and weakening her knees.

'I ... I was just going,' she told him breathlessly, and before he could reply, she had edged past him, her flying feet making for the sanctuary of her room.

She had no idea how long she sat there, trying to control the chaotic whirl into which her thoughts and emotions had been thrown. Marlowe was back! What did it mean? It didn't necessarily mean anything, except that he had chosen to visit his home ... his uncle. But she couldn't help the treacherous little spurt of hope that he had wanted to see *her* again ... to see her before she left.

Her heart sank with terrifying, sickening rapidity. Of course, that was it! Yuji Hirakawa would have notified his nephew that his guest was sufficiently recovered to depart. Now, with his innate courtesy, which all her hostility had been unable to dispel, he would escort her back to Tokyo to collect the remainder of her belongings, before putting her on the plane for England.

When the time came for the evening meal, which usually she ate alone, she scarcely dared to leave her room. Had Marlowe forgotten the anger of their parting? Would he be joining her, or would he, perhaps, eat with his uncle? She wondered if she could plead fatigue, lack of appetite ... and that was true enough, now, and stay in her room.

But she knew Akoya would be concerned, and she did not want to make extra work for the goodnatured housekeeper, who would undoubtedly insist upon serving tempting morsels in her room. Besides, if she claimed indisposition, she wouldn't put it past Marlowe to come there, as he had done before, and she didn't think she was equal to the potentially tense atmosphere his presence might engender in the more intimate surroundings.

So, summoning up all her courage and pride, she made the best of her appearance, putting on a dress he had not seen before, a simple figure-hugging style in a flame-coloured material, which drew attention to and emphasised the red lights amongst the copper tendrils of her hair.

Head very erect and blue-grey eyes unknowingly wary, she entered the room, to find him already seated. He rose politely and waited until she had taken a chair, before resuming his own place. So far he had not uttered a word, and the silence stretched unbearably between them, as Akoya served their meal . . . slices of raw fish in a piquant sauce, together with boiled rice served in the customary sticky consistency, warm rather than hot.

At last, as the housekeeper discreetly withdrew, Cinnabar could bear it no longer.

'What are *you* doing here?'

The words blurted themselves out, with no consideration for their context or tone of voice.

The hazel eyes stared at her impersonally. 'I *was* under the impression that I lived here.'

She flushed painfully. 'Yes, I . . . I didn't mean . . . It . . . it's just that I thought I'd never see you again.'

Hastily she looked down at her plate, to disguise the sudden, over-bright sheen the thought had brought to her eyes.

His voice softened perceptibly, as he asked: 'Would that have mattered very much?'

She fought for control before answering, her voice only very slightly husky, as she strove to meet his quizzical gaze.

'I should have been sorry to leave without an opportunity of thanking you for all you've done.'

His face hardened into impassivity. 'Of course,' he said.

The silence threatened to become uncomfortable once more.

'Have . . . have you seen anything of the others?' she asked desperately. 'Gary? Magda?' She would *not* ask if he'd seen Michiko.

He nodded, speaking between mouthfuls of the excellent fish.

'The assignment at Gifu was completed last week. Gary seems very satisfied. I understand he persuaded Magda to pose with a cormorant.'

Cinnabar fought back the desire to laugh. The elegant Magda loathed all forms of furred and feathered life, convinced that they carried parasites, which would be transmitted to her immaculate person.

'They're in Nara this week,' he added.

'Does . . . does Gary intend to keep to the original plan . . . to come to Kyoto?' she asked.

'Still anxious to see him?' Marlowe asked, his tone edged with contempt. 'Haven't you given up on him yet?'

'Why? Is Michiko coming with him?'

Cinnabar had to know ... not whether Michiko was accompanying Gary, but whether he, Marlowe, had the temerity to bring his mistress to his uncle's house.

'No,' he said shortly. 'She's remaining in Tokyo, to continue with her studies.'

'That must be very frustrating for you,' Cinnabar said sweetly.

'We will not discuss Michiko, if you please.'

She shrugged. 'Just as you like.'

'I've invited Magda and Gary to stay here while they're in Kyoto. I thought that now you're recovered from your accident, we might accompany them. Of course, you won't be able to handle your camera yet, but ...'

'Thank you,' she interrupted him, 'but I really think I ought to leave. I've trespassed on your uncle's hospitality long enough. In fact I told him yesterday that ...'

'And he asked you to stay a little longer.' Marlowe interrupted in his turn. 'Have you no sympathy, then, for an old man's whim?'

She stared at him.

'Y—yes, but ... but I thought he was just being polite. I ...'

'My uncle tells me that he has become very attached to you. He finds your mind lively and intelligent, receptive to his descriptions of our heritage. He's a little disenchanted by modern youth, their gradual departure from the old ways. It's comforting to him to know there are still people, albeit of a different culture, who still have some respect for tradition ... that there are young people still willing to show deference to the aged.'

'How pompous you sound,' Cinnabar said, 'and you make me sound a horrible little prig.' She rushed on impulsively, ignoring his affronted frown. 'I love your uncle Yuji. I think he's the sweetest, most learned old man I've ever met, and I don't listen to him from a sense of duty or respect, but because I *am* fond of him, and I find his stories fascinating ... and beautiful.'

Marlowe's stern countenance had gradually relaxed as she spoke, and now he actually smiled, something she had never thought to see again. Its impact struck her with the full force of all his sexual magnetism and her eyes widened, her lips parting unconsciously, as she passed her tongue over their sudden dryness, an unwittingly sensuous provocation to the man opposite.

'Cinnabar,' he said, his normally smooth tones slightly jerky, 'let's go out this evening . . . have some time together, just the two of us, before the others arrive?'

For a second or two she hesitated, knowing that to accept, to be alone with him once more, would inevitably bring back to life the flames of her feelings for him. It would be playing with fire, and yet, suddenly, she was in a mood to burn her fingers . . . reckless, fatalistic.

'All right, I'd like that,' she murmured, her eyes on her hand, as it toyed nervously with the chopsticks it held.

It was still wet outside and she needed to put on a raincoat over her dress. But Marlowe garaged a car on the premises for use when he was at home, and it was only a short run, across the rain-brilliant cobbles, to the side-gate.

Laughing and breathless, she subsided into the passenger seat and turned to look at him, filled with a sudden urge to lean over and brush the raindrops from the smooth, bronzed texture of his face.

Marlowe returned her gaze and his eyes narrowed, as though he had sensed her desire, and for a moment she trembled, thinking that he was going to reach out for her. But the moment passed, as he turned the key in the ignition and the superbly maintained engine sprang into instant life.

'Wh—where are we going?'

Absurd how difficult it was to articulate the most ordinary words, when she was this close to him.

'To the theatre.'

'Theatre? Oh!' She was dismayed. 'But I'm not dressed for that.'

Amused, he gave her a brief, sideways smile.

'You don't need an evening dress and furs for this kind of theatre. Just relax . . . wait and see.'

She did as she was told, stretching out in the comfort of the front seat, languorously content just to be with Marlowe again in this enclosed intimacy lulled by the sweep of the windscreen wipers, content to smell the distinctive scent of his favourite cologne, to sense the male warmth of him, to hear his voice, free from the cold censure it had held when they had parted.

The theatre Marlowe had chosen was one devoted solely to the presentation of Kabuki.

'The word "Kabuki", roughly translated, means "deviation from normal behaviour". It was once an entertainment for the lower classes.'

'And now it's attended by descendants of the Samurai,' she teased, feeling ridiculously lighthearted, warmed by his responsive smile, the touch of his hand, guiding her to her seat.

She was enthralled by the interior of the building. The sumptuous stage curtain, decorated with a pattern of pheasants, woven in opulent colours, highlighted with silver and gold, rose to reveal yet another curtain, striped vertically in black and green. As they watched, a man dressed all in black ran across the stage, pulling the striped curtain to one side.

'According to the convention of Kabuki, anyone dressed in black is invisible,' Marlowe whispered, using the occasion to move nearer, his arm, apparently of its own volition, curving about her.

'Oh!' was all her tightened vocal chords would allow her to say.

The stage was enormous, wide but low, the scenery magnificent, depicting a hillside, a gateway, a villa and the inevitable cherry blossom. In the middle of the stage, a young lady sat upon a tatami, slit-eyed, rosebud-lipped, with mothlike brows painted near the top of her whitened forehead.

'She's beautiful!' Cinnabar breathed.

'*She*,' Marlowe murmured, a trace of laughter in his voice, 'is a man. All female parts are played by men.'

Cinnabar was a little disappointed, but, as the play proceeded, it was surprisingly easy to forget that the very convincing heroine was a man. Though she could not understand the dialogue, Marlowe seemed only too happy to provide a whispered translation, an exercise which involved bringing his face dizzyingly close to hers in the darkness of the auditorium, his warm breath fanning her cheek. She was aware that she was sitting tensely erect, afraid to move her head even by the merest fraction, in case her mouth should encounter his and be irretrievably lost.

On stage, the chanter-narrator explained the plot, as a

troop of soldiers interrogated the "lady" as to the whereabouts of her lover, threatening to torture her. Then the lover appeared, while "invisible" assistants removed scenery, to clear a space for the battle sequence.

One by one, the soldiers fell to the hero's symbolic posturing. Though the scenery and costumes were picturesque, Cinnabar found the movements to be both grotesque and yet oddly graceful.

'Kabuki is an acquired taste,' Marlowe told her during the interval.

'I think I could soon acquire that taste,' she said laughingly, a little more relaxed, now that it was not necessary for him to sit quite so close to her. 'But tell me, why *are* all the female parts played by men? I thought that sort of thing went out after Shakespeare's time.'

'In Western countries perhaps, but not in Japan. Maybe the Oriental clings more closely to his traditions than his Western counterpart.'

'But men playing women!' Cinnabar protested.

'It's quite simple, when you know the reason,' Marlowe assured her. 'Kabuki originated in a Shinto shrine, when a female dancer gave a performance which included an erotic dance, parodying a priest's devotions. Her performance was a great success and developed into "Pleasure Woman's Kabuki", all the performers being prostitutes. But eventually this became so flagrantly immoral that all women were banned from the stage, and men undertook all roles.'

'They're terribly convincing,' Cinnabar admitted, thinking of the graceful gestures, the femininity of the actor's movements.

'It takes a lifetime of training to become a Kabuki actor. Before he is good enough to play a leading part ... a beautiful and innocent maiden, for instance ... a man may be as much as fifty years old.'

The play was divided into two acts, with interludes consisting of comic scenes and dance items, the dancers accompanied by the music of gongs, bells, hand drums, bamboo flutes and samisen.

Cinnabar emerged from the theatre, dazed by exotic colours and sounds.

'That was a tremendous experience,' she told Marlowe, as they made their way back to the car.

'I'm glad you enjoyed it,' he said gravely, as they drove away. 'It is good to find that we have so many things in common. Do you know, Cinnabar, I believe you could be very happy, living in Japan.'

Cinnabar was silent, knowing wretchedly just how correct he was in his belief, but knowing too that there was only one set of circumstances under which such an event would be possible; and she recalled Michiko's words ... 'Marlowe say much in common very important between man and woman'. There were far stronger ties, of ancestry as well as taste, between Marlowe and the young Japanese girl.

She waited as he garaged the car, then strolled with him across the courtyard. The heavy rain had finally stopped and the moon was full, painting with silver the puddles that lay between the cobbles.

It was such a perfect night, the air redolent of damp earth and foliage scents, that Cinnabar was reluctant to end the evening by going tamely inside.

'Could ... could we walk around the garden for a while?' she asked diffidently. 'Somehow I'm not tired yet.'

Marlowe agreed, but she thought his manner held a hint of reluctance.

'It ... it doesn't matter,' she added, 'if you're tired.'

'I'm not tired,' he said curtly. 'We'll walk.'

Cinnabar never wearied of the inner garden. It was not the one she could see from her bedroom window and was entirely different in concept, being divided into two very separate halves. One section was river gravel, raked into parallel lines, straight at first, but resolving into a series of loops, ripples and whirlpools. The other half was composed of stones, grass, shrubs and even a few flowers, the two halves being divided by a path of smooth, round cobblestones.

'I always think it's so peaceful here,' said Cinnabar, as they walked ... not touching, but close enough that any unwary move might cause them to brush against each other.

But the peace of the garden was disrupted for her tonight. Instead, it seemed full of restless currents, as wild and complicated as the patterns in the gravel. Yuji Hirakawa had told her it was a place designed for quiet contemplation. Yet there was no quietude in her, and her thoughts, far from being contemplative, were confused and chaotic.

'I suppose you've guessed that this all means something?'

Marlowe waved an arm in a comprehensive gesture. 'In Japan, nothing is without meaning.'

Yuji had already explained his garden, but: 'Tell me,' she invited. Anything to delay their return to the house . . . the end of a perfect evening.

He stopped, as though the better to choose his words; and with Cinnabar only a pace behind him, the inevitable occurred. Instinctively she steadied herself, with a hand on his arm. With a sound that might have been speech, or simply an utterance of extreme feeling, he pulled her into his arms and stood, his face resting against her hair, his words half muffled in the bright curls, silver-tipped now by the moonlight.

'The garden is a symbol of wholeness . . . one side the desert, where man must be tested . . . on the other side, the earth, the world where life must be lived.'

She pondered his words, as his hands began to make little tentative caressing movements along her spine. Was it true, this Zen Buddhist concept that every life had a time of testing? If so, she fancied that she was being tested now, weighed in the balance . . . poised between the completed past and the unknown future. Would *she* be permitted to cross the stony path from the desert, into the garden of life, or was her heart destined to remain barren, arid, lacking the nourishment of love?

She looked up at him. She had to know, however much the knowledge might wound.

'Does . . . does Michiko ever come here to Kyoto?'

In the moonlight, his teeth gleamed whitely, wickedly.

'I would say she spends more time here than anywhere else.'

'Oh!'

Galvanised by his words into attempted withdrawal, she felt herself imprisoned by arms like steel bands, relentless, constraining.

'You may as well stop struggling,' he told her, 'because I'm not going to let you go . . . yet.' She found herself being lifted from her feet, his great body arched backwards to balance her weight, so that she was aware of the hardness of the sinews against which she was being moulded, compressed, as though somehow he would make her one with himself. 'Don't fight me,' he whispered. 'I want to make love to you . . . here, now . . .'

Her mouth, half-opened to deny him, was enclosed, stifled

by his, and he took advantage of her parted lips to probe, to explore, in a moist, provocative duel. The devastation he was creating within her rose to intolerable heights, so that she cried out, pressing herself even closer to him, feeling him tremble as she did so ... his chest rising and falling violently beneath the hardening of her breasts.

'Cinnabar!'

Her name on his lips, he swept her completely into his arms, one hand beneath her slender legs, carrying her with rapid strides towards his own part of the house.

Mindlessly she clung to him, her arms tightly wound about the hard muscularity of his neck, her lips pressed to the slight roughness of his jaw. Breathlessly impatient, he struggled with sliding doors, until finally they reached his room and he put her down on the quilt that served him as a bed, set ready for the night on the tatami.

He lowered his great length beside her.

'Cinnabar!' He said her name again, the quiver in his deep voice duplicated in the tremor that ran through his whole frame as he strained her to him. 'Oh, Cinnabar! It's been so long!'

She wanted him to stop talking, to go on kissing her, drugging her with the hypnotic sensuality of his mouth, his caresses, so that her mind would be unable to function, unable to reason her out of this shaking desire to accept every experience he was prepared to share with her. But desire seemed to have loosened his tongue and instead of the insidious persuasion she longed for, he continued to murmur her name, his hands shaking, suddenly clumsy, as they struggled with the fastenings of her dress.

'Have you missed me, Cinnabar?'

He'd asked her that question once before ... then as now he had spoken no words of love. It seemed to her that he only wanted her for one thing ... something he probably hadn't been able to obtain, while Michiko had been travelling the countryside with Gary and Magda. Well, *she* wasn't going to keep his mistress's place warm!

With a swift, angry twist of her body, she was out of his arms and on her feet.

'No, Marlowe,' she lied, 'I haven't missed you ... but you're apparently missing something else. Michiko's back in Tokyo now. Why don't you go to *her* for what you want?'

She ran from the room, without waiting to hear his answer, half fearing, half hoping that he would pursue her, deny her accusations. But there were no sounds of pursuit and her feet slowed draggingly, as she entered her room, safe ... and lonely.

CHAPTER EIGHT

MARLOWE greeted Cinnabar with cool civility during the next few days, on the rare occasions when they encountered each other; and she found herself bitterly regretting the outburst on her part, which had caused the resumption of their hostilities. Maybe, if she had not spoken as she had, things would have been very different now, she mused. She had been given . . . or so she felt . . . an opportunity to oust Michiko from Marlowe's affections. Shouldn't she have taken it?

No, she decided; for to do so would have involved taking the Japanese girl's place in his bed, and that was not necessarily the way to his heart. Cinnabar had always been determined that when . . . and if . . . she married, she would come to her husband untouched, inviolate. Even on the slim chance that, by relaxing her standards, she might obtain her heart's desire, she knew she could never bring herself to anticipate the marriage ceremony, unless . . . unless . . .

So why didn't she just pack up and go home, she asked herself drearily . . . save herself more heartache? Surely, in time, though she would never forget Marlowe Hirakawa, the pain *would* lessen? It was not a bit of use, of course, telling herself that she would meet someone else. Cinnabar knew now that she was a one-man woman, that once her heart had been bestowed, it would never be hers again to give elsewhere. All she had ever given to Gary, she realised, was friendship and affection. But irrevocably, for all time, she was Marlowe's; and if she did leave Japan, never to see him again, she would have to return to being a career girl, to dedicate the rest of her life to it, sublimating the urges of her body and mind in hard work.

No, she knew what she *ought* to do . . . the sensible thing to do, but, weakly, she allowed optimism to overcome common sense. Just a few more days, she pleaded with her better judgement, just until the Oriental assignment is finished . . . *then* I'll go home with the others.

Gary and Magda arrived as planned, Gary in high spirits, full of enthusiasm for the work completed and the work still

145

to be done. Magda had not been in the house five minutes, Cinnabar noticed resentfully, before she had attached herself to Marlowe's side, making a constant play for his attention. Not that it made much difference to her. Marlowe was barely speaking to her these days, though on occasion she had encountered his eyes fixed upon her with a brooding intensity.

'What's the plan of campaign?' Gary asked briskly over breakfast, on the first full day of their visit. 'You're the boss, Marlowe. You're on home ground here.'

His words made Cinnabar itch to be behind the camera once more; *she* would never have let Marlowe dictate *her* schedule, she thought scornfully, conveniently forgetting the occasions when he had taken charge.

'I thought perhaps Nijo Castle, followed by a temple?'

A hire car had been arranged, to avoid parking problems, and Cinnabar found herself sitting with Gary, forced to endure the spectacle of Magda opposite, exercising her not inconsiderable feminine wiles on an unusually responsive Marlowe.

He had always been polite and attentive to the model, openly admiring of her appearance ... had always censured Cinnabar's criticisms of her companion, but he had never gone beyond the bounds of common courtesy. Now, Cinnabar thought with disgust, he was positively encouraging Magda, his arm thrown around her narrow shoulders, his face very close to hers, as they talked and laughed.

Jealousy clawed at Cinnabar like the rending talons of a wild beast, but she had sufficient spirit left to hide the misery that engulfed her. Thank goodness she had not given in to Marlowe's importuning the other night! Judging by the play he was making for Magda, he had found a substitute; the model would soon be the next recipient of his favours.

To disguise her feelings, Cinnabar chatted animatedly to Gary, until they reached the castle, making a point of slipping her hand through his arm and smiling into his eyes.

She couldn't help noticing that Gary seemed a little discomfited by her attentions, and she did not need to be unduly perceptive to realise that he was no longer interested in her. Poor Gary! They were in the same boat really ... both doomed to unrequited love.

Accustomed to looking over the stately homes of England and the lavish national monuments of other Western

countries, Cinnabar had at first been a little disappointed by
the smallness and plainness of the ancient buildings of Japan,
until she had discovered that simplicity too could be beautiful.
But Nijo Castle was an exception in its size and splendour, she
thought, as, leaving the car, they approached it, via a wide
boulevard then through a gate in the eastern wall.

'The castle was built in 1603, as the Kyoto residence of the
Shogun Iesayu,' Marlowe told them, as they passed under a
second gate, roofed in Japanese cypress bark, richly
ornamented with woodcarving and metal.

Cinnabar paused for a moment or two to run her fingers
over the carvings, finding amidst the design, as she had
expected, the sixteen-petalled chrysanthemum. How this
flower seemed to haunt her, everywhere she went. Guiltily she
looked around to see if anyone had noticed her absorption,
but the others had strolled on without her. Probably none of
them had even missed her.

As she caught up with them in the first building, composed
of a number of lavishly decorated rooms, following one upon
another, Marlowe took something from his pocket, holding it
out towards her.

'I thought this might ease the frustration you must be
feeling . . . at not being able to use your camera.'

He placed a miniature camera in her hand and for a
moment she looked down at their hands, linked by the
instrument, blinking back the tears produced by his
thoughtful gesture. How penetrating his insight could be
sometimes, how accurately he had gauged her feelings. If only
it were possible . . . as easy . . . for him to alleviate her greater
need . . . the need of him.

Shyly she raised her eyes to the square, handsome face.
'Thank you,' she said simply.

He nodded and turned away, his face still wearing the cold,
impenetrable mask it had assumed since her rejection of him.

Cinnabar recognised just how thoughtful Marlowe's
inspiration had been, when she saw the many splendid murals
decorating the rooms through which they passed . . . tigers
lurked amongst bamboo trees; pine trees and cherry blossom
swayed realistically in painted breezes; a mythical lion seemed
to glare at the onlookers, no matter where in the room they
stood.

As Magda posed and preened for Gary, Cinnabar was

happy to snap away, like the veriest tourist, she thought, as if, indeed, she had never heard the words 'professional photographer'.

There were five buildings in all, and by the time their group emerged, Cinnabar was dazzled with a surfeit of beauty and extremely footsore, glad to find the car waiting to collect them once more.

The afternoon was not so successful. Marlowe and Gary seemed tireless, but Cinnabar was weary and Magda was visibly wilting, hard put to it to keep a smile on her face even for Marlowe; and Cinnabar heard her snap at Gary once or twice, when Marlowe was out of earshot.

'Temples . . . temples . . . I'm sick of temples! See one and you've seen them all!'

For someone who had claimed to be so tired, Magda had recovered surprisingly swiftly, Cinnabar thought later that evening.

Marlowe had issued a general invitation for them to accompany him to a puppet theatre, but when Cinnabar found that Gary planned to spend his evening developing films, she made a hasty excuse herself. The idea of making an unwanted third did not appeal to her. Magda's satisfaction had been unconcealed and she had departed in high spirits, clinging to Marlowe's arm and looking very lovely.

'How do you intend to spend your evening?' Gary asked. 'Want to help me?'

The offer was made without much enthusiasm, and Cinnabar shook her head. Besides, there was not as much satisfaction in developing someone else's photographs.

'I think I'll look in on Uncle Yuji,' she said. 'I haven't been to see him today.'

She did not stay long with Yuji Hirakawa. The old man retired early and Cinnabar thought she might as well do the same. She had no idea what the plans were for next day, but since her accident, she had not regained her usual stamina for long hours.

She was almost ready for bed when she heard Gary's voice and heard his fingers scratching tentatively on the panels of the sliding door.

'Bar? Bar, are you there?'

Quickly she pulled on the chrysanthemum-patterned kimono which she had purchased in Tokyo.

'Come in.'

Gary looked a little disconcerted. 'Sorry! I didn't realise . . .'

'I thought I might as well have an early night,' she explained.

'I rather wanted to talk to you,' Gary said hesitantly, 'while the other two are out of the way.'

Cinnabar opened the door wider. She was glad that her room was furnished Western style; somehow the floor did not seem suitable for serious discussion, and she had an idea from Gary's manner that this *was* to be serious.

It took him some time to come to the point, however, as he looked around the room, studied his fingernails with intense concentration, unable, seemingly, to meet her eyes. Finally, looking somewhere past her left ear, he began.

'Bar—just how keen are you on . . . on us getting engaged?'

She knew what was coming, but she couldn't think of the right words to help him and there was silence, until, drawing a deep breath, Gary tried again.

'Bar, I'm not in love with you. I'm sorry, it sounds an awful thing to say, but . . .'

'It's all right, Gary,' she interposed hastily. 'I know you're not. I've known for some time. It's Michiko, isn't it?'

He nodded. 'I'm going to ask her to marry me. I would have asked her before, but I felt I had to straighten things out with you first. You're . . . you're not mad at me, then, Bar?'

'No . . . no, I'm not annoyed.' She laughed awkwardly. 'In fact, it's a load off my mind. You see, I'm not in love with you either.'

'Oh!'

It was obvious that Gary's relief was mingled with pique. Men! Cinnabar thought. It was all right for *them* to fall out of love, but to suit their insufferable egos, the girl was supposed to be devastated.

'Gary,' she began diffidently, 'about Michiko . . . I . . . I don't want to be a wet blanket, but what makes you think she'll marry you?'

Gary frowned.

'Well, I can't be certain, of course, until I've asked her. But I'm pretty sure she likes me . . . likes me a lot. A fellow can tell these things—you know?' His expression became complacent.

Strange that Gary's instincts had not told him that *she* was not in love with him, she thought a trifle cynically.

'But she may not be able to marry you,' she persisted.

'Oh, stuff! Honestly, Bar, anyone would think you were jealous! I know that years ago a Japanese girl's marriage would be arranged; but things are different now.'

'Gary!' Cinnabar said desperately, hating to disillusion him, yet feeling bound to issue the warning. 'Have you forgotten what I told you when you first arrived, about Michiko being . . . being Marlowe Hirakawa's mistress?'

'Oh, that! I remember you telling me, but frankly I didn't believe it. For one thing, she's . . .'

'You mean you've never asked her?'

'Good lord, no, Bar. What do you take me for? I wouldn't insult Michiko by asking her a question like that!'

Cinnabar sighed. She was very much afraid that Gary was in for a shock. She only wished she weren't so sure about Michiko's relationship with Marlowe, but she couldn't allow Gary to be deceived, any more than she could deceive herself.

'Michiko *is* Marlowe's mistress, I'm sure of it. But you'll just have to ask her to marry you, if that's what you really want, and see what she says.'

He nodded. 'That's just what I intend to do. Tomorrow should just about see the Oriental collection wrapped up. I've finished a couple of weeks ahead of schedule, which should please Vyvyan. Then I'm off back to Tokyo, to see Michiko and pop the question.'

This was the second assignment he had finished early, Cinnabar reflected. She couldn't help wondering if Gary was as serious about his work as he used to be. Once upon a time, he had erred on the side of excessive care, frequently being behind schedule.

He stood up and moved towards the door.

'I'm glad we've had this little chat, Bar . . . cleared the air. Thanks for being so decent about it.'

What a relief it would be, Cinnabar thought inconsequentially, not to have to spend the rest of her life hearing Gary call her Bar!

He paused in the doorway.

'Wish me luck, Bar?'

'Of course I do!'

Perhaps the Japanese girl would give Marlowe up for Gary. Cinnabar couldn't imagine any girl in her right mind making such a choice, but if Marlowe was not the marrying kind, perhaps Michiko would prefer to settle for a more permanent relationship, albeit with a less attractive man ... a less wealthy one too, if it came to that.

Impulsively, she stood on tiptoe to kiss Gary.

'I hope it works out for you, honestly I do.'

The kiss was not prolonged or particularly enthusiastic on either side, but that was not the impression received by the man who came upon them suddenly, his tread, for all his size, remarkably light and soundless.

It was rather the instinctive knowledge that someone else was present which made Cinnabar look beyond Gary's shoulder, to meet the implacable contempt in Marlowe's hazel eyes.

'Excuse me for intruding, but I think it might be a good idea, Cinnabar, if you went to Miss Llewellyn.'

'Magda wants *me*?' Cinnabar found the eventuality unlikely.

'I didn't say she wanted you,' he said drily, 'but I think it might be advisable if you had a chat with her, nevertheless.'

Mystified, Cinnabar stepped out into the corridor and saw the rapid play of expression across Marlowe's face as, for the first time, he saw the chrysanthemum kimono. He made no comment, however, and she could not be sure if he was scandalised by the fact that she had received Gary so informally dressed, or whether it was the pattern of the garment which had caused his reaction. She had never intended that he should see her impulsive buy, in case he thought her choice had been in any way influenced by his own obsession with chrysanthemums.

'I'd like to see you ... after you've spoken to Magda,' he told her, one hand briefly restraining her, as she brushed past him.

Fervently Cinnabar hoped that the interview with Magda would keep her so late that he would give up waiting.

Her tentative knock at Magda's door elicited only a peevish:

'Whoever you are, go away, damn you!'

The model's voice sounded oddly muffled, and Cinnabar,

though she had no liking for the girl, was immediately concerned.

'It's Cinnabar, Magda. Are you all right?'

'Hell! Oh, O.K. Wait a minute.'

It was considerably more than a minute before Magda opened the door, and Cinnabar received the distinct impression that Magda had just renewed her make-up, more heavily than usual. But she must be mistaken. Magda wouldn't go to all that trouble just for her.

'What do you want?' Magda asked ungraciously, closing the partition.

'Well, I'm not sure,' Cinnabar admitted. 'I got the impression that you might want to see me.'

'What makes you think that?' The model's tone was sharp.

'Marlowe said . . .'

'Marlowe! You've seen Marlowe? When?'

'Just now . . . he . . .'

'What's he been telling you? Did . . . did he say anything about . . . about . . . well, anything?'

For Magda, the poised, the self-assured, she sounded remarkably incoherent, her eyes over-bright, her usually graceful movements jerky, restless.

'He didn't say anything. Just that I ought to come and have a talk with you.'

'I see. Well, since you're here, you may as well sit down.'

Cinnabar watched Magda expectantly, as the other girl fidgeted about the room.

'Are you sure there's nothing wrong, Magda?'

'Of course,' the model said brightly . . . too brightly. 'What should be wrong? I've just come to a decision, that's all. I'm leaving.'

'Leaving?' Cinnabar was incredulous. 'But why . . . when?'

'In the morning, first thing.'

'But . . . but tomorrow's photographic session? Gary said . . .'

'To hell with Gary, with photography, Vyvyan, the Oriental collection . . . the whole boiling lot! I'm sick of it . . . up to here!' Her thin hands gestured expressively.

'But why . . . why so suddenly?'

Magda hesitated, her dark eyes regarding Cinnabar narrowly.

'You're quite sure Marlowe didn't tell you anything?'

'Quite sure,' she said in exasperation. 'You must have noticed . . . we're hardly on speaking terms at present.'

'I'm going to New York,' said Magda.

'To . . . to New York? But . . .'

'Before he left, Hank Schuster asked me to marry him. I . . . I hadn't quite made up my mind then.' Her manner became defiant, truculent almost. 'But now I have. I'm going to say yes . . . and I'm going to New York to tell him so.'

'Isn't that a bit drastic?' Cinnabar asked. 'Wouldn't a telegram do? Then you could finish the assignment. Surely another day won't make much difference?'

'Another day!' The model's voice rose hysterically. 'If you think I'm going to stay in this place another day . . . I don't know how I'm going to endure the next few hours. I can't wait to get away. If I never see any of you again it'll be too soon, especially that . . . that . . .' Magda seemed to be having difficulty breathing, 'that arrogant, two-faced, two-timing swine, Marlowe Hirakawa!'

She turned away, but not before Cinnabar had seen the over-bright eyes spill their angry tears. Magda might be anxious to join Hank Schuster, but it was equally certain that a disagreement with Marlowe had given impetus to her decision. What on earth had Marlowe said or done to upset the model like that? She had accused him of two-timing her. Surely it hadn't taken this long for Magda to find out about Michiko?

Cinnabar hovered in the doorway. It would be hypocritical to say she was sorry the model was leaving, but she had to say something.

'I . . . I hope things work out for you . . . with Hank,' she said diffidently.

'Why shouldn't they?' The model was certainly in a very strange mood. 'I suppose you think you're the only woman capable of attracting a man? Well, let me tell you . . . any man who fancied you wouldn't be worth having . . . not in *my* book!'

Magda obviously didn't realise that Cinnabar's friendship with Gary was now finally over, she thought, and she saw no reason to enlighten the model. It wasn't as if they were close friends and confidantes.

'I suppose I'd better go and tell Gary,' she said. 'This is goodbye, then, Magda?'

The other girl did not deign to answer, and Cinnabar slid the panelled door shut and made her way along the corridor towards Gary's room, which lay beyond hers. She hadn't gone far before she encountered Marlowe, loitering, as though accidentally, in the vicinity of her room.

'Where are you going?' he asked sharply, as she nodded and made as if to pass by.

'To see Gary.'

'Why?'

'I imagine you already know the answer to that.'

'So that you can take up where I interrupted you?' His normally lazy tones were incisive. 'Why don't you let him go, Cinnabar? You must know by now he's not for you?'

'My relationship with Gary is none of your business,' she said coldly, 'but as it happens, I merely wanted to discuss Magda with him. I assume you know she's leaving in the morning?'

'Is that all she told you?' The question was asked with a strange intensity, and Cinnabar stared at him.

'No, she told me something else.'

'What?' He towered over her, his hands coming out as if to grasp her arms, but she evaded him.

'That she's going to marry Hank Schuster. That's why she's leaving . . . to go to New York.'

His good-looking face had become suddenly bleak.

'She didn't tell you anything else . . . nothing at all?'

What did he want her to say? Light suddenly dawned. Magda had questioned her closely too. They'd had a row, and he was upset because Magda was leaving, but he was too proud to plead with her himself. He'd hoped that the model would confide her love for him to Cinnabar, and Magda had been hoping for the same thing . . . in reverse. It must have been a pretty dreadful disagreement for Magda to give up all her ambitions of marrying a man who was both rich and attractive. Perhaps Marlowe had refused to give up Michiko, and if this was the case, Cinnabar could understand and respect Magda's reasons for leaving.

Cinnabar was aware of a gnawing jealousy of Michiko and, for once, a fellow feeling for the model.

She realised that Marlowe was still waiting for an answer.

'No,' she said shortly, 'Magda didn't say anything else—and if you'll excuse me, I want to talk to Gary. He ought to be told, and we'll have to discuss the effect on tomorrow's schedule.'

'The morning will do for that. I've already told Reid that his model is leaving.'

'Gary knows? What did he say?'

Marlowe shrugged. 'He didn't seem unduly concerned.'

No, he wouldn't be, Cinnabar thought furiously. All Gary could think about at the moment was Michiko. But this had originally been *her* assignment, and now that there was nothing else here for her, all her professional instincts were rearoused.

'The rest of the designs must be photographed somehow,' she insisted.

'I have an idea about that,' he said, his tone impatient, 'but we'll discuss it over breakfast. There are other, more important things to be discussed.'

'I disagree,' she told him. 'Nothing is more important to me than my work.'

'Cinnabar, kindly listen to me! Your assignment *will* be completed. But first of all, I have to talk to you.'

He gestured towards her room. But Cinnabar stood her ground. No way was she going to invite Marlowe Hirakawa into her room even to talk about Magda. Because that was his intention, she felt sure. He'd been hoping . . . was probably still hoping . . . that she would persuade the model to stay. That was why he was so sure the pictures would be taken.

'I'm too tired to discuss your problems tonight. But I wouldn't worry too much about losing Magda. You may not agree with me, but I know you're better off without her. After all,' she added, unable to conceal the bitterness in her voice, 'you've still got Michiko . . . unless Gary's plans work out.'

With that she entered her room, wishing fervently that there was a lock on the door. But after a while she relaxed, hearing him move slowly away towards his own section of the house.

Cinnabar tossed and turned all night in an unhappy, restless frustration that was both mental and physical, falling asleep finally from sheer exhaustion. Consequently, she overslept; and by the time she had showered and dressed, it was to find Magda already gone.

Gary was in the garden, hands thrust into his trouser pockets, as he studied the convolutions of the raked gravel.

'Blessed if I can understand this sort of thing! But I suppose I'd better get used to it, if I'm going to marry Michiko and stay here in Japan.'

'You're going to stay here?' Somehow Cinnabar hadn't expected this. 'But what about Mr Lamonde ... your work ... how will you earn a living?'

'Oh,' he shrugged, his fair skin a little flushed, 'I fancy that will be taken care of ... but I can't discuss it with you. It's ... it's sort of confidential at the moment.'

How young Gary seemed, how immature. She supposed it must be by comparison with Marlowe.

'What are we going to do about today's photos?' she asked.

He looked at her doubtfully. 'I'm not sure how you'll feel about this, Bar, but Marlowe suggested that *you* model for me.'

'Me?'

Her first instinct was horrified refusal. But then she shrugged fatalistically. What did it matter? The job had to be done, the clothes had to be modelled by a European, and Vyvyan would never hear of flying a second model out for one day's filming. The sooner the assignment was finished the sooner she could get away. With Gary obsessed with plans for his future and Marlowe hankering after the departed Magda, there was no place for her here any longer.

With a tinge of regret, she contemplated the moment when she must bid farewell to Yuji Hirakawa. She would miss their absorbing discussions and she felt sure the old man would miss her too.

'Has ... has Marlowe taken Magda to the airport?' she asked.

'No, she called a taxi. I think Marlowe's with the old boy ... his uncle. What's he like, Bar? I haven't met him yet, but I believe he's incredibly ancient. Make a good subject, would he, for a photo?'

'He probably would,' Cinnabar said absently. 'But I'm not asking him. He's such a dignified old man, he might not like being thought of as an object to be photographed.'

While she spoke, her mind was busy with other matters, surprised that Marlowe had not accompanied Magda, made the most of his last chance to persuade her to stay.

'You know, I feel sorry for Hank Schuster,' she mused.

Gary stared at her.

'How the devil did *he* get into the conversation? And why should you feel sorry for him, for heaven's sake? I gather he's rolling in money ... and at his age too! I wouldn't mind changing places.'

'I'd feel sorry for anyone Magda married,' Cinnabar said with feeling, unable to suppress a glow of satisfaction that at least it would not be Marlowe who had to suffer the model.

'What on earth are you talking about, Bar? Who's Magda going to marry?'

'Hank Schuster,' she repeated patiently.

Gary guffawed. 'She most certainly is not! At least, only over Hank's dead body!'

It was Cinnabar's turn to stare. 'But she told me he'd asked her to marry him before he left. She said she was going to New York, to say yes.'

Gary shook his head. 'I had a couple of drinks with old Hank while he was here. Nice chap, actually. In fact I pulled his leg about Magda, and he told me in no uncertain terms that she wasn't his type.'

'He *did*?'

Gary was positive.

'Said he'd met plenty like her back in the States ... gold-diggers. He knew he wouldn't have stood a chance of squiring her round Tokyo if he hadn't been practically a millionaire. Said she was useful company ... for making whoopee, he called it ... but nothing more.'

The bit about making whoopee was so obviously Hank that Cinnabar could no longer doubt the truth of Gary's statement.

'But why should she tell a whopping great lie like that?' she puzzled.

Gary shrugged. 'Search me? Why do you girls do these things? You should know better than me.'

And Cinnabar thought she did know. Magda had hoped that Cinnabar would repeat the information to Marlowe, as she had done, to arouse his jealousy, hoping that it would bring him back to heel. But it still didn't explain why Magda had gone through with her threatened departure. Knowing the model, Cinnabar would have expected her to capitulate, rather than lose everything she had worked for. She shook her head.

'I thought I *did* understand Magda, the way her mind ticks ... but this time I'm as puzzled as you.'

Marlowe didn't look particularly downcast that day, Cinnabar thought, as at intervals she stole surreptitious glances at his bronzed attractive features. But he had had a few hours in which to master his feelings; like anyone else he must have his pride, and in any case she felt sure he was not a man who would wear his heart upon his sleeve.

All that day Cinnabar posed for Gary, inside and outside of temples and shrines, in front of statues inside, and under gigantic ginko trees outside. Although Marlowe had accompanied them as their guide, he took very little part in the proceedings, offering no comments or suggestions on their choice of subject, not entering into their amicable wrangling as to how a shot should be posed.

He was no more communicative over the evening meal, concentrating on his food, as Gary and Cinnabar discussed the day's work.

'I suppose there's nothing to keep you here now?' Gary asked.

Cinnabar agreed.

'As soon as I can book a flight, I'll be off. When are you going back to Tokyo?'

'Tomorrow, first thing. If I develop this last batch tonight, will you post them off to Vyvyan?'

Marlowe showed a faint spark of interest.

'You're not going back to England immediately then?'

'No.' Gary fumbled for words. 'Actually, I . . . I have some unfinished business in Tokyo, and a . . . a couple of days should see it sorted out.'

'And then?' Marlowe enquired politely.

'I . . . I'm not sure. It depends,' Gary said vaguely. 'If you two will excuse me, I think I'll go and get on with some work.'

It was obvious to Cinnabar that he did not want to reveal his reasons for returning to Tokyo. So he wasn't as certain as he pretended of Michiko's non-involvement with Marlowe.

'Shall I come and help,' she offered, 'if you want to get them finished tonight? I could . . .'

'I'm sure Reid will work faster without distraction,' Marlowe foiled her desperate attempt not to be left alone with him, for, to her annoyance, Gary agreed.

'You know we don't work the same way, Bar. We'd only get on each other's nerves.'

'Oh, then in that case, I'll go and visit Uncle Yuji. I shan't have many more opportunities before . . .'

'I'm afraid that won't be possible.' Smoothly, Marlowe destroyed her last refuge. 'Akoya tells me he's already gone to bed.'

'He's not ill, is he?' Cinnabar was concerned, her own problems forgotten.

'No, just very tired. But I should be grateful for your company this evening. After all, you won't have many more opportunities to talk to me either, will you?'

'No.' Cinnabar tried to make her answer casual, to hide the pain which the thought gave her.

Marlowe had asked for her company, but once Gary had left them he seemed to fall into a fit of abstraction and Cinnabar began to feel the restless tension she always experienced when alone with him. After a while, she could stand it no longer and getting up, began to move around the room, re-examining objects she had studied a dozen times before.

'My Uncle Yuji claims to find your company restful,' Marlowe commented. 'I can't say the same.'

But then Uncle Yuji didn't disturb her the way his nephew did, she thought.

'I'm sorry! If you want a peaceful evening, perhaps I'd better leave you alone. I don't feel particularly . . .'

'Relaxed?' he asked. 'No, you're never relaxed when you're with me, are you, Cinnabar? I wonder why?'

Oh, the unmitigated hypocrite! He knew very well how he affected her . . . knew only too well his own powers of sensuous provocation.

'Perhaps you're not a very restful person to be with either,' she said lightly, trying to keep the conversation on a superficial level.

'I might be . . . with the right company, and in certain circumstances,' he suggested.

'Then it's obvious I don't fulfil those conditions,' she told him, 'so, if you don't mind, I think I'll . . .'

She had not realised that he could move so fast. For all his size, he was light on his feet and graceful. Now he had interposed himself between her and the door . . . the only route to safety; the door to the garden was secured for the night.

Helplessly she backed away from him, at a loss for words
. . . even those with which to protest.

'We never really had that opportunity to get to know each
other better,' he said conversationally, 'a chance to
understand each other.'

The trouble was, she thought, that she understood him only
too well!

'You can't blame me for that,' she returned. 'You were the
one who dashed off to Tokyo and stayed away for three
weeks.'

'Was it as long as that?' Marlowe's tone was mocking, and
she cursed her glib tongue for giving away the fact that she
had recorded the length of his absence.

'Perhaps it may have been more . . . or less. I didn't really
notice,' she lied.

And he knew that she lied, his smile devastating even in its
irony.

'Well, suppose we try again?'

Imperceptibly, he had moved closer to her, away from the
door, and surreptitiously, she estimated her chances of
gaining it. But he anticipated her intention.

'You don't stand a chance,' he told her. 'Well, what do you
say, Cinnabar? Shall we work towards a better understanding?'

'It's hardly worthwhile,' she said coldly, 'for the short while
that I shall be here. Two days at the most, I imagine.'

'A lot could happen in two days.'

And a lot could happen in two minutes . . . as it had in the
first two minutes of her very first encounter with Marlowe
Hirakawa. Even then, on the day of their arrival in Tokyo,
she had sensed that this man spelt danger for her.

'Besides, I don't think you'll be leaving quite that soon,' he
said.

He sounded so arrogantly certain that Cinnabar determined
to make enquiries first thing next morning as to just how soon
she *could* leave. In the meantime, she had a more immediate
problem.

'How much longer do you intend to keep me in this room,
against my will?'

'As long as it takes to make you change your mind.'

She attempted a laugh . . . a poor effort, but the best she
could manage.

'I think I told you once, I never change my mind, and I don't believe even you could endure being confined to one room for a lifetime.'

'Is that how long it's going to take me to persuade you?' His laugh held real amusement and she turned her back on him, putting the width of the room between them.

The next moment she had swung wildly round, running towards him, clinging to him, shaking with fright, as the floor seemed to lift and sway beneath her feet, with a lurching, terrifying rumble.

'You changed your mind rather suddenly,' Marlowe murmured, as his arms closed around her.

'Oh, you beast,' she moaned, as the room continued to sway and shake. 'You know it wasn't that. It ... it's an earthquake ... isn't it?'

'Only the merest tremor,' he reassured her. 'We're quite accustomed to them. See, it's over now.'

The earth tremor might have passed, but the disturbance within her was far from settled. She had sought his arms as a refuge from her fear, but now that its cause had passed, he offered a present danger almost as terrifying as the quake itself; and, moreoever, he seemed in no hurry to release her from the embrace *she* had initiated.

'L-let me go,' she begged. 'I'm ... I'm all right now.'

'You know, I'm inclined to disagree with you.' His lips were moving among the tendrils of the hair framing her brow. 'I think things are far from right in your world.'

'Wh-what do you mean?'

She couldn't look up at him to ask the question; it would mean bringing her face ... her mouth ... far too close to his. Instead, the words were muffled, somewhere about the centre of his chest.

'Well, for one thing, you've lost Gary ... surely even you have to admit that now?'

'I don't admit anything of the kind ... and anyway, even if I did, you've no room to talk. *You* couldn't hold on to Magda, and if you're not very careful, you may even lose Michiko. I ...'

His hold tightened threateningly.

'Cinnabar! One of these days I'm going to ...'

But whatever he had been about to say was lost in Gary's noisy, exuberant entrance.

'I say, Bar! Just look at these photos of you! I'd no idea you could look so stunning. Look, Marlowe . . . Vyvyan's going to be over the moon about them, or my name's not Gary Reid. Bar, you could knock spots off Magda any day!'

CHAPTER NINE

THE old house was very quiet without Magda's loud voice and Gary's cheerful noisiness. To Cinnabar's chagrin, Marlowe had not resumed their conversation where Gary had interrupted it, and two days later, he too left for Tokyo.

Their party dispersed, Cinnabar decided she might as well make her own plans for departure, and it was only due to persuasion from Yuji Hirakawa that, once more, she postponed her return to England.

She had not seen so much of Marlowe's uncle while Gary and Magda had been in Kyoto, and she was shocked by the old man's increasing frailty.

'It would please me if you would consent to stay a little longer,' he said, when she told him she had booked her flight. 'This house would seem very empty without you now.' He smiled with a gallant attempt at humour. 'I do not think *my* earthly body will remain here much longer. The two great universal principles are no longer in accord.' Cinnabar looked at him questioningly. 'You have not heard of Yin and Yang?' She shook her head. 'They are the two universal principles which control everything in nature. Yin and Yang play their part also in the health of an individual. If the two principles are in balance one is healthy.' Yuji sighed. 'Ageing, it is thought, is caused by a gradual lack of Yin.'

'You don't really believe all that, do you?'

Yuji's expression was whimsical.

'Can you deny, however, that I am very old . . . would you call me a fit man?'

He was too proud to plead with her, she realised, but her soft heart was touched by his loneliness and his courageous facing of the inevitable. Politeness, she knew too, prompted all Japanese to mask any show of deep emotion, for fear of distressing others.

'But I'll have to go some time,' she said gently, as she conceded his request.

'Maybe . . . maybe not,' he said cryptically. 'At least wait until Marlowe returns?'

Too many of her decisions lately had rested on Marlowe Hirakawa's actions and she had promised herself that, this time, when he returned, she would be gone. But Yuji Hirakawa was watching her, his sunken eyes full of the pleading his lips refused to utter.

'All right, just till Marlowe comes back . . . but then I *must* go, Uncle Yuji, much as I've enjoyed my stay. I have a job waiting for me back in England; and my employer must know by now that I'm completely recovered from my accident.'

Afterwards, when she had cancelled her flight, Cinnabar regretted her acquiescence. She had no idea how long Marlowe would be away this time. She could be kept kicking her heels almost indefinitely. Yet she could not enquire the probable date of his return, for fear it should make her seem eager for that event.

She wondered how Gary was getting on. Had he proposed to Michiko yet . . . and what had her response been?

The news came in a telegram. Evidently, Gary's excitement had overcome his usual caution where money matters were concerned, for his message was lengthy and exuberant.

'What ho, Bar! Am about the happiest man on God's earth at this moment. Michiko and I are engaged. Stay right where you are. On my way back to Kyoto. Want you at our wedding. Cabling Vyvyan my resignation. Gary.'

Cinnabar reflected wryly that there could not be many girls, thrown over by their boy-friend one week, who received an invitation to his wedding the following week. Of course it was ridiculous to expect her to wait for the event, but at least she would be here when Gary got back, would be able to hear his account of his successful proposal. But what on earth would Vyvyan Lamonde say when he found he was losing one of his best fashion photographers? Why *was* Gary throwing up the security of an established career? Surely Michiko, if she loved him, would be willing to live in England?

She was wildly curious, too, to know Marlowe's reaction to Michiko's engagement.

She was with Yuji Hirakawa the next afternoon when she heard unmistakable sounds . . . the noise and bustle of arrival and Akoya's voice raised excitedly in her own language.

Yuji had stopped in mid-sentence, his head tilted to one

side, a smile of ineffable pleasure irradiating his parchment-taut features.

The door opened, with less care than was usual in the old man's house, and Cinnabar's eyes went straight to Marlowe's face. He was smiling more broadly than he had for a long time. Then she was unable to suppress her gasp of astonishment, recognising his companion, as Michiko ran across the room with small, dainty steps, to fling herself into Yuji Hirakawa's arms.

Cinnabar stared accusingly at Marlowe. He must know that Michiko was now engaged to Gary. How *could* he bring her here now, and Michiko ... how could she treat Gary like this? From the air of rejoicing it was almost as if ... as if ... her heart began to pound furiously ... as if it was Yuji's nephew that Michiko had promised to marry. Could Gary be mistaken? Had Marlowe ... She felt faint and dizzy.

Yuji and Michiko kept up their flow of continuous, incomprehensible conversation until, at last, the old man turned to Cinnabar.

'My apologies! In my happiness, I forget my manners. Cinnabar, my dear young friend, this is Michiko ... my daughter.'

'Your ... your *daughter*?' Cinnabar repeated the words in a strangled voice. Then she turned on Marlowe, still standing in the doorway, his hazel eyes deliberately mocking her discomfiture. 'You lied to me,' she hissed, 'you deliberately misled me into thinking ... let me make a fool of myself! Oh, I hate you, Marlowe Hirakawa! I *hate* you!'

Ignoring the little sounds of surprise and protest from Yuji and his daughter, she brushed past Marlowe and began to run.

But there was nowhere to run to. She hadn't even the satisfaction of being able to lock herself in her room. There were no locks on the inner doors of the house. There was only one place she could think of, where Marlowe wouldn't expect to find her ... in *his* rooms.

She was beyond tears, flinging herself flat in an agony of unhappiness upon the tatami of his bedroom floor. It was cruel, the way he had deceived her, allowed her to go on thinking that Michiko was his mistress. What was the point of such a deception? Cinnabar was mortified, as she remembered the accusations she had made. Michiko was his *cousin*! This was something else Cinnabar could not understand. She was positive that Marlowe had referred to his uncle as being childless. A dreadful thought occurred to her. Suppose ... suppose Marlowe, or Gary for that matter, had told Michiko about *her* insinuations? Michiko would be sure to tell her father, and what would Yuji think of *her* then? ... the girl to whom he had extended his hospitality, his friendship, his affection even. It was all Marlowe's fault, she decided. How she loathed him!

The creak of a floorboard told her that she was discovered. She tensed, still face downward, hoping that it was only one of the servants, that whoever it was would go away. But the warmth of the long body being lowered to the floor beside her, the unmistakable masculine fragrance of him, gave the clue to who had found her.

She lay rigid, determined not to move, not to be the first to speak. But resistance was impossible, as two large hands, none too gentle, rolled her over on to her back and held her prisoner there, by the simple expedient of pressing her shoulders to the tatami.

'How did you find me?' she asked sulkily, deliberately avoiding his gaze, her eyes fixed on the buttons of his shirt ... the topmost one undone, to reveal a broad expanse of flesh, as bronzed as his face and shadowed by a mat of strong, dark hair.

'Akoya saw you come this way.'

Of course. So simple. She had forgotten the silent unobtrusiveness of Yuji's servants. Besides, she had probably made a considerable amount of noise in her angry, precipitate flight.

'I'm sorry if I'm trespassing,' she said stiffly, 'but I thought you wouldn't expect to find me *here*. There's ...' she stifled a sob, 'there's no privacy anywhere in this house.'

'I'm glad you came here,' he said softly. 'It gives us the opportunity to talk ... a conversation that has been deferred too many times, gives us a chance to straighten out a few things.'

Wearily she moved her head from side to side.

'I don't want to do any more talking. We've talked enough. It always ends up the same way ... arguments, misunderstandings.'

'Yes,' Marlowe said thoughtfully, 'you could be right. Maybe we should skip the conversation.'

Cinnabar looked at him then, surprised at his ready agreement. But what she saw in his bright, wide-apart eyes made her look away again, licking lips suddenly dry with apprehension.

'Let me go,' she whispered.

'No talking, remember?'

As he spoke he moved closer, so that his body almost covered hers, his great weight resting on his forearms, otherwise, she felt, she must have been totally crushed by him; and suddenly she wanted to be. Regardless of any pain or discomfort, she wanted to be annihilated beneath him, to feel her whole body constrained by his.

His kiss sent shock waves of ecstasy through her, and as he felt her involuntary response, he relaxed his punishing grip on her shoulders, rolling over, taking her with him, so that now she lay on top of him; and all the time, his mouth did not release those willing hostages, her lips.

Belatedly, Cinnabar struggled to free herself. She was making this too easy for him. She would not permit herself to be a mere outlet for his sexual appetites.

'I didn't come here for this,' she protested, as she succeeded in evading his marauding mouth.

'Maybe you didn't,' he agreed, 'but now that you *are* here . . .'

'Now that I am here, I still feel the same. You . . . you made an utter fool of me.'

'No,' he contradicted her, his eyes laughing at her. 'You didn't need my help to do that.'

'Oh!' Furiously, with clenched fists, she beat at his chest. 'Let me go! Why did you lie to me . . . and to Magda? You told us your uncle had no children, that you were his heir.'

He let her go so suddenly that she rolled to the tatami with an undignified thump, wounding her pride more than her person.

'Why did you do that?' she asked indignantly, sitting up to glare at him, forgetting that a second before she had demanded her release.

'Because you disappoint me . . . no, more than that . . . you disgust me.'

'*I* disgust *you*?'

Marlowe had risen to his feet, and while it was obvious that, physically, he was still aroused, he was master enough of himself to speak coldly.

'When, originally, I explained my family circumstances to you, I told you that my uncle had no son to succeed him. In Japan this is of great importance, especially where a business is concerned. My uncle wouldn't dream of taking his daughter into the firm—making her his heiress, yes, but a woman in business, never. *My* position is virtually that of a caretaker, until Michiko marries, when the responsibility becomes that of her husband.'

An awful suspicion was growing within her. Had Gary known all along that Michiko was Yuji Hirakawa's daughter? Was that the reason for his determination to give up his career with Vyvyan, because he would have the certainty of a place on the board of Messrs. Hirakawa?

Right now, she didn't know whom she despised most ... Gary for his cupidity, herself for her jealous assumption concerning Michiko's relationship with Marlowe, or Marlowe himself, for allowing her to continue in error.

She stood up, the better to outface him.

'Why didn't you tell me Michiko was your cousin?'

'You were so determined to think ill of me. Why should I justify myself to you?'

Why indeed? Only if he had some lasting personal interest in her would he have sought to set her mind at rest on that score. Well, at least she could put one thing right.

'I'm sorry,' she said stiffly, 'for the remarks I've made about your cousin, but ...' and here indignation superseded contrition, 'I think you might have told me, instead of letting me go on insulting her!'

'Yes, I could have told you, but as I said, why should I? At first I credited you with more insight ... I had hoped that you would eventually realise for yourself that I was not that sort of man, the kind of man who makes love to one girl while keeping another as his mistress.'

'I'm sorry,' Cinnabar repeated miserably.

There seemed to be nothing more to say. She had totally misjudged Marlowe and in so doing had forfeited all chance of his good opinion.

But there was more to be said, apparently. Marlowe had not concluded his condemnation of her.

'I *had* placed you in a different category from Magda. It seems I was mistaken about that too.'

'I don't understand.'

Was there more misery to be endured?

'Magda is totally mercenary. She had no interest in me, only in what she thought I represented . . . I recognised that straight away.'

'Then why did you always shut me up when I . . .?'

'Because,' he said sternly, 'your criticisms of her diminished you, while telling me nothing that I couldn't see for myself. When Magda discovered, amongst other things, that I was not Yuji's sole heir, she couldn't get away fast enough . . . to pursue poor old Hank Schuster, who really *is* a rich man.'

For once Cinnabar disagreed with this assessment of Magda's character. Magda, it was true, had set out with the intention of ensnaring what she considered to be a wealthy husband; but Cinnabar could not forget the model's very real distress, the night before her departure, and she knew . . . which Marlowe did not . . . that Hank Schuster had never proposed marriage to the model. Magda, she considered, had for once been really in love . . . with the man, as well as the material things she thought he had to offer. She wondered fleetingly what the 'other things' were that Magda had discovered, to Marlowe's apparent discredit.

'You reacted in just the same way as Magda,' Marlowe continued inexorably, 'when you discovered that Michiko is Yuji's daughter. Your first words were the same as Magda's . . . "Why did you lie to me, tell me your uncle had no children, that *you* were his heir?" '

Cinnabar stared at him, comprehension beginning to fill her with a sick realisation of his unfounded belief.

'Of all the foul, unjust accusations!' she whispered, when she finally found her voice. 'I don't give a damn whether you're as rich as Croesus, or as poor as a church mouse. Why should I?' Hastily, pride asserted itself, before she could give herself away . . . her true reasons for her lack of concern over his financial state. 'I haven't the slightest interest in you, or your money . . . or lack of it. It's just that, if you'd told us right from the start about your relationship with Michiko, it would have avoided all this unpleasantness . . . the embarrassment.'

And the heartache, she thought. Without this misunderstanding, she might not have rejected Marlowe's overtures quite so vigorously; things might have been very different between them now.

He was regarding her broodingly, assessingly, and for once there was nothing in his gaze to alarm her senses. He seemed to be looking at her, not as a man looks at a woman he desires, but as though he would penetrate her mind, probing for any hidden insincerity beneath her words.

'Magda wanted to marry a rich man . . .' he said slowly, his eyes never leaving Cinnabar's face. 'At least *she* made no secret of the fact.'

'Well, I don't want to marry a rich man,' Cinnabar asserted. 'You needn't judge my values by hers. When I marry, it's going to be for the right reasons!'

'Which are?'

She hesitated. How could she speak to this man of tenderness, of spiritual commitment, of a chemistry that outweighed all promptings of common sense? Swiftly she riposted:

'If you don't know the answer to that, then you're as bad as Magda. Besides,' she added . . . a rider which she felt must clinch the argument, 'you must know I had no intention of marrying a rich man. I was going to marry Gary.'

His face darkened.

'Yes . . . yes, I keep forgetting your alleged tendresse for young Reid. You know, I suppose, that he's now asked Michiko to marry him?' As Cinnabar nodded, he added: 'And do you suppose his reasons are the correct ones?'

Helplessly, she lifted her shoulders.

'I hope so . . . I do believe that he fell in love with Michiko at first sight, before he even knew who she was, but . . .'

'But he likes the idea of wealth?'

'Who doesn't!'

Her flippant reply brought down censure upon her.

'You . . . so you've just alleged.'

'Oh, don't turn my words against me,' she snapped. 'Of course I don't like the idea of poverty . . . of course money has its place. What I said was that I wouldn't marry for money. I . . . I would have to be in love . . .'

'As you were in love with Gary Reid?'

Why did he keep asking such awkward questions? If she now denied that she'd ever been in love with Gary, he'd know that all along she had lied to him and he would wonder why. If she said yes ... But she was tired of deception. She settled for a silent shrug.

'And would you have him back, if that were possible?'

This was getting worse. By her very silence she was compounding her falsehood.

'I ... I ...'

'Suppose my uncle and I didn't want Michiko to marry Reid? Suppose we too doubt his motives. Do you think he could be bought off?'

Blue-grey eyes wide with incredulity, Cinnabar stared at him.

'You ... you'd give him money not to marry her?'

'He might turn back to you then, and with the money he'd be able to support you in comfort.'

Cinnabar's volatile temper had been rising slowly within her, and now it exploded in contemptuous condemnation of his insulting suggestions.

'Do you really think I'd have a man on those terms ... a man who'd been bought back for me? I wouldn't marry Gary Reid now, if he were the last man on earth. I'm not in love with him, but I *do* like and respect him. I know he's ambitious, but he's not the ... the despicable gigolo you're trying to make out. I'm sure he loves Michiko for herself ... and if you don't believe that, you and your uncle can always cut her off without a penny and see what happens.'

'Your loyalty to your ex-fiancé is quite touching,' Marlowe said drily. 'And of course I would expect you to deny any feeling for him *now*. Such fervour stems, I've learnt, from a woman's pride, reluctance to admit ...'

'Nothing of the sort! I ...'

'Would you admit to a man that you loved him,' Marlowe interrupted her, 'if he hadn't first made some declaration to you?'

Again she was bereft of words. He seemed to have a knack of formulating questions which were quite unanswerable ... unanswerable to him. To anyone else she would have admitted the truth of the words, but to him ... never!

She was relieved when he seemed content to let the matter rest.

'I think, despite your reluctance to talk to me, we've reached some degree of understanding?'

Cinnabar wished she thought so. It seemed to her that the rift of misunderstanding between them widened at every encounter.

'What are your plans for the future?' Marlowe asked, as they left his rooms and walked across the courtyard to the main house.

Cinnabar was anxious to be free of his disturbing company, but his firm grasp on her elbow slowed her pace.

'Gary did ask me to stay for his wedding, but I don't think I . . .'

'Why not?' he said. 'It's to take place very soon. Michiko is anxious to be married while her father is still strong enough to attend the ceremony.'

Cinnabar stopped in mid-stride. 'So you never intended to try and stop the wedding?' she accused. 'That was all . . .'

'An experiment on my part,' he said smoothly.

An experiment? What sort of experiment . . . to find out more about Gary, or about *her*? But why should he want to know more about her? A little bubble of excited speculation rose within her. He had not, by his own account, been deceived by Magda . . . Michiko was not his mistress. Was it possible that his approaches to her had been sincere?

His next words pricked the bubble before it had time to expand, to reflect the rainbow of hope in her heart.

'You'll be glad to get back to work, I suppose? With Reid resigning from the House of Lamonde, there's not much doubt that you'll be sent on the Indian assignment?'

'Yes.' She did not attempt to keep the quiver out of her voice, guessing rightly that he would take it for excitement.

At the entrance to the main house it was Marlowe's turn to pause, looking down at her with a curiously enigmatic expression in the normally expressive hazel eyes.

'But you'll stay for the wedding?'

She wanted to refuse, knowing that to stay was only prolonging her own agony. But it would be selfish to spoil Gary's pleasure, churlish not to be there to wish him and Michiko good luck.

'I . . . suppose I must,' she said reluctantly, evading his eyes, her toe demolishing the careful pattern of the raked gravel.

'And until then, for the sake of others, do you think we could manage to suspend our own private hostilities?' he probed.

She did not, could not reply, and immediately his hand shot out, lifting and twisting her chin, so that she had to face him. 'Well?'

His touch, the ordeal of meeting his eyes, were effecting strange, disturbing reactions within her ... reactions which she hoped were not relayed to him by her external appearance. Lids lowered once more, she murmured:

'I ... I suppose so.'

'Look at me, Cinnabar,' he commanded. 'I want to see your eyes, to judge whether you mean what you say.'

'I do mean it.'

For a brief instant, blue-grey eyes met intent hazel ones, and before she had time to glance away again, his dark head was lowered and his firm, full lips had brushed hers in a fugitive caress, tantalising, unsatisfying.

'The pact is sealed,' he said lightly.

His tone betrayed no emotion of any kind, so that she could not guess whether her assent had pleased him or not. But in case he should feel that he had scored too easy a victory, she added a rider to her promise.

'I suppose my last few days here might as well be peaceful ones.'

Gary returned that evening, ebullient, delighted with himself and with life.

'The last of the photos are on their way to England, and so's my resignation,' he told Cinnabar.

He and Michiko were obviously happy, Gary noisily so, she with a quiet, serene joy, their wedding planned for a couple of weeks hence.

The full heat of summer had descended upon Japan like a stifling moist blanket. Cinnabar found the humidity almost stupefying, blessedly dulling her mind to the fact that these really were her last few days in that country ... near Marlowe.

The sky, pearly grey and glaring with diffused light, dazzled the eyes; the air and the ground were alive with creeping, crawling things, swarms of mosquitoes and gnats invaded the garden ... and, if allowed to do so, the house.

No one felt inclined for exertion, and the days passed in a lethargic haze. Michiko and Gary spent much of their time talking to Yuji Hirakawa, sharing their happiness with him and discussing their plans. Marlowe had left for Tokyo once more, promising to return in time for something which he briefly referred to as 'the Summer Festival.'

'Presumably that, and Michiko's wedding, will be your final experiences of Japan,' he told Cinnabar ... a parting shot which added considerably to her already stifling depression, for he seemed totally unmoved by the thought of her imminent departure.

Despite the fact that he had his beloved daughter with him, Yuji Hirakawa still welcomed Cinnabar's visits, and it was he who enlightened her about the festival.

'The festival of the Gion shrine is probably the most spectacular in Japan,' he told her. 'Until recently, I went every year to watch the processions. You must make sure that Marlowe *does* take you.'

'I'd rather be going with you,' she said truthfully.

His laugh, politely covered by his hand, was pleased but disbelieving.

'Sooner go with an ancient man? That I find hard to believe, but I thank you for the compliment. You must know, Cinnabar, that I have come to look upon you almost as a second daughter ... a niece, perhaps?'

'And I think of you as an uncle,' she said with spontaneous warmth.

If only Marlowe were in love with her, she thought wistfully, she could in reality have become Yuji's niece.

'And soon I will be losing both my daughters,' he said sadly. Cinnabar looked at him uncomprehendingly, and he nodded. 'Michiko and Gary will be leaving Japan shortly after the wedding, to live in New York.'

'New York? But ... the firm ... Hirakawa ... I thought ...'

'You thought I would put an untried and untested young man in charge of my head office?' His smile was wry. 'Physically, I may be diminishing, but not mentally. No, Gary will learn my business in New York and eventually, I hope, take charge of that branch.'

'And ... and Marlowe?' There was agony and ecstasy in saying his name.

'Stays here, naturally. I need his support in my last weeks ... oh yes ...' as she would have protested, 'I know I have not long to live. I would not have it any other way. My body has become a burden I long to lay down.' He leant forward, one ancient finger touching her cheek. 'Tears? For me? Unnecessary, my child! But Marlowe will be very alone, when I am gone,' he added, as if reflectively.

'You ... you were telling me about the festival,' Cinnabar said hastily, forcing back the signs of grief he forbade.

Yuji smiled. 'You wish to distrust an old man's thoughts, but I assure you I am not afraid of death.'

Guiltily she admitted to herself that the distraction had not been wholly intended for Yuji, but to take her own mind from the dangerous thought of his nephew alone ... lonely. She could not really believe that state of affairs would last very long. Marlowe's personal magnetism would soon draw a new crowd of friends around him, many of whom would be the beautiful, soignée women he seemed to favour.

'I really do want to know about the festival,' she told Yuji.

So, when Marlowe returned from Tokyo, Cinnabar was able to accompany him, his cousin and Gary to the festival of the Gion shrine, with some idea of what to expect ... not, as when they had gone to Gifu, totally ignorant of what she would experience.

Not that the Summer Festival could hold the same sensations, the insidious magic of Gifu, she thought, shuddering as she recalled their proximity in the gliding boat, that oasis of darkness, under the cover of which Marlowe had made sensuous, provocative love to her.

Since then, their encounters had taken place in an atmosphere of flaring antagonism, as when he had accused her of being as mercenary as Magda ... or, since their truce, in one of restrained civility.

'The festival lasts for nearly three weeks,' Yuji Hirakawa had told her. 'And during the whole period, all of Kyoto is en fête. Scarcely a day passes without some interesting ceremony, but the high spot is the great procession of the floats.'

Before the festival was over, then, she would be gone, Cinnabar told herself firmly. She would witness the procession and the following week attend Gary and Michiko's wedding. Then she must be strong ... her logical brain had granted her treacherous heart too many reprieves.

The night before the commencement of the festival, the four of them had gone out into the crowded streets of Kyoto, where street vendors made the most of their opportunities of trading. Barrows piled high with baubles, trinkets and hideous

jewellery stood cheek by jowl with fruit stalls, sellers of ice
cream and fireworks. Children clustered round large, shallow
tanks filled with goldfish, selecting their purchases, to be
transferred to waterproof plastic bags, no different from
children at fêtes the world over. From time to time a
firecracker exploded and flaring rockets lit up the night sky.
The many shrines of the Gion area were lavishly decorated
and crowded with people buying amulets wrapped in bamboo
leaves ... the religious charms said to ward off illness.

By tradition, so Yuji had told Cinnabar, on this night all
the houses in the neighbourhood were left open to public
view, the rooms facing on to the street exhibiting special
flower arrangements, while the inhabitants themselves
lounged on their tatami, watching baseball on television, or
drinking iced beer, accustomed to being part of the annual
spectacle.

Somehow, in the crush, Cinnabar and Marlowe had
become separated from the others ... a development
Cinnabar regretted. She wished *she* might evade him too, but
realised it would be foolhardy to do so in such a crowd of
humanity. As it was, she was forced to endure the grip of his
guiding hand at her elbow, as they moved nearer and nearer
to their goal, the main shrine.

Here an attendant barred their way, for no one might pass
while the deity was being transferred from his home in the
shrine to the Mikoshi, or ceremonial palanquin, in which he
was borne during the procession.

Darkness enfolded them, as, with a startling suddenness, all
illumination was quenched and silence fell over the watching
crowd. In the faint glow of the moon, the only light which the
hand of man could not extinguish, the white-robed priests
could just be discerned, as they emerged bearing a white, tent-
like structure, which concealed the Kami, or god.

The god transferred to his new home, the lights went on
again and the crowd, bearing Cinnabar and her companion
along in their midst, hurried to witness the ritual of exorcising
evil spirits, which took the form of a dance before the
assembled priests, by men wearing grotesque demon masks.

Tremulously, Cinnabar had wondered what would happen
when the evening's entertainment was concluded, fearing the
strained silences that fell between them these days, the awful
searing longing which possessed her in Marlowe's presence,

physically so near and yet spiritually so far removed from her.

But she need not have worried. Chance brought them in contact with their friends again and they returned home together; and she was not sure whether she was sorry or relieved that there was no opportunity for their parting to take place unwitnessed.

But now it was the morning ... the first day of the festival proper, the sky a blazing blue, the humid heat broiling and, together with an enormous crowd, they had returned to witness the procession.

Cinnabar had taken immense pains over her appearance, her sleeveless dress in one of the autumn-leaf shades which always complemented her aureole of bronze hair exaggerating its chrysanthemum-like qualities. But Marlowe had given her no more than a cursory glance and she thought with painful nostalgia of a time when he would have made the analogy she now craved, likening her to the flower which symbolised so much for him.

'The parade dates back over a thousand years,' Marlowe explained, 'to the time when a great plague devastated Kyoto and the religious leaders of the time ordered a carnival to sweep away the lingering spirits of the dead.'

The floats were of two kinds, Yama and Hoko. The Yama carried sacred symbols or life-sized dolls, representing famous characters from history and legend, borne palanquin-wise on the shoulders of husky young men. The Hoko were enormous, tower-like constructions, weighing up to fourteen tons, carrying orchestras of flutes, gongs and drums and surmounted by a mast rising as high as a hundred and thirty feet. The whole structure was mounted on gargantuan wooden wheels, two metres wide, and drawn along the wide roads and narrow passageways by teams of forty or so young athletes, urged on by fan-brandishing charioteers. This drawing of the floats was no mean feat, since the ancient wheels had no axles and had to be forced around corners by sheer muscle power, their contents rocking perilously.

Both kinds of floats were decorated with gorgeous antique hangings ... Gobelin tapestries flanking Ming brocades and the formalised floral pattern of Turkey carpets. It was noisy, it was gaudy, but it was immensely impressive.

And so the procession proceeded, hour after hour, amidst

the heat, glare, colour and excitement of a crowd in holiday mood, but so orderly and respectful of official signs and barriers that the watchful police had little to do.

Cinnabar was very silent as they made their way home through the still teeming streets. How dull and ordinary London would seem after all this exotic pageantry ... even the Changing of the Guard, the Trooping the Colour, would seem mundane.

But was it just the spectacle, or the company in which she had witnessed it? With Marlowe at her side, wouldn't even a Girl Guide parade take on the mystique of romance?

'You enjoy our festival?' Michiko asked, as they strolled, four abreast, along the quieter roads leading to the Hirakawa family home.

Cinnabar nodded.

'Japan has many festivals,' Michiko continued. 'In time, perhaps, you will see them all?' There was a note in her voice Cinnabar could not interpret ... was it of hope?

But before she could speak, Marlowe answered for her, his voice brusque, repressive.

'Cinnabar will not be here that long. Immediately after your wedding, she's returning to London.'

CHAPTER TEN

THOUGH that was Cinnabar's declared intention, it was not pleasant to hear the words on Marlowe's lips, as if he actually welcomed the idea that soon she would be gone ... for there was no trace of regret in his voice that she could discern.

'Is that right, Bar?' Gary asked. He sounded surprised. 'Somehow, I thought ... we thought ...'

'Yes,' she interposed hastily. 'I've been lazy long enough. Vyvyan will be giving me the sack if I don't go home soon.'

'And this would matter very much?' Michiko asked.

'Cinnabar is a career girl,' Marlowe said curtly. 'That's a fact which has been impressed upon us often enough since her arrival in Japan.'

Michiko nodded understandingly.

'Once I too wished to be career girl.' She turned to Cinnabar. 'But my father, he wish to arrange my marriage to young man of good family, in the old way. Instead, Marlowe persuade my father that these days girls given more freedom. My father not like very much, but he love me and he give in. I attend college in Tokyo to study to be secretary, but now ...' her soft brown eyes turned lovingly on Gary, 'now I not want career. I make good wife ... home for Gary.'

Cinnabar could understand now Yuji's deep sadness at the dying out of tradition. It had been his own daughter who had disappointed him. But, being a wise man, and perhaps influenced by Marlowe, he had allowed Michiko to move with the times. Now all Michiko's enthusiastic references to the help Marlowe had given her were comprehensible. It had been cousinly interest and not, as her jealous heart had supposed, the concern of a man for his mistress.

'You do not wish to make a good wife ... a home?' Michiko persisted.

Cinnabar could feel her colour rising, three pairs of interested eyes upon her ... Michiko's and Gary's frankly curious, and Marlowe's ...? His were enigmatic as always, giving away nothing of what he thought.

'I ... perhaps, some day,' she mumbled.

179

'Let's hope that "some day" will not come too late,' Marlowe observed.

Mercifully, this uncomfortable discussion was terminated by their arrival at the front door of the Hirakawa dwelling, where they were met by an agitated Akoya, brandishing an envelope.

'This come for Forester-San, while you all out. I hope not bad news?'

Like women the world over, Akoya associated telegrams only with disaster, Cinnabar thought, as she ripped open the flimsy container. Vyvyan had spared no expense, but his message, though full of enthusiasm and information could be condensed into a few brief words. Cinnabar looked at the others, her eyes expressing mingled emotions of incredulity, pride and . . . regret.

'Vyvyan is over the moon about the Oriental portfolio and . . . and he especially likes the last few, the ones I posed for. He . . . he wants me to go to India, not as the photographer, but . . . but as the model!'

'Told you so, Bar. Didn't I tell you so?' Gary's reaction was triumphant. He turned to Marlowe. 'You saw them, you agreed with me . . . stunning, weren't they?'

Cinnabar scarcely dared to look at Marlowe. What would his reaction be to this startling news?

Irritatingly, his face remained impassive. He might have inherited the features of his European ancestors, but he was also endowed with the inscrutability of the Oriental, she thought.

'The opportunity of a lifetime,' he said, 'the beginning of a whole new career.'

'One she'd be a fool to pass up, too,' Gary agreed enthusiastically.

'Indeed!'

Well, if that was how he felt, what he thought, then it was obvious that Marlowe Hirakawa didn't care two hoots if he never saw her again. Only furious pride dispelled the stinging sensation beneath her eyelids. She'd go to India . . . she'd *show* them . . . show *him*. By this time next year, her face and figure might be as well known as Magda's. She would be fêted and sought after by more handsome and wealthy men than she could count; and she tried to convince herself that this would compensate for the absence of the one in the world whose admiration really mattered.

It was the day of the wedding. To Cinnabar it had seemed to approach with frightening rapidity, heralding as it did her own subsequent departure.

She did not know what she had expected, but it had been nothing as lavish and extravagant as this. Michiko, now that she had abandoned her ideas of a career, seemed to have completely reverted to the traditions beloved of her father, insisting on a traditional wedding, with formal Japanese clothes for herself and all the trappings of the Oriental wedding.

The clothes, she had told Cinnabar, would be expensive to buy, particularly her ceremonial kimono, which instead had been hired. The hire firm also sent out a dresser, to help the bride put on her special wig and make-up.

Out of consideration for Yuji's frail state of health, the wedding was conducted in the grounds of his home, as was the reception. Most of the guests were men and custom decreed that women sat at a separate table. Thus Cinnabar found herself among a gossiping group of strangers, totally unable to understand their excited chatter, her eyes again and again drawn irresistibly to the table where Marlowe sat, head and shoulders above the other men, never once, apparently, glancing in her direction.

Western music was played throughout the reception and Western food served, which Cinnabar found strange in view of the close adherence to Oriental dress and custom. After much food and wine, the now euphoric guests made speeches, sang songs and recited poetry ... unfortunately all in Japanese, so that Cinnabar felt increasingly restless and out of things, found herself beginning to wonder if the day would ever end.

She felt sorry for Gary too, formally dressed in a Western morning suit and seated in the place of honour beside his bride, as unable as she to understand what was going on, yet forced, for the sake of politeness, to look interested. But at least he had Michiko to translate for him, to press his hand beneath the table, her soft eyes sending him messages ... promises of more enjoyable moments to come, moments to be repeated throughout a lifetime together.

She had nothing of that nature to console her for her mounting boredom. Cinnabar knew that she was becoming maudlin, but irritatingly could not shake off her depression.

But at last ritual and formality were over and Michiko

had gone to change back into Western dress. The couple planned to spend a few days here, in Michiko's childhood home, before flying to New York to take up their new life together.

Marlowe, Cinnabar supposed, would return to Tokyo, leaving the newlyweds alone ... except, of course, for Yuji, who would be glad of these last bitter-sweet days of his daughter's presence.

Cinnabar wondered if Michiko realised that she might not see her father again, and guessed not ... or the girl would never have consented to leave him. Knowing the courtly, sensitive old man, Cinnabar guessed that he had forbidden anyone to reveal the extent of his frailty to his daughter.

The last guests had drifted away, the caterers were clearing up the debris of the reception, and Cinnabar drifted aimlessly towards the inner garden. Unsure how to spend the remaining hours of the evening, she had thought to find a measure of tranquillity there. But she paused in dismay, for Marlowe was already in possession, leaning against a gnarled tree, contemplating with some intensity the complex whorls and patterns of the gravelled area. She turned to leave, but the movement caught his eye and he said her name.

'I ... I'm sorry,' she faltered, 'I didn't mean to disturb you. I didn't know you were here. I'll ...'

'No! Don't go.' He spoke jerkily. 'I have something for you.'

He moved towards her and she shrank back a little, filled with panic. It was so long since they had been quite alone and she could feel herself trembling with emotion it was difficult to conceal.

It was the wedding, she decided, which had revived in her all kinds of longings, which she had believed crushed ... dispelled by Marlowe's obvious indifference to her imminent departure, smothered by her own determination to accept Vyvyan's offer of a modelling career, to put Japan and all that it meant to her firmly in its place, the irredeemable past.

He held out a small package, wrapped with the care and taste that was an essential part of Japanese present giving.

'I want you to have this ... no,' disturbingly, his hand closed over hers, 'don't open it now. It's a memento of your visit. Perhaps ...' he hesitated, 'when you look at it, it will remind you of Japan, of ... of the friends you've made here.'

As if she could forget any of it ... ever. Did he count himself amongst those 'friends'? When she thought of him, it would not be by so lukewarm a description.

His voice was still oddly staccato, his hand releasing hers, slowly, reluctantly.

'You've made your plans for departure?'

She nodded. 'I'm going back to Tokyo, the day after tomorrow, to collect the rest of my things from your hotel. I ... I fly back to England the day after.'

'And you're not likely to change your mind ... about this new career?'

It was not the words, but his tone of voice, which gave her an odd feeling of breathlessness. She must not imagine things, must not read anything into this conversation, and that was all it was ... polite conversation.

'I ... I don't ...'

'I'm going to Tokyo myself, early in the morning, if you would rather not travel alone?'

'Oh no,' she gasped. 'No, thank you. I ... I'll stick to my arrangements.' It would be unendurable to travel with him, to count off the miles, knowing that each one brought them nearer to their final separation.

'Then we must make our farewells this evening ... now?'

She felt a quiver run over her, as Marlowe held out one large, tanned hand and fearfully she entrusted her own to it, expecting nothing more than a brief handshake.

Perhaps that had been all he intended, but once her hand was in his grasp, he seemed reluctant to release the slender fingers again and she felt a pulse begin to beat in her neck, as he tightened his hold. Nervously she looked up at him, surprising a wry twist to his lips as he looked down at their joined hands, his jaw tight, his expression unreadable. Suddenly, before she could anticipate his movement, she found herself imprisoned between him and the gnarled bark of a tree, and she experienced intolerable sensations of painful longing, at the sudden pressure of his body, his straining thighs moulded against her.

'Marlowe, please ...' She managed to whisper the words.

'You wouldn't deny me my last goodbye?' His voice was throaty, the words almost indistinguishable, and the heat of desire scorched through her as he shifted against her.

She was immobilised, helpless to deny him, as physical

awareness overcame the restraints she had imposed upon herself with the aid of intellect ... common sense, so that it seemed right, natural, to be crushed by him like this, his hands moving over her, sapping all remaining willpower, her lips burning under the pressure of his demanding mouth.

She abandoned herself to the ecstasy of his touch, telling herself that this was the last time, that she must have this memory to carry with her on her long, lonely journey, almost delirious as his hands increased the urgency of their caress and the pressure of him became more intimate, creating a knot of physical anguish within her.

The imprisoning weight of his body shifted a little, as he raised his head, the expression in his eyes just visible in the waning light.

'Come with me to my room, Cinnabar ... now ...?'

The crescendo that had built inside her waned at his words, the blatant directness of his invitation ... an invitation to what? She thought she knew, only too well. He had said he wanted to bid her a last farewell, but if that was the kind of leave-taking he had in mind ...

It was as if he anticipated her refusal, for once more his sheer weight restrained her, the proximity of him extorting a response she was powerless to hide, even while her brain sought to control the pulsating of her feverish body. She could not, would not submit to what he had in mind, and exerting all the remaining power of her seduced and weakening flesh, she began to fight him.

Miserably, she felt that the love she bore him had been profaned by his suggestion; and his importuning was becoming brutal in its intensity, the hitherto tender torture of his hands turned to a compelling agony, as he initiated intimacies that she had never even imagined, much less experienced ... intimacies which given and received in love would have been pure heaven.

She *had* to break free, before it became totally impossible to control the urges of his virile body, before Marlowe overcame her by sheer physical strength. It would not be love ... for her, sex with no involvement of mind or spirit could not be love. *He* was not mentally or spiritually attuned to her ... it would be rape.

With a tortured gasp she succeeded in dragging her mouth from his, her bemused brain seeking the words with which to repel him ... to ensure her freedom.

'You're behaving like an animal!' she told him, the words coming painfully through her tortured breathing. 'You're drunk, of course. Men always drink too much at weddings.'

It was not so, she knew, for there was not the slightest trace of alcohol upon his warm breath, in the intimate taste of his mouth, but it was the best she could do.

'I'm a guest in your uncle's house,' she continued, 'yet you insult me!'

'Insult you?' There was anger and some other emotion in his strangled tones. 'Insult you, when I . . .'

'When you try to lure me to your room . . . to your bed. What kind of girl do you take me for? Do you really think I'm the sort who spends the last night of her holiday . . .'

'Enough!' He had released her now. 'You've said enough. I had intended . . . but no matter. I have my answer.'

His movements as abrupt as his words, he turned and strode away, leaving her shaking and distraught, the gift he had given her all this while still clutched, unknowingly, in her hand.

Absentmindedly, in the light of the stone lanterns that edged the path to the house, she unwrapped it. The paper opened to reveal a Kikkaishi . . . a patterned stone. Cinnabar had seen one before, Yuji Hirakawa owned one, but this was slightly different in tone and texture. Known as a 'Miracle Chrysanthemum stone,' its patterning took the form of a stiff petalled flower.

So this was what she must take with her, as her memento of Japan. Not just a memento of a country, but of a man. How could she ever forget Marlowe, when every time she looked at this she would think of a deep voice speaking caressingly, as his fingers touched the bronzed curls of her head, likening them to his favourite flower?

She was tempted for one moment to hurl the thing from her, to be lost forever amongst the rocks and stones of the garden, but she knew she could not do it. It was all she would ever have of him. Instead, she walked into the house, the stone cradled against her breast, while the tears that, for the past ten minutes, had threatened, flowed unheeded down her cheeks.

As though automatically, her feet led her to Yuji's room. Excited and over-stimulated by the events of the day, the old man had not yet retired, and he was pathetically glad to see her.

'You cannot sleep either?' he asked, then, observing the ravaged state of her tear-stained cheeks, added with concern, 'You are unhappy?'

Cinnabar nodded, slipping almost naturally into a kneeling position at his feet, her hands holding out the Chrysanthemum Stone for him to see.

'So he gave it to you?' Yuji observed, running one frail finger over the pattern. 'And yet these are not tears of happiness?' he queried.

'Why should they be?' she asked bitterly.

He looked puzzled. 'Tell me, child, just what has passed between you?'

Brokenly, she told him ... of her encounter with Marlowe in the garden, his impassioned embrace, his gradual loss of control, the invitation he had issued ... her indignant rejection.

Yuji listened gravely.

'And this is all my nephew said?'

'Isn't that insult enough?'

'Insult? My nephew did not seek to *insult* you.'

'You don't consider it insulting to invite a woman to his room, with ... with the intention of ...'

'With the intention of proposing to her,' Yuji interrupted, 'in the privacy a man and a woman desire at such moments, where servants, however discreet, are certain not to be present.'

'Pr—proposing?' She knelt up, staring earnestly into the sunken eyes. 'Don't joke, Uncle Yuji, not at a moment like this!'

'It is no joke,' he assured her. 'This morning, before the wedding, my nephew came to me and told me all that was in his mind ... his fear that the promising new career before you was still the most important thing to you, his reluctance to come between you and success in any way ... and yet tonight he intended to ask you to marry him, as he has always intended.'

'Always?' She said the word faintly, shaking her head.

'You do not believe me? But I tell you, it *is* so. In the early days of your visit to Japan, my nephew came home briefly, to tell me that he had met the girl whom, above all others, he wished to marry.'

'He had a strange way of showing it,' she muttered, still disbelieving.

'Despite his European ways and appearance, my nephew still has much of the reserve, the pride of his ancestors,' Yuji reminded her gently. 'Always he sought to know your feelings for him, before declaring himself, but he found you an enigma, sometimes passionate, sometimes hostile ... suspicious.'

'I was jealous,' she whispered. 'At first I thought he and Michiko ... until I found out she was his cousin. Then there was Magda ...'

The old man hissed expressively through his teeth.

'That ... no, it is not gentlemanly that I say such a word.'

'What am I going to do, Uncle Yuji?' she whispered. 'I misunderstood again ... rejected him. He ... he's going away in the morning. I ... I may never see him again ...'

'Go to him, child.' The old man seemed surprised that the idea should not have occurred to her.

'To ... to his room?'

'Why not, if you are to be married ... wish to be married?'

'I ... I couldn't,' she demurred.

'Are you going to let pride stand once again in the way of your happiness?' Yuji asked sternly. 'One of you must relent, and I know my nephew. He will never descend to begging. We Hirakawa are of the Samurai blood. There was a time when, rather than sacrifice his pride, the Samurai would commit Seppuku.'

For a long moment he held her gaze, until her lids flickered submissively before him. It was true what he said ... *her* pride, *her* jealousy had been the cause of all her misunderstandings with Marlowe. It was up to her to admit herself in the wrong.

Yet her feet moved slowly as she left Yuji's room and crossed the courtyard; it was always hard to apologise, to admit error to the person one had wronged, but when it was also the man you loved, feared to lose ... and when you feared now that *he* might reject *you* ...

The other wing of the house was silent, oppressively so, as if its occupant had imbued it too with the gloom of his emotions. Softly, Cinnabar moved along the polished wood of the corridor, with its subdued lighting. She hesitated, before stretching out her hand to slide the panel that opened upon Marlowe's living room. But the room was unoccupied, showing little sign of occupation, except for a few glossy

photographs strewn carelessly upon the lacquered table, as if
tossed there by an impatient hand.

Curiously, she examined them. Some she had seen here
before . . . one or two shots of Magda, sleek, seductive in
Vyvyan's exotic costumes, but last time she had seen them she
had not noticed what lay below. There were several
photographs of herself . . . those Marlowe had taken of her
wearing the golden robe, posed against the haloing petals of
the chrysanthemum, carved on the doors of the Kannon
shrine.

So he hadn't just taken copies of Magda's photos . . . and
the thumbprints on the glossy surfaces of those which
featured herself showed that they had been much handled.

She heard a slight sound from the adjoining bedroom.
Taking courage from the presence of the photographs, their
implication, she moved towards the source of the sound, then
paused in the doorway, her hand going to her throat in panic
at the sight that confronted her.

Marlowe stood, profile towards her, against the Tokonoma
alcove, wearing only a thin kimono, the delicate silk seeming
to emphasise rather than detract from his masculinity. In his
hand was the short Wakizashi sword . . . the sword of
Seppuku, of suicide, and as she watched, he ran an
exploratory finger along its edge.

With the scream she uttered, her immobilised limbs were
released from their temporary paralysis, and as he turned
towards her in surprise, she flew across the room, snatching
the sword from his hand, throwing it aside and flinging herself
into his arms, hers tightly around his waist.

'Oh *no* . . . oh no, my darling, you mustn't! I couldn't live
without you!'

With a quick intake of breath, Marlowe grasped her upper
arms, holding her firmly away from him, looking at her
searchingly, noting the trembling of the full lower lip, the tear-
filled blue-grey eyes that looked entreatingly into his.

'*What* did you say?' His tone was incredulous.

'I said you mustn't. Oh, Marlowe, you mustn't . . . nothing
is worth *that*. Besides, there's no need . . . I . . .'

Incredibly, he began to laugh.

'Little idiot! What stories has my uncle filled you with? Did
you really think I was about to kill myself?'

Mutely, she nodded, a blush beginning to spread itself

across her face and neck, as she realised how ridiculous she had made herself. She tried to turn away from him, but he would not let her go.

'And what else did you say?' he asked, his voice infinitely tender, but stern too.

Cinnabar shook her head. Nothing could induce her to say another word. Standing there in the doorway, she had recollected, vividly, Yuji's words . . . 'rather than sacrifice his pride, a Samurai would commit Seppuku.' And for one moment she *had* thought . . . How incredibly stupid, how conceited of her, to think that Marlowe would do something like that, because of *her*! This was the twentieth century! And suppose . . . suppose Yuji had been wrong about other things, had misinterpreted his nephew's intentions regarding herself?

'Have you nothing else to say to me?' Marlowe queried, pulling her closer, until she was entirely confined by his arms, aware just how thin, how sensuous to the touch was the silk fabric of the kimono, moulding itself to his sinewy body.

A long tremor invaded her body, as her imprisonment seemed to deny her breath and her senses whirled in chaos. His strong fingers pressed along the length of her spine, forcing her to arch towards him, every curve of her fitting to the muscled hardness of him.

'Then it seems I must say it for you?'

With the sense of the desire mounting between them, recognising that his equalled her own, courage returned to her. After all, was this not why she had come here?

She shook her head, looking up into his eyes, shyly at first, then with mounting confidence.

'No, let me . . .' Her voice faltered.

'Yes, my little unawakened bud?' His voice was deep, softly encouraging.

Not unawakened now, she thought, with leaping pulses.

'I love you,' she told him, with only the faintest tremor in her voice.

As his gaze held hers, she saw his eyes fill with a hot darkness, turning their hazel to molten brown, and her mouth trembled, pleading for the comfort of his touch. He drew an unsteady breath and she felt emotion stir his body anew, as one hand came up to to touch her hair.

'You mean this?'

She nodded, speechless now with the desire that filled her

throat with liquid sweetness, her limbs heavily lethargic, so that her brain felt disembodied, floating as though outside herself.

'And you would marry me? Give up your chances of a new career, of fame?'

He was taking nothing for granted, she thought, making sure of her, as his uncle had said, before committing himself, but she did not begrudge him this right, and again she nodded.

'When?'

She could feel his strong frame beginning to tremble now and he was hot, vibrant, through the thin material of the kimono.

'Whenever you want me to,' she whispered, 'tomorrow . . . yesterday!' She tried to laugh, but the sound came out as a little sob of agonised need.

Marlowe held her a little away from him and turned his eyes towards the quilted bed behind him. She followed his gaze, her heart doing strange, impossible things, as she anticipated his next words.

'Tonight?'

'Yes, please . . .' The words were a thin, breathy sound, which barely reached him.

His eyes held hers, while his hands slid the simple dress from her shoulders, to fall in a silken pool about her feet.

'You know now that I love you?' he asked simply.

She nodded, unable to take her eyes from his face.

'I think I've always loved you,' he said unsteadily, 'from the moment I walked into my office and saw you standing there, with your fiery curls framing that adorable little face. But you were so spiky, so hostile.' He laughed throatily, as he removed the last of her garments. 'More like a thistle than my chrysanthemum! I told Magda, before she left, that it was you . . .'

'You told *Magda*?'

'Yes,' he confessed. 'I had hoped that she might tell you and . . .'

'Not Magda,' she sighed. Oh, if only she had known then! How much time had been wasted. But they would make up for it, she vowed.

His kimono slid easily from his broad frame, then he carried her, walking slowly, as one who fears to spoil a pleasure by anticipating it too soon, laying her down almost reverently, coming down slowly to cover her, the touch of his flesh on hers like a magnet, drawing her . . . making her arch towards him.

Still he did not hurry her, as his hands searched out the intimate, responsive places of her body, stroking, touching with caressing appreciation, causing ecstasy to flood her being, so that she moved restlessly, provocatively, inviting his possession.

It was not an invasion, but an intense, mutual urgency, abandonment . . . sweet fulfilment, as he taught her the secrets of her body and his, until the tenderness of his desire climaxed into the ecstatic, sword-like thrust of explosive consummation.

Lax in lazy contentment, he smiled at her, that smile that had tugged her heart from her so many times, as he whispered:

'At last my chrysanthemum has flowered for me.'

Harlequin ® Plus

A WORD ABOUT THE AUTHOR

Annabel Murray was born in Hertfordshire, England, and now lives in Liverpool with her two teenage daughters and her husband, who is a college teacher. He has always actively encouraged her in pursuing her hobbies, which have been legion, with writing foremost among them. Annabel had ambitions to be an author from the time she was in school.

In the interim, other hobbies captured her attention and energy. Involvement in arts and crafts led to her participation in the foundation of a local arts group. Drama, too, intrigues her, and she has appeared in many plays, produced others and even won an award for a historical play she wrote. Hiking and gardening allow her to enjoy outdoor beauty and healthful air.

None of her interests, though, is truly separate from her writing activity, for she uses all her experiences to flesh out her heroines' backgrounds. Not even her holidays are exempt. Like every serious writer, she keeps her eyes open for the unusual detail that can be transplanted into fiction from the life around her. Annabel's several novels attest to the acuteness of her observation.

Yours FREE, with a home subscription to
SUPERROMANCE™

Complete and mail the coupon below today!

- -

FREE! Mail to: SUPERROMANCE

In the U.S.
2504 West Southern Avenue
Tempe, AZ 85282

In Canada
649 Ontario St.
Stratford, Ontario N5A 6W2

YES, please send me FREE and without any obligation, my
SUPERROMANCE novel, LOVE BEYOND DESIRE. If you do not hear
from me after I have examined my FREE book, please send me the
4 new **SUPERROMANCE** books every month as soon as they come
off the press. I understand that I will be billed only $2.50 for each book
(total $10.00). There are no shipping and handling or any other hidden
charges. There is no minimum number of books that I have to
purchase. In fact, I may cancel this arrangement at any time.
LOVE BEYOND DESIRE is mine to keep as a FREE gift, even if
I do not buy any additional books.

NAME _____ (Please Print) _____

ADDRESS _____ APT. NO. _____

CITY _____

STATE/PROV. _____ ZIP/POSTAL CODE _____

SIGNATURE (If under 18, parent or guardian must sign.)   **134 BPS KAJ6**

SUP-SUB-1

This offer is limited to one order per household and not valid to present
subscribers. Prices subject to change without notice. Offer expires July 31, 1984